What in the world was she going to do about John Gunner?

Tessa *couldn't* be attracted to him n an instantaneous, pure simmering sex a girls gush and old lad t, of course. Not se wasn't a committe us, one of life's quinte

But how could *she,* of all people, be attracted to his cocky animal magnetism? It had nothing to do with morals, with common sense, with all the rules she'd grown up believing in. It was elemental. Gunner's laid-back charm was something that simply *was.* A mature, sensible, moral person acknowledged it and walked around it.

At the moment she was wondering if she had a mature, sensible, moral bone in her body....

SAFE HAVEN

BEVERLY BIRD

The Marrying Kind

Published by Silhouette Books

America's Publisher of Contemporary Romance

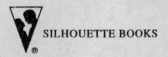 **SILHOUETTE BOOKS**

ISBN-13: 978-0-373-36192-2
ISBN-10:   0-373-36192-0

THE MARRYING KIND

Copyright © 1996 by Beverly Bird

Visit Silhouette Books at www.eHarlequin.com

Printed in U.S.A.

BEVERLY BIRD

has lived in several places in the United States, but she is currently back where her roots began, on an island in New Jersey. Her time is devoted to her family and her writing. She is the author of numerous romance novels, both contemporary and historical. Beverly loves to hear from readers. You can write to her at BvrlyeB@aol.com.

For The Dude—my reason for everything.

Chapter 1

Tessa Hadley-Bryant threw her pen onto the desk in frustration. It skidded to the edge and teetered there.

If it stays on, I'll win this. If it falls off, he'll win.

It fell off. She had been partnered with John Gunner for something like nine hours now, and already she wasn't surprised.

"You know what your problem is, Gunner?" she demanded.

He was standing at the coffee machine directly behind her desk. Tessa didn't turn around to look at him. She didn't have to. She already knew that he would glance over his shoulder at her, and the left corner of his mouth would lift halfway into a grin that could melt the socks off a nun. And now one of his brows would go up. At any moment, he would chuckle.

John Gunner was the sexiest, best-looking man she had ever laid eyes on. *Sorry, Matt,* she added silently, then she flinched. Matt Bryant had been dead for nearly a year now. But talking to him was an old, dear habit, one that was very hard to break. He had been her husband, and they had worked together. They had shared everything, and his loss was still a gnawing hole in her heart.

Unfortunately it didn't gnaw quite deeply enough anymore to keep her from shivering when Gunner's laughter finally came. The sound reminded her of warm, callused hands moving slowly over her skin.

Tessa swiveled around in her chair hard and fast.

"You have no imagination," she went on accusingly.

"Are we talking personally or professionally?" He settled one hip on their shared desk, still grinning. "Because if we're talking personally, I guess I'd have to argue with you."

Tessa kept her eyes deliberately on his face, well above his thigh, which was now inches from her right hand.

"Pardon me?" she managed to say, her mind suddenly blank.

"Is my lack of imagination a personal liability or a professional one, in your esteemed estimation?" he repeated. Damn it, did he *know* the effect he had on her?

Probably, Tessa answered herself. After all, he had the same effect on every woman in the department.

"I wouldn't touch your personal life with a ten-foot pole," she said finally.

Gunner's grin widened. "Too bad."

She shot out of her chair to get her own cup of coffee. She could hear him sipping behind her, could feel his eyes following her with that speculative glint. She had noticed *that* look long before today. She had noticed it before Matt had died, when she had worked in the Homicide Unit of the Philadelphia Police Department side by side with Gunner and his then partner. She hadn't seen a lot of Gunner back then, just enough to be able to recognize and anticipate that glint.

Then again, Gunner tended to reserve that look for blondes, which she definitely was not, so maybe it was just her own imagination this time. Her hair was short and thick and nearly black. She raked a hand through it self-consciously and spilled her coffee.

"Damn." She grabbed a paper towel to try to blot the stain from her sleeve.

"Professional then," Gunner prompted. "Tessa, I'm a *cop*. I deal in facts, not speculation. And don't go getting that stubborn look on your face. You look like a mule getting ready to kick."

"Thank you very much," she said stiffly.

They faced off for easily the ninth or tenth time in as many hours.

Actually it was a mighty intriguing look, Gunner thought. Her chin came up and her eyes got heated enough to sparkle. He had decided first thing this morning, upon being assigned to her, that he liked it. But he didn't think she'd appreciate him telling her so. Tessa was...different. She didn't seem to be the type a man could easily horse around with.

Maybe it was those high-brow Hadley genes, Gunner thought. By his reckoning she was related to just about every politician in the city, past and present. Or maybe it was the fact that she had been widowed last year. Either way, she had a quiet class about her that he didn't know quite how to handle. Yet.

He took in her flawless skin, her short, black hair tucked behind seashell ears, the clear blue eyes. She was tall and trim, without that overly athletic hard look that so many female cops seemed prone to. Not, Gunner thought, that there weren't a few very nice bodies among them. But this one was—

"Huh?" He realized that she was still talking to him.

"I said, don't talk to me about being stubborn. Not when you won't even entertain the possibility that Christian Benami might have killed his own wife."

It was the first file to land on their shared desk, the reason Tessa had finally been reassigned to Homicide. She shared the victim's blue blood, was well acquainted with her social circle. In spite of that, or maybe because of it, she and Gunner had been at odds over the case all day.

"I've entertained it plenty," Gunner argued. "You've been yakking my ear off about it nonstop."

"*Yakking?*" Tessa fought hard not to sputter, and ended by clamping her jaw shut.

"I just want some solid reasoning before I accept that he did it."

"He *must* have."

"Now there's solid reasoning." He grinned again. "Why? Because Daphne Benami was rich and Christian wasn't? That's not motive. And it would take a *big* stretch of imagination to put him in two places at one time, no matter how much of a social climber you seem to think he is."

"Not necessarily. I mean, maybe he *wasn't* in two places at one time. Maybe he just manages his time exceptionally well."

Gunner moved away from their desk. When he paced that way, he reminded her of a caged animal—restless and dangerously unpredictable. She tried not to watch him and failed.

He was a rugged-looking man, with a lopsided grin that made him appealing rather than intimidating. He had incredible shoulders—they could well be the sexiest thing about him. Other than his eyes. They were the color of smoke, and they usually seemed to hide a laugh. He had dark hair that was just shaggy enough to make a woman's fingers itch to straighten it out. Tessa had never seen the back of his neck or his collar.

She knew that their captain didn't like that, and their chief inspector probably liked it even less, but somehow Gunner kept squeaking by without getting a haircut. Even if they had written him up, Tessa knew it would be his most mild infraction to date. In his six years with the department, Gunner had gone through three other partners, three unmarked cars, one service revolver, and—reportedly—every female employee the city had to offer. All things considered, Tessa figured that their superiors had decided they could live with his hair just fine.

Also, she allowed, for all his eccentricities, Gunner was supposed to be good, *very* good at what he did. So what were a few shaggy locks as long as he kept getting his convictions?

She finally managed to find something fascinating about the coffee in her cup, but then she looked up sharply again when she smelled smoke.

"Do you have to do that?" she cried as he inhaled on the cigarette. "Why do you have to do that at my desk?"

"It's *our* desk." He looked genuinely surprised.

Point taken, Tessa thought. Philadelphia was a very big city with one Homicide Unit having jurisdiction over all of it. A *big* Homicide Unit, in keeping with the size of their turf. Many large cities had detectives assigned to each precinct or district, but in Philly, they were all squeezed in here, on a single floor of the Police Administration Building.

Both space and funds were at a premium. Ergo, partners shared their desks, supplies, city cars. About all they had to call their own were their guns.

That didn't mean she had to give up without a fight.

"If I die of lung cancer, I'm coming back to haunt you."

He flashed her another of those grins. She'd make one hell of a ghost, he thought, and couldn't imagine that he'd mind having her keep him awake nights. But he went and sat on someone else's desk, a respectable distance from her.

"Anyway," he went on, "here's my problem. Christian Benami would need wings to get back and forth between the Four Seasons Hotel and his home fast enough to kill his wife without any one of fifty people noticing that he was missing from that party."

"One hundred people," Tessa muttered. She was scrupulously honest, even when it wasn't to her advantage. The district cops who had first caught the case had taken statements from close to a hundred people putting Christian Benami at the Heart Association Ball on the night of December 26, two nights ago now.

Allegedly, Daphne had stayed home on the night of the Ball, complaining of a migraine. Christian had gone ahead to the charity function. When he'd gotten home shortly before one o'clock in the morning, he'd found his wife dangling from their dining room chandelier.

The coroner's report wasn't in yet, but their captain, Roger Kennery, had a hunch that it was going to be interesting. The hunch was strong enough that he had finally called Tessa back from her exile on desk duty in the Fifth District to work on it.

"He could have done it *before* he went to the party," Tessa insisted. "He could have hung her from the chandelier, put on his tux and hightailed it a few blocks to the Four Seasons where he was fashionably late."

"It's possible. Hell, anything's *possible* in this business. But probable? I think you're reaching, Princess."

Tessa stiffened instinctively at his lazy use of her nickname.

Before Matt had died, nearly everyone in the Homicide Unit had called her that at one time or another. She understood it even as she hated it. She was certainly the only detective among them with a law degree, a multimillion dollar trust fund, a brother who was the D.A., an uncle who was a Superior Court judge and a grandfather who had been the governor. It had taken her a long time to win over her co-workers, to get them to accept her for the woman she was and not for her name. And even then, some of them still spoke the nickname rather bitterly and disparagingly.

Gunner didn't say it that way. He said it in a...warm way. An intimate way that made her belly roll over.

Gunner watched her with both brows up as she began to whip back and forth beside their desk. "You're just being a snob," he went on equably.

"I am not!"

"Sure you are. Your Hadley is showing. You're bothered because Daphne Benami was a snooty little rich girl who married beneath her—"

"Well, Christian never had a dime to his name! She met him in Paris and married him there before her family knew what was going on. And Daphne was always *very* wary about men wanting her for her money. You forget that I knew her."

"Nope, you haven't let me forget it for a minute. That's why I say you're irrationally obsessed with this case."

"I am *not*."

He shrugged lazily, a gesture that she was already learning was pure Gunner.

Tessa crossed her arms over her chest to face him.

"Christian married her for her money," she said obstinately. "Then he killed her so he could have it all to himself. There's over a million dollars in insurance money at stake here, plus the rest of her estate. Gunner, her estate's got to be worth—"

"Oh, don't be such a cynic."

"Damn it, Gunner—"

She wasn't so proper or blue-blooded when she got frustrated, he noticed. He watched a faint flush creep up her neck into her cheeks, ever so gently staining that ivory skin. He decided he liked the effect.

"Look," he said calmly. "We haven't turned up anything, not one shred of evidence, not one single rumor, that their marriage was anything but blissful. So even if he *did* marry her for her money, then why not just *stay* married to her? There was no reason for him to kill the goose to get to the golden eggs—he had full access to them anyway. And let me tell you, given those pictures of Daphne we got in this morning, I'd have to say she'd be a lot more use to him alive than dead. *I'd* sure prefer to have her warm in my bed rather than cold and six feet under."

Incredibly Tessa felt her mouth dry out. It wasn't that she was a prude. She had shared squad room humor with the best of them. She had survived the Police Academy. Anyone else could have made the same observation and she wouldn't have thought twice about it.

It was just...something about Gunner, she realized. It was something about the *way* he said it. She ran a manicured finger inside the neckline of her silk blouse. Suddenly it felt warm and very tight.

"Well, I don't think Christian agreed with you," she said finally.

"A hell of a lot of people say he was at that party, Tess," Gunner said quietly.

She sat down again and sighed. "I don't like the way he looks, Gunner," she admitted quietly. "Did you notice the way his eyes shifted when we went over there this morning? He wouldn't quite meet mine dead-on. Because he knows who I am, and he knows that I'm not likely to believe his marriage was purely some kind of fairy tale. Daphne was a *Carlson*, Gunner. Do you know what that means?"

He cocked a brow. "Nope, but I guess you're going to tell me."

Damn right she was, Tessa thought. "The Carlsons don't marry men like Christian Benami. And they definitely don't marry men like that then immediately write them into their will as sole beneficiary. He *had* to have twisted her arm somehow."

"Maybe with some prime loving?"

Her heart hitched again at the slow, intimate drawl he rolled the words out with.

"What about the Hadleys?" he asked suddenly.

Tessa blinked. "What about us?"

"Would a Hadley be expected to marry someone like Matt Bryant—a *cop*, even one with a law degree?" Matt had had one, too, Gunner remembered. In fact, he was pretty sure they'd met in law school.

Tessa paled. "You don't pull any punches, do you?"

"It's a big, bad world out there, Princess. Best way to fight it is to be honest with yourself and your partner. I was just trying to make a point and get a handle on your motivations here. I'm trying to figure out why you want to go after Benami so damn badly. And you know what I'm starting to think? You're already too emotionally involved in this thing. You're thinking that Daphne could have been you, I'd bet. *Did* you write Matt into your will as sole beneficiary?"

Tessa flinched. "Yes, but—"

"So what are you thinking here? That there but for the grace of God goeth you?"

It was true, she admitted uncomfortably.

"You're letting it skew your judgment, Princess. You're not seeing the forest for the trees."

That *wasn't* true. "It's a gut instinct," she argued. "I really think Christian did it."

Gunner blew out his breath and studied his coffee. "All right."

"All right?" Her jaw dropped. They'd been going around in circles on this all day. Why was he suddenly giving in now?

"Maybe," he amended. "I'll make a bet with you."

"What kind of bet?" she asked warily.

"The Medical Examiner's report should be in anytime now," he went on, then he cocked his head a little bit as though he was trying to remember something. "As a matter of fact, I know her. Doc Byerly is a fine lady."

Tessa groaned and rolled her eyes. "Most women are, Gunner, where you're concerned."

"Nah. You're letting that imagination of yours get away with you again."

"Go listen in the women's bathroom."

He grinned. "Really? They talk about me in there?"

"Often," she said dryly.

He shook his head. "That's amazing." He wondered privately what they could be saying. All he knew for sure was that *their* imaginations had to be top-notch, because he honestly hadn't been to bed with any of them.

He shook his head to clear it. "Anyway, about Angela."

"Angela?"

"Byerly. The Medical Examiner. Get with the program, Princess."

She continued to eye him suspiciously. "Okay. The M.E. So what's this bet that has to do with her?"

"If Angela gives us any physical evidence whatsoever that Christian did this, then I won't smoke in your presence and contaminate your pretty little lungs for a whole week."

"And if she doesn't?"

He thought about it. "You can buy me a beer. At the establishment of my choice."

Her eyes narrowed. Already she knew him well enough to guess that he probably had a card up his sleeve.

"You've never said who *you* think did it," she realized aloud.

"All day you've just kept saying that it wasn't Benami. Don't tell me you're buying into the suicide angle."

He looked at her levelly. "Nope. If it was suicide, you'd still be uptown filing reports on dog poop."

Tessa flushed. She had badgered their captain for months to let her come back to Homicide. She had been exiled—she still couldn't think of it in any terms but that—to the Fifth District after Matt had been killed.

"I'm just warning against closing our eyes to other possible scenarios." Gunner hesitated. "You're rusty, Princess. That's all. And you're letting your heart rule your head here. It's no big deal," he added quietly when he watched her stiffen. "Hell, I'd be rusty, too, if I'd spent nearly a year on desk duty. But I didn't, so I'm suggesting that we make this bet just for the hell of it, just to see where it takes us."

Rusty? He was right and she knew it, but she hated it. She looked at her watch in a deliberate attempt to end the conversation.

It was past six o'clock. She made a move for the coat tree. "I'm going home."

Gunner stepped quickly in front of her, blocking her way. "Come on, Princess. What have you got to lose?"

Tessa shrugged, dodging around him.

"I'll sweeten the pot. If Angela gives us the evidence you want, I'll go *two* weeks without smoking."

Tessa hesitated. Now *that* was a deal. She had nothing to lose but a few bucks for a beer. Still, the people who had dubbed her "Princess" had vastly underestimated her.

"Forever," she countered.

"Huh?" He looked disbelieving.

"No cigarettes in my presence *ever*. Certainly not at my—our—desk."

"You drive a hard bargain, Princess."

Her chin came up a notch. Something in her eyes grinned. It was fascinating, he realized.

"Take it or leave it, Gunner."

"Or what?"

"Or I'll *yak* all day tomorrow, too."

"I'll take the bet."

"Wise man." Actually, Tessa thought he was either a bone-deep gambler, or dead sure that she was wrong.

He held her coat out for her. Tessa took it from him rather than let him help her on with it. That might have meant touching him in some fashion. And she had decided at nine o'clock this morning that that was going to be a definite do-not-do with John Gunner. The Homicide Unit walls had eyes. If he so much as touched her, the department gossips would sink their teeth into it and run with it in a hurry. Tessa had decided right off the bat that the best and only way to maintain a good working relationship with Gunner was to keep him at a personal arm's length.

She wondered how buying him a beer would fit into that, and her heart did something that almost felt like a skip.

Gunner pulled his own jacket—comfortably worn black leather—off the tree. "I'll call the M.E. tonight and see how close they are to finishing the autopsy. Maybe we can run over there first thing in the morning."

Tessa thought about it, about how much running they would actually have to do. The M.E.'s office wasn't far. She nodded.

Granted, she thought, Gunner had only actually *wrecked* one of the cars whose demise was listed in his file. He had parked another in the wrong place in a city lot and it had been tagged as inoperable and towed off and destroyed. And Tessa thought she'd heard that the third car had been bombed by an ex-felon convicted on Gunner's testimony.

Gunner held the office door open for her just as Becky Trumball, their captain's secretary, appeared there. Gunner winked at the woman and strolled off down the hall, and Becky pivoted to watch him appreciatively.

"My, oh my," she murmured.

"He pulls his pants on one leg at a time, just like every other man. Trust me," Tessa responded tightly.

Becky looked back at her fast. "You've *witnessed* this?"

Tessa was taken aback. "No! Nor do I want to."

Becky studied her a moment, then she shook her head. "You won't stay immune to him for long, honey. Mark my words." She handed her a file. "It's that hooker who was killed up in North Central last night. Kennery says to give it to Mel and Jeffrey."

Tessa took the file and hugged it to her chest for a moment. "So have you...uh, witnessed it?" Tessa didn't care, of course. She was just curious.

"What?"

"Gunner putting his pants on." She already regretted that she had asked. Becky seemed to be struggling with herself.

The woman finally shrugged. "A lady's got to have some secrets." But Tessa thought her voice sounded pained.

No, she guessed, Becky had probably *not* witnessed it, and she was undoubtedly the only one in the department who hadn't, with the exception of Tessa herself.

Becky spun out the door again. Tessa went to put the file on Melanie Kaminski's desk.

Immune? It didn't feel like it. It didn't feel like it much at all.

Chapter 2

It was snowing when she got outside, small, stinging flakes that wouldn't amount to much, but they would definitely make her walk a miserable one. Tessa pulled her collar up and lowered her head into the icy wind instead. Her brownstone was in Elfreth's Alley, five blocks from the Police Administration Building. She'd be halfway there before she found an empty cab at this time of night, she thought. Besides, even at its worst, she loved Philadelphia.

She passed a vendor on the corner of Seventh and Race Streets, smiling at the smell of the soft pretzels the city was renowned for. Fragrant steam rose off them in the frigid air. A teenage boy waved a copy of the *Daily News* at her, but she wasn't much of a sports fan, and that was the paper's forte. Further on she had to step around a homeless person who was already bunked down for the night on one of the sidewalk grates. The P.D. had a separate, special detail for vagrants. She knew someone would be around to collect the man shortly and take him to a shelter.

Philadelphia was...Philadelphia, she mused. A little less hostile than New York, much less transplanted than L.A. The weather was fractionally better than in Chicago, and the people were less affected than in San Francisco. Some obscure, nonsensical survey had recently revealed that the merchants and the cabbies here were the most honest of any major American city. Tessa grinned crookedly. If that was the case, then she *definitely* didn't want to live anywhere else.

Drivers blared their horns just as loudly as those in Manhattan, and people rushed through center city with the same determination, but Tessa was convinced that there was a gentler mingling of smells, sounds and impressions here. There was a stronger sense of history. Her brownstone was half a block from Betsy Ross's house, two blocks north of Penn's Landing. It was another handful from the Liberty Bell and Independence Hall. When the weather was good, she sometimes detoured by that way, if only to watch the tourists.

But the weather wasn't good. She kept an eye out for a cab, but she had been right—she was a block away from home before she saw one that was available. She jogged the rest of the way, rushed up the stoop and fumbled for her keys in her briefcase.

Maxwell, her cat, was just inside the door. He greeted her with a highly insulted squawk and she grinned down at him. "It was for a good cause." She hung her coat up and dropped her briefcase into the antique Louis XIV chair in the entryway. "I'm back, Max. I really worked today. And you ought to get a gander at the guy I'm working *with*."

She started for the kitchen at the back of the house. Maxwell forgot his temper to trudge after her curiously.

"No," she went on, "you haven't met him, and you never will." She reached into a cabinet for a can of cat food. "But he was why I was late, so I thought you might care."

She spooned food into his bowl, then she went still, the can suspended over the dish. *Oh, God, now she was talking to the cat.* Not that there weren't thousands of people—probably *hundreds* of thousands—all over Philadelphia talking to their cats right about now, but when you had been widowed less than a year, and you were only twenty-nine years old, every response, every impulse, became suspect.

That was perhaps the only thing she had learned in grief counseling after Matt had been killed. The therapists had jumped on every moderately unusual reflex she possessed. Which was why she had stayed with the counseling less than three months. Their badgering still left her a little bit paranoid about almost every move she made, and she hated living that way.

She straightened away from the cat's bowl and tossed the can into the trash compactor. She decided she wasn't hungry herself, but then she had to pause to examine *that* reflex, too. Was she depressed, or was it merely that obscenely loaded hot dog Gunner had talked her into at three o'clock?

Probably the hot dog.

She shook her head and looked briefly at the canister full of odd and exotic tea bags she had collected over the years. For one of the rare times in her life, she went into the dining room for a bottle of wine instead. She was celebrating, after all.

She poured herself a careful half glass of cabernet and took it upstairs. She turned on the tub in the master bath, generously adding some bubble bath. As she passed back through the bedroom, she scowled. The grief counselors had urged her to sell the brownstone, but she was stubborn and she loved the place. She *had* changed the bedroom since Matt had been gone. The bed they'd shared was in the guest room now, and she'd bought cherry antiques and brass for this room. But Matt still lingered somehow. Tessa closed her eyes for a moment, letting herself remember him.

Suddenly she panicked.

Her heart started pounding hard. For a second, maybe only a fraction of a second, she had a hard time calling back his face. She didn't *want* to lose him...but on New Year's it would be a whole year since he had been gone.

She slipped quickly out of her clothing, grimacing again at the coffee stain on the sleeve of her silk blouse. She went back to the bathroom and slid into the hot, foamy water, and this time when she closed her eyes, Matt's face came to her more easily, if only because she worked at it.

Unfortunately it was as she had last seen him. Dying.

She shivered, though the water hadn't had a chance to cool yet. It had happened at Tommy's Grill after a quiet New Year's Eve dinner last year. Matt had been working, but she was off. He had used his meal break to meet her at Tommy's because it was a special occasion.

They had left the restaurant, replete and happy, talking about what they planned to do when Matt got home. Then they'd stepped outside onto the sidewalk into the middle of a mugging. Matt had interceded. It hadn't been immediately apparent whether or not the perpetrator had had a gun. Matt had hesitated going for his own under the circumstances. And then the bullets had started spitting. Cracking. Whining.

By then, it had been too late. Tessa hadn't had her own gun with her. She'd only been able to watch and scream. And scream.

She missed him, she thought, her throat closing hard now. Sometimes she still missed him abominably. But she had thought she was over the worst of it when she had ditched the therapists after three months. She had finally stopped dreaming about Matt by then. She had even stopped waking up in the night, her heart slamming, her palms sweating, the sheets wadded up in her hands. She had come to terms with it. Her husband had been a cop. And sometimes cops got shot. Life went on. Matt would have *wanted* hers to go on without too many missteps.

Tessa had always prided herself on her common sense. She'd told the Department psychologist—Gale Storm—that she could deal with it. What she hadn't told her, what she had never admitted to anyone, was that she secretly wondered if she could have shot that night when Matt was killed, if she'd had a gun. She didn't tell her that she often tore herself up inside wondering if there had been something—*anything*— she could have done to save him, and that when she thought about that part of it, her heart still slammed and her palms still sweated. When Gale had suggested that she might harbor such feelings, Tess had denied it vehemently, with all the haughty disdain and dignity of a Hadley.

But perhaps Gale had guessed. To Tessa's utter horror, the woman had recommended against letting her go back on active duty in Homicide. And that was the other reason she had stopped seeing her—pure resentment and anger.

"Matt was down almost before you stepped through the door. The whole department knows it." That was what Gale had said. *"Still, I'm concerned that you'll freeze up the first time somebody fires again if you come back too soon, or worse, you'll start shooting blindly out of rage. Either one would be an understandable reaction."*

Kennery and her chief inspector had listened to Gale. They'd put her on desk duty in the Fifth, the district with the lowest crime rate in the entire city. She'd spent nine months writing up reports of neighborhood spats and she-said-he-saids. Then Daphne Ben-ami had died.

Tessa's mouth curved into a smile as she sank a little deeper into the bath. Her exile was finally over. But now she had to deal with John Gunner.

The department maverick, she thought, the Don Juan of detectives, destroyer of automobiles, loser of service revolvers, forever on probation. To be fair, though, he hadn't seemed all that bad today. And his personal reputation was his own business. She would simply keep him at a personal arm's length so that *his* horrible reputation didn't become *hers.*

The phone began ringing in the bedroom, jolting her. She thought about letting the machine pick it up, but the water was getting cold and the wine was making her drowsy. She got out of the tub, grabbing a towel on her way into the bedroom, carrying the last of her wine. Gunner's slow chuckle answered her breathless hello.

"Am I interrupting something? Do you have some erotic secret life going on over there, Princess?"

"Of course not. I was in the tub." She felt her face go hot and was glad he wasn't there to see it. She took a quick gulp of the wine.

His silence was just a little too long, as though he was trying to picture it.

"Well, listen," he said finally, his grin in his voice. "I just talked to Angela. We can see her at nine o'clock tomorrow morning. She'll have the results of the autopsy tonight sometime. How about if I pick you up at eight-thirty?"

Nice, straight, strong lines, keeping him at a personal distance. She had absolutely no idea where he lived and she wouldn't invite him to her brownstone.

"I— No. I'll, uh...I'll meet you at the office."

"Tomorrow's Saturday, Tess," Gunner reminded her. "We don't have to report in."

"This isn't a nine-to-five job," she snapped, then she sighed. "Speaking of which, that makes this Friday night. Don't you have something better to do than nitpick with me, Gunner?"

"Yeah," he said finally. "I've got somewhere I'm supposed to be."

"So go be there. I'll see you in the morning."

"Right."

There was a click as he hung up, but Tessa stood for a moment with the phone in her hand. She wondered why the brownstone suddenly sounded so quiet. Wondered why she felt as if she were the only person in the city who was home alone on a Friday night.

What a way to celebrate being back in the fold.

She drained the last of her wine and stared thoughtfully and sadly down into the empty glass, then she decided on another.

"Here's to Homicide," she murmured quietly.

Maxwell meowed.

Tessa stared into her closet the following morning for a long time before she settled on black jeans, a turtleneck sweater and a heavy wool jacket. If Gunner's driving was as bad as everyone said it was—bombs and bad parking notwithstanding—then she reasoned it would be easier to scramble from a wreck if she wasn't wearing heels.

She fed Maxwell and read most of the morning *Philadelphia Inquirer,* all before seven o'clock, and refused to think what that might mean.

She walked into the Homicide Detectives' office at a quarter to eight. Gunner had beaten her there anyway. He was sitting on the corner of Melanie Kaminski's desk. Tessa picked up scraps of their conversation as she crossed to them, and realized that they were talking about the new North Central case.

She was more interested in Mel's faint but discernible blush.

How could Gunner have that effect on *every* woman? Tessa wondered wildly. We don't all go for the same type of man, she reasoned. Some liked blond, aristocratic types. Others went for the rough, dark looks. But it was beginning to seem that *everyone* got hot and bothered over John Gunner.

Then, watching him, she realized what it was. It wasn't just his looks, though they certainly had impact. It was the way he used them, with lazy, unstudied sex appeal. When he smiled at a woman, he made her feel as if he had never smiled in just that way for anyone else before.

Potent stuff, she thought. She wished she hadn't worn a turtleneck. Suddenly it felt tight around her throat, and that gaze wasn't even directed at her.

Gunner looked up at the sound of her footsteps. "Hey, Princess."

A tremor scooted through her. He said it so...intimately.

"Hey yourself," she answered carefully. "Ready?"

He nodded and slid off the desk, then he stopped to get a cup of coffee to take with him. While his back was to her, Tessa let her gaze coast over him again. There was something about Gunner on the morning of an official day off that was both comfortable and titillating. He hadn't shaved. He wore very tight jeans. It was below freezing outside, but he seemed comfortable in a T-shirt that outlined every broad, hard inch of those shoulders and his biceps. He smelled like something woodsy, she thought, sniffing, as though he had just stepped out of the shower, which he probably had. The ends of his hair were still wet.

Immune? she thought again, then added an extra warning to herself. *Don't look at him.*

He grabbed his jacket. Tessa moved fast to catch up with him, and he held the door wide for her.

They picked their car up in the garage and Gunner swung it south on Eighth Street. Tessa buckled her seat belt. She started to ask him why they were heading south, but Gunner was apparently a morning person and that distracted her. He switched the radio on to a rock station and began singing, pausing now and again to drum his hands energetically on the steering wheel.

"Has anyone ever mentioned to you that you're tone deaf?" she muttered.

"Can't hear myself. Doesn't matter."

"Ah." She slid down a little in her seat so that she wouldn't have to watch the parked cars rushing at them. "I'd feel better if you kept both hands on the wheel, Gunner."

He stopped drumming, but only long enough to speed through an intersection while the light was still marginally yellow.

"So how do you know Dr. Byerly?" Tessa asked. She really didn't care. She was just making conversation, she told herself. If he was talking, he couldn't sing.

Gunner seemed to think about it. "We go way back," he answered finally. He was discreet, she'd give him that much.

"Did you know her before you joined the department?"

"Yeah."

"So what does she look like?" Angela Byerly had taken over

the post while Tessa had been at the Fifth. She hadn't had occasion to meet her yet.

Gunner shot her an amused glance. "What difference does it make?"

"I'm just curious."

"She looks sort of like a young Dyan Cannon."

"So she's blond."

"Last time I saw her. You got a thing about blondes, Princess?"

"I think *you* do."

This time when he looked at her he was grinning fully. "As a matter of record, I've gone out with just as many brunettes." And one memorable, natural redhead, he mused, but that had been a very long time ago.

"Gunner!"

His gaze shot forward again. He was bearing down fast on a garbage truck. He swung around it and narrowly missed an on-coming cab.

"Oh, my God," Tessa groaned. Then, in spite of herself, she laughed. The reflex shimmered through her, feeling good, whispering all the way down to her toes.

Gunner grinned. "Angela's a good kid," he went on without missing a beat. "Well, not a kid anymore, I guess. She's my age."

Which put her at about thirty-six, Tessa figured.

"She's from the old neighborhood."

"So you've remained friends with her all this time?"

"The best."

Well, she had asked, Tessa thought. "What were you doing then?"

"Doing? When?"

"For a living, before you joined the department." She wasn't sure why she was asking. She really was convinced that she didn't need to know that sort of thing in order to work with him. But if he hadn't joined their ranks until six years ago, he would have been about thirty then and presumably he'd had another career. Besides, talking seemed to keep his mind off the radio.

Gunner passed a slow-moving car. "I worked for my father-in-law."

That startled her. "Father-in-*law?* You're married?"

"Not anymore. Why? Interested?"

She blushed and decided to ignore that question altogether. "What did you do for your father-in-law?"

"He had an accounting firm."

"You were an *accountant?*" She couldn't help laughing again, this time until her stomach hurt, then she sobered abruptly.

She hadn't laughed a lot since Matt had died. She felt an odd, uncomfortable queasiness in the pit of her stomach that she should do so twice in five minutes this morning.

She just couldn't see John Gunner behind a desk, though, in a suit and tie, no matter how she tried. Granted, their partnership was only a day old, but so far all she'd ever seen him do was sit *on* desks.

"Don't tell me," she said finally. "He fired you."

"Nope, she did."

Tessa sobered. "Why?" Given Gunner's reputation, maybe he had cheated on the woman, she thought. And if that were the case, she decided that she'd really prefer not knowing.

But Gunner looked sad and thoughtful. "Elaine wanted to grow up to be just like you."

"Like me? How?"

"I don't know. Rich."

"I live off my salary," she said indignantly. He shot her another glance. "Would you please keep your eyes on the road?"

"You didn't buy a place in Elfreth's Alley on a cop's salary," he observed finally.

Something skittered through her blood. "How do you know where I live? I'm not in the phone book."

"Nope. Hadley-types usually aren't," he agreed, "at least from what I've been able to tell. It's in your file."

"You read my file?"

"I wanted to know what I was getting into."

"Personnel isn't supposed to give out that sort of stuff," she said stiffly, then she sighed. He was right, of course. "Hadley-types" tended to be very private. A certain aloofness had been drummed into her from the cradle. Silly, really, she thought, and a regular nuisance when you stepped down into the real world, a world she had positively ached to rejoin for months now.

"I guess it sort of depends on how you ask them," Gunner was saying.

Them, Tessa thought, was Nancy Hart, the woman in charge of employee records. She decided she didn't want to know what methods Gunner had used on the woman...and she definitely didn't want to feel the flutter that came from realizing that he had been curious enough about her to use those methods.

"Matt and I bought the brownstone together," she said suddenly, then she scowled, feeling the beginnings of a headache. She wondered why she felt so compelled to pull Matt into this conversation.

Gunner nodded unconcernedly. "Well, Elaine wanted a place just like that. Or one in Society Hill. And she wanted me to work eighty hours a week to take her there. I just couldn't see the point."

"Because you loved her, maybe?"

Gunner scowled at her. "Hell, Princess, I was twenty-five. I didn't know love from baloney."

"Do you now?" *Why was she asking this?* "Never mind. Go back to singing."

He switched the radio off instead. "I haven't had cause to think about it in a good long time," he said honestly. "But no, I'd kind of have to doubt if I've ever been in love. Maybe I'm just not capable of it. Maybe love's just too confined, too stringent for my tastes. Marriage definitely was." He paused, obviously giving it a great deal of consideration. Then he shrugged. "Anyway, there's no sense in trying to pretend that a relationship is something it's not. So I let Elaine go with no hard feelings, and since then, I just keep things simple."

She wanted to pursue the subject—and knew it was far wiser not to.

A moment later she realized that he drove as if he knew South Philly with his eyes closed. It was a colorful area, settled heavily by Italian-Americans. The whole city had pockets of strong ethnic culture, but South Philly had the Italian Market with its delicious smells and startling bursts of sound, and some of the best pasta she'd ever encountered anywhere. It also had its share of organized crime hits. She had been down here a few times before she'd been relegated to the Fifth.

She wondered if this was the area of the city Gunner lived in and bit her tongue against asking. She had already crossed over her lines enough this morning.

And what the devil were they doing in *South* Philly anyway?

Gunner darted the car through back streets and finally screeched to a stop on Oregon Avenue, in front of a long line of middle-class row homes. "What's this?" she asked dumbly.

"Angela's place."

"Angela's...her *house?* Why did we come here? What was wrong with her office?" She'd felt as though she'd suddenly opened her eyes to find they'd landed on the moon. She'd been so preoccupied with their conversation that she hadn't even wondered what they were doing driving so far.

"She's off today, Princess," Gunner said patiently. "It's Saturday."

"She's a medical examiner!" Tessa protested senselessly. "She doesn't *get* days off!"

"Nope, not when there's an autopsy requiring her personal attention. But this one's done, and there's no reason why she should have to go into the office today just to talk to us. If she were anyone else, she would have pushed us off on one of her assistants or held us off until Monday. As it is, she brought the Benami file home with her last night as a special favor to me."

"I...oh." There wasn't much she could say to that.

She got out of the car. It was still early enough that there weren't many children around, but there was evidence of their presence—bicycles chained to stoop railings, and a basketball sat on top of an overturned trash can.

"This way," Gunner said. Then one of the doors opened and Angela Byerly bounded out.

Tessa felt her stomach tighten hard. She had already known that the M.E. was going to be blond and beautiful. But she wasn't prepared for someone so...exuberant. Given her job, Tessa had expected the woman to be more grim and subdued. But Angela fairly hurled herself at Gunner. She wrapped her arms around his neck and he gave her a quick spin before he put her on her feet again.

Tessa buttoned her jacket self-consciously and forced herself to walk up the sidewalk to join them. She offered Angela a hand and a weak smile.

"Hi. I'm Tessa Hadley-Bryant. It's a pleasure to meet you."

"Hadley?" Predictable things happened to the woman's expression. "As in—"

"That's right," Gunner supplied, interrupting. "She's a real

blue-blooded princess.'' It would have stung, Tessa thought, except he winked at her. God, he was good.

They went up the steps together, hand in hand. Tessa followed
behind them, feeling awkward and uncomfortably hot in her wool
jacket. She wondered for the first time if she hadn't made a big,
big mistake coming back to Homicide under these circumstances.
What was another month or two in the Fifth District? If she had
waited awhile longer, Kennery would have brought her back eventually, and surely another partner would have become available
for her.

But then again, she had *laughed*—twice. And she had been a
good five miles into the south part of the city before it had even
occurred to her to wonder what they were doing there.

She was suddenly convinced that no matter how many rules she
devised for herself, working with John Gunner was not going to
be a good idea.

Chapter 3

Angela led them to her kitchen. Her hips swayed in a perfect, sultry rhythm that Tessa had never quite been able to master, certainly not in a private, Catholic school where the nuns were always poking at her spine and reminding her to stand up *straight*. The woman wore a long yellow skirt that probably wouldn't have made it past the sisters, either. It was filmy and vaguely sheer, swirling about her calves.

Tessa realized that something about the woman was positively jingling. She scowled, then she saw that underneath Angela's cascading blond curls, tiny strings of bells dangled from each ear.

Tessa decided that she had never felt so plain, so colorless, in her life.

She wished desperately that she had worn something else, something besides jeans and wool. Then again, there wasn't a thing in her closet that would even come close to the outfit that Angela Byerly wore, and she couldn't imagine why she should care. Matt had liked the way she dressed.

She hugged herself as Gunner made himself comfortable at the breakfast bar. He looked over at her and she realized that he was wearing that dangerous half smile again.

"Problem, Princess?"

Tessa's spine snapped straight, as though one of those nuns had just run her ruler down it. "No, of course not." She slid carefully onto the stool next to his.

Angela went to the coffeepot and Tessa looked at Daphne Benami's file on the bar. She itched to open it, to *know*.

"So," she prompted as Angela deposited a pair of mugs on either side of the folder. "What did you find out?"

"First of all, I had Ed Thackery do the actual cutting," Angela began, leaning prettily against the opposite side of the counter.

Tessa nodded, noticing the woman's vibrant pink fingernails.

"Ed found that the cause of death was asphyxiation due to strangulation," Angela informed.

"No surprise there," Tessa responded. She was relieved to find that her tone was short and professional. "She hanged. But was it her idea, or did somebody decide it for her? And if so, *what* somebody?"

"Oh, I'd say someone definitely decided for her. Ed also found rope fibers on both of her wrists," the M.E. explained. "Since she didn't hang by her wrists, and the fibers didn't match those we found on her neck, we sent them on to Forensics."

"So somebody tied her up first before they tied her *up?*" Gunner asked, thinking aloud.

"That would be my guess," Angela agreed. "We found pretty high levels of two different sedatives in her blood as well."

Tessa's mind began working. She forgot what Angela looked like. She forgot about Gunner and how he had made her laugh. Her thoughts veered, picked, considered...and it felt *so good.*

"So Daphne fought," she said aloud.

"Or her killer just expected she would," mused Gunner.

"I wonder if he might have thought that he could just lift her up to that chandelier, or maybe he even did it by gunpoint to coerce her, but she went wild," Tessa said. "Or at least much more wild than he had anticipated. Daphne was always...quiet," she remembered. "Docile. Complacent. So maybe she surprised him and he had to tie her hands to keep her from striking him, and sedate her to make her drowsy enough that she couldn't use the rest of her body to fight him, either."

"Could be," Gunner agreed.

Tessa finally looked at Angela again. "How long before her

death was she given the sedatives? Were they the kind she could have administered herself because of her headache?"

"Librium and Seconal."

"Not necessarily headache stuff, but maybe she was in enough pain that she just wanted to sleep," Gunner observed.

"My best guess says that she took the stuff—or it was given to her—about an hour, maybe an hour and a half prior to her death," Angela told them.

Poor Daphne. Had she genuinely loved that man, or had she just been swept off her feet by him? Either way, oh, God, she must have felt so betrayed!

"What else?" she asked Angela a little too sharply. "Did you find anything else?"

"Lots of little things, maybe important, maybe not. I made a copy of the report for you guys," Angela answered. "But I tend to agree with your assessment that she fought pretty hard, at least on an evidentiary basis. I don't think binding her was merely a precautionary thing. For starters, the fibers were embedded, like on her neck—indicating that her assailant was angry, or at least that a good bit of force was used. There were also traces of skin and blood beneath the nail of the middle finger of her left hand."

Tessa went still. "Did you type the blood?"

"Of course," Angela said. "It was AB-Negative."

"And Daphne was..." Gunner prompted.

"B-Positive," Angela said triumphantly.

Tessa's heart began beating hard. This was almost too easy.

"So we get a blood type on Benami, and then I guess you can throw out your cigarettes."

"Not so fast, Princess." Gunner patted his pocket. Angela's gaze moved curiously between them. "We've got a little way to go on this yet. It'll still keep us occupied for a while."

Tessa felt her blood chill. He was so cocky, so confident. Had he set her up?

She remembered thinking yesterday that Gunner would never make a bet that involved not smoking if there was any real chance that he could lose it. He had already known the autopsy results, she decided. After all, Angela was some kind of a...a personal friend. Suddenly, Tessa would have bet money that Gunner already knew that Benami did not have AB-Negative blood.

Except that didn't make sense, because he really didn't stand to gain much if he won this deal. A *beer?*

Then she thought she understood.

The room grew immediately, cloyingly hot. "You...you orchestrated this," she managed to say.

Gunner shot a brow up at her.

"You don't care about this stupid bet," she said. "You were just...playing with me. Keeping me preoccupied with it so I wouldn't—" What? she wondered wildly. Then she knew that, too. *Be assailed with memories of Matt.*

He had done it so she wouldn't be crippled by remembrances of the last time she sat in that Homicide Unit and of the man who had often stopped by to sit on the corner of her desk *then.* That was the only reason Gunner had argued with her all day yesterday, keeping her preoccupied. It was the reason he had kept throwing her curves—*you're rusty, Princess*—and why he had challenged her at nearly every turn. The bet was just part and parcel of keeping her on her toes so that she wouldn't feel, hurt, remember.

She shot to her feet.

"Let's get one thing straight, Gunner, right now, right from the start." She was vaguely aware of Angela's gaze flying back and forth between them now, and that her hands were trembling, but her temper couldn't let her care. "I don't need a keeper."

"Chill out, Princess," he said mildly. He leaned lazily against the wall behind him. "I never said you did."

"You—"

"I was just trying to spiff things up a bit. It's damn awkward being thrust onto a new partner."

Awkward? For him or for her? "You knew—"

"I didn't know diddly," he snapped, getting angry.

"But—"

"You're thinking that I got the results from Angie last night, right? Get real, Princess. The work wasn't even done when I talked to Angela. Ed was still cutting."

He shot Dr. Byerly a look. The woman nodded.

"I didn't know the results until right now, sitting here with you," Gunner said, and his face finally softened. "If you're going to get ticked off at me for something, then for God's sake, do it because I thought this bet thing would challenge you a little, get your mind off...you know. I thought it might get you to think like a Homicide cop again.''

She had been right about that part, then. Oddly his admission took the wind out of her sails.

''I...the whole department has been expecting me to grow horns or fall apart for a year now, ever since Matt went down,'' she said more softly. ''I really am fine.'' She *was*.

''Is that Hadleyese for 'I'm sorry for flying off the handle, you miserable peon'?''

Tessa glared at him.

Gunner finally nodded. ''Yeah. You'll be just fine, Princess.''

Her heart thumped too hard. It was the first vote of confidence anybody had really given her. Even Kennery had seemed a little cautious when he'd brought her back.

She stood up abruptly and made a swiping move for the car keys on the breakfast bar. She got them before he could react.

''Yes,'' she agreed firmly. ''I'm going to be fine. And your little game is going to cost you, partner. I'd suggest you do some heavy smoking now, because when we get back to the office, your cigarette days are numbered.''

''One more thing that might help,'' Angela said hurriedly, handing Gunner their copy of the autopsy report. ''AB-Negative is extremely rare. Roughly two percent of the entire population has it. If you can find a suspect with it, then I'd bet my entire life savings that the DNA will match as well. Of course, it's going to take six weeks or more for the DNA work to come back.''

Gunner looked down at the report absently. Then he glanced up again and watched Tessa stride elegantly—and still a little angrily—down the hall.

''Wow,'' Angela said, watching her go, too.

Gunner's gaze shot to her. ''Wow, what?''

''There's a lot boiling in there, John, just looking for a place to explode.''

Gunner's face hardened again. ''She'll be fine.'' And he wondered why in the hell *he* sounded defensive all of a sudden.

He leaned sideways to watch her go out the front door.

''She's also out of your league, John,'' Angela warned, watching his expression. ''You could get your heart broken really badly here.''

Gunner let out a bark of laughter. "All those fancy college degrees, and you're way out in left field on this one."

But Gunner thought about it. As far as he was concerned, Angela was the kind of woman who made him think of a cold beer—thoroughly enjoyable, and she certainly had her place at the end of a hot, hard day. He had dated her briefly, when they had been teenagers. But Tessa...well, Tessa Hadley-Bryant was more like eighteen-year-old Scotch.

And *that* had its place anytime, anywhere.

Unfortunately, he had a beer budget. He couldn't afford good, eighteen-year-old Scotch unless he saved for it, and that wasn't his fiscal style. But Angela was right about one thing. Tessa Hadley-Bryant had a lot going on in there. She wasn't ready. As thorny as she could be on any subject related even remotely to Matt Bryant, Gunner knew she wasn't anywhere near ready for romance, not with him, not with anyone at all.

"Thanks, Angie." He threw the words over his shoulder and went to catch up with his new partner.

Tessa was waiting behind the wheel of their unmarked car. He stopped beside her window and tapped at it.

Tessa lowered the glass. "What?"

"Damn it," he growled, looking down.

"What's wrong?" she asked again, alarmed now.

"Pop the trunk, Princess. We've got a flat."

She groaned and pulled the keys out of the ignition. She pushed open the driver's side door and stepped out onto the sidewalk. Before she could take even a single step toward the trunk, Gunner had slipped the keys out of her hand.

"Hey!" She whipped around, but not fast enough to stop him from sliding behind the wheel in her place. He started the engine again.

"Damn it, Gunner! That was sneaky!"

"Sure it was. Five seconds to blast off, Princess."

She hurried around the car and scrambled into the passenger seat. She wasn't entirely sure that he really wouldn't drive off without her.

Gunner pulled out into traffic again with a slight squeal of rubber. "I'm all for equal opportunity employment," he explained easily, "but I like to do my own driving."

She slouched in the seat, moderately angry. "That's ridiculous."

"Not really. Men are good at some things, women at others. And men have better reflexes than women behind the wheel of a car."

"Tell that to the cabbie you just barely missed driving down here."

"But I *did* miss him, didn't I? Because I'm a man, and men are better drivers."

"Of all the chauvinistic, superior—"

"Easy, Princess. By the same token, I can't type worth a damn. In fact, I can't do anything that requires delicate work with my fingers." He thought about it. "Well, hardly anything."

Her eyes widened and she looked across at him to see if he meant what she thought he meant. He was grinning again. Heat seared into her face and she fidgeted in her seat.

Don't think about it. But, of course, once the idea was planted in her mind she couldn't help but think about it. In minute detail. She was widowed, not dead. She watched Gunner's hands as he began drumming on the wheel again, and his fingers were long and strong and...well, capable, she thought. She imagined them sliding and probing into secret places of a woman's body, and she fidgeted some more and tried to find her breath.

She was blushing to the roots of her hair, Gunner thought, fascinated. He wasn't actually sure he had ever seen a woman do that before.

"Something going on with that seat that I don't know about, Princess?"

Tessa gasped.

Gunner laughed aloud, but then he found it hard to hold onto his grin. He knew exactly what she was fidgeting about over there, and he thought again about what Angela had said.

He took a deep breath. He'd seen Tessa around, of course, back before Matt had died. Maybe once in a while he had appreciated the way she walked with that unstudied, unconscious, built-in class. He remembered her from the funeral, as well. Damn near every cop in the tristate area had turned out for Matt Bryant's viewing. It had been hard to miss his widow, her face chalk white, that wild-animal, pleading kind of desperation in her eyes, as though she were just waiting for someone to wave a magic wand and make it all be a terrible mistake.

Though Gunner had barely known her, for a moment there he would have given body and soul to have possessed such a wand…and he doubted very seriously if he was the only man there who had felt that way.

Angela was right. She was pure class, a purely good woman, and she was out of his league.

He'd gotten married all those years ago because Elaine had pushed and wheedled him into it, because she'd said it was the natural progression of things, and she had largely been right. They'd been going together for several years. They'd been good together, in a way old friends were, as he and Angela were. But that, of course, was absolutely no basis for a marriage.

Afterward, when he'd acknowledged regretfully that marrying her had been a mistake, Gunner had given that some thought. He'd decided that if there really was such a thing as love, then it undoubtedly involved the kind of woman who made thunder roll and lightning strike. The kind of woman who made your life pass before your eyes at the thought of losing her. An actual relationship should be saved for a woman to kill for and die for. Since he was reasonably sure that such a woman didn't exist, he played the field. Anything less would be shortchanging himself—again— and the woman, as well.

The bottom line was that if, through all the dating he had done, thunder had never rolled, lightning had never struck, well, then, it wasn't likely to start happening at this late date. He didn't have it in him, he thought again. No big deal. He'd accept it, and live accordingly.

Which brought him back to the woman who was still squirming in the seat beside him. He thought again how she had looked at the funeral. *She* knew how to love.

She could fidget her way clear out the car door, Gunner thought, but Tessa Hadley-Bryant sure as hell wouldn't let anything develop between them. Nor did *he* think it was a good idea. And conversely, that was his only real concern about their partnership. Partners needed a certain rapport to work truly well together. And Tessa was very busily building walls between them. Already he knew that she had no intention of letting him get too close, platonically, romantically, or otherwise.

That worried him far more than any aftershocks she might still be feeling over Matt Bryant's murder. Partners needed to think with one brain. They needed to feel, to sense, to *know* what the other guy was going to do before he did it. Gunner felt reasonably certain that he was never going to develop that kind of link with Tessa Hadley-Bryant. She wouldn't allow it.

Oh, well, he'd ride it out. He still had the strong feeling that she was far better off with him right now than with a partner who either overlooked her past or placed too much weight upon it.

He glanced over at her again. She had little diamonds in her ears this morning, and they caught the sun, winking and sparkling when she moved. She smelled good, too, he realized, like something subtly floral. He moved his own head just right to catch a whiff.

"What are you doing?" she asked curiously.

For the first time in his memory, Gunner felt his own skin heat a little in something that might have been a blush if he had been any other man.

"Huh?" he asked, deliberately obtuse.

"Nothing," she muttered. "I just thought you were...nothing."

She had been thinking about something, he realized. A little frown still touched her forehead.

"Okay, let's hear it," he prompted. "What has your mind going at ninety miles an hour?"

"*You're* going ninety miles an hour."

"Fifty-two."

"The speed limit is twenty-five!"

Gunner tapped his foot on the brake and reached into his pocket for his cigarettes. She rolled down the window and stuck her head out. *Soon,* she thought, *soon.*

"I was just thinking that the guys who first caught this Benami thing—the precinct cops who took Christian's initial call—didn't notice any additional rope around the house," she said finally.

"Having second thoughts about whodunit?"

"I'm just wondering how well Benami covered his tracks."

He nodded and veered into the city garage, whipping the car around the turns up to the eighth level. They made their way back to the Administration Building in thoughtful silence.

Melanie was gone. Gunner went to her desk—sitting on the edge of it again—and immediately picked up the phone, tapping out a number with those fingers. It seemed to Tessa that they did reasonably well with delicate work after all.

She took a deep breath and shrugged out of her jacket. She hung it neatly over the back of her chair, pushed her sleeves up and went to work. She sat down at their desk to begin making her own set of phone calls.

Ten minutes later, Tessa heard Gunner swear. She was on hold with Hahnemann Hospital.

"What?" she asked quietly, looking over at him again.

"I can't find any record of Benami with any branch of the armed forces." He hitched his weight around to face her. "So what have you got?"

"Nothing, yet." Then her eyes sharpened as someone came back on the line. She spoke briefly, then hung up the phone.

"Well?" Gunner prompted.

"Benami's definitely our man."

"He's AB-Negative," he said resignedly. He dropped his cigarettes in Mel's trash can, wincing painfully.

"Not exactly."

"Blood types either are or they aren't, Princess."

"I mean...I don't know. I can't find out, either. According to all the area hospitals, Daphne's family physician, the IRS and the Social Security Administration, a man named Christian Benami doesn't exist at all."

It took Gunner only a split second to dive for the trash can again. Tessa moved fast and instinctively, shooting out with one foot to kick it clear of his reach.

His smoky eyes came back up to her face slowly.

"A deal's a deal, Gunner."

"Not if we can't get a blood type on Benami."

She leaned back in her chair, crossing her arms over her chest. "This lack of a paper trail is *very* suspicious, so don't split hairs."

"I said no cigarettes if Angela gave us anything that pointed to Benami," he argued.

"Sure, and Benami erased all traces of his past because it seemed like a fun thing to do at the time."

Gunner's expression twisted.

"Angela told us about the blood type, which led us to find out that Benami apparently doesn't exist. There's got to be a glitch in there somewhere. It'll just take further digging." She paused, smiling sweetly. "I hear they make nicotine patches for what ails you, Gunner."

"Damn sissy things," he muttered. "I'm tough."

"Good. So stop your complaining."

She grinned at him. Gunner surprised himself by chuckling when all his instincts were already craving nicotine.

She might be busily building walls between them, he thought, but every once in a while she forgot to. Every once in a while, she smiled that way, jumped back at him, surprised him, and he thought their partnership might work out all right after all.

He liked this lady, he thought. He really did.

Chapter 4

Gunner found himself continually revising his initial opinion of their rapport as the day wore on. It was Saturday, they were on their own time and neither of them gave a single thought to going home. They organized their priorities without conscious debate. He stayed on the phones, searching for some record of Benami, while she went to consult Igor.

The computer system was nearly phenomenal, Tessa thought, sitting down to tap her way into it—*nearly* being the operative word. It collated Pennsylvania's criminal proceedings, convictions and DMV records with the other states in the union—or it tried to. Not all states had the financial wherewithal to purchase the system. Unfortunately, with such vast stores of data to sort through, Igor was slow. Sometimes he simply went down, for hours, for days, overwhelmed by the sheer number of queries made of him.

Tessa set him to work and went back to the Unit office. Gunner covered the phone by tucking it against his shoulder as he looked up at her. "What've you got, Princess?"

"Nothing, yet. We have prints on Benami, right?"

He fished through the file and pushed them at her. "They were all over the house. No surprise there. It's *his* house."

"Now it is," she agreed grimly, then she was gone again.

When she returned the second and last time, she brought two cold soft drinks from the machine in the hall. His was the standard, sugar-laden variety. Hers was diet. Gunner raised a brow, leaned back and put his feet up on their desk. He decided that he was going to enjoy hearing this explanation.

"So how come I get the calorie-packed one? Trying to fatten me up for the slaughter?"

"You don't strike me as the type who thinks his body's a temple to be preserved," she muttered.

"So you think I'm flabby?"

"Of course not! You're—" She broke off, flushing. He hooked his hands behind his head and waited for her to go on, his T-shirt stretching tautly over his incredible chest and torso. There was nothing there that could even remotely suggest flab.

No, she thought, there was no way she was going to point *that* out.

"Actually," Gunner said after a moment, "I'm not."

"What?"

"The type who treats my body like a temple." He took a deep swig from his can. "I just kind of use it the way God meant it to be used, and enjoy the hell out of it while I'm about it."

"I—oh." She wasn't going to touch that one, either, Tessa decided. "So what did you find out through more outmoded, conventional channels?"

"Nothing."

Her heart thumped, though she wasn't surprised.

"Christian Benami doesn't live in the state of Pennsylvania, that's for sure," Gunner declared. "No way, nohow."

"It's an alias," Tessa said. She sat on the corner of their desk this time.

"Oh, yeah," Gunner agreed. "Somewhere out there, he's got a social security number, all right—"

"And he probably registered for Selective Service—"

"And he votes and he drives, but he sure as hell doesn't do it as Christian Benami."

"They were married in Paris," she mused. "I guess he wouldn't have had to have shown proof of identity there."

"Must not have," he agreed. "At least not of the same sort that we do. He doesn't seem to have any fake ID as Benami, not in this country, anyway."

Tessa rubbed a headache behind her eyes. Gunner scrubbed a hand over his unshaven jaw.

"I can't decide if it's sloppy or brilliant," she admitted. "He's hiding *something*. He was *somebody*."

"Somebody who probably vanished off the face of the earth as far as his old friends and associates were concerned," Gunner agreed. "I'll go with brilliant. He didn't take a chance on resurrecting himself as someone else, at least not record-wise."

"But *why?*" She thought about it. "Witness Protection?"

Gunner snorted.

"Well, that's always got to be considered when somebody just disappears," she said indignantly. It was a thorn in the sides of police departments everywhere. The Feds didn't even let local authorities in on those particular proceedings. It resulted in miscellaneous missing persons cases all over the country that would never be closed, where the cops were as much in the dark as the bad guys.

"Princess, we don't got a missing person, we got a *dead* person," Gunner said pointedly, and Tessa almost smiled.

She sighed and drank from her own can. "Well, I gave Igor Benami's prints. If Benami's being investigated for anything else, anywhere else, we'll hear about it."

Gunner grimaced. "Maybe. Sooner or later."

That was another of Igor's drawbacks. He could tell them if Benami's prints matched any others in the state of Pennsylvania. He could check them against *convicted* criminals elsewhere, but if Benami was merely being investigated somewhere else, if his file was still open, then it would take a strong stroke of luck for Igor to do them any good. Some other police department would have to notice the query she'd put in with Benami's prints. They would have to be currently investigating Benami through Igor to realize that Philadelphia had their man. Without even an accurate name or social security number to go on, it was something of a long shot.

Still, stranger things had happened in police work, Tessa knew.

"He's our man, Gunner," she said quietly.

"You won't get an argument from me now." Tessa watched his gaze go longingly to Mel's trash can again. Then he yanked open the center drawer of their desk. "Didn't I see you put Life Savers or some sissy thing in here?"

Tessa smiled. "In the back, tough guy."

He flashed her a look, one brow not quite up, one corner of his mouth not quite smiling. He found them and popped one into his mouth. "You know, I've got to warn you. This could get ugly. No cigarettes, no charm. You'll be lucky to get civility. I'm going to be a bear."

"I'll pick up a whip on my way home."

"Brings some interesting images to mind."

Tessa closed her eyes against a rush of embarrassment. *Damn* him.

"Gunner, look," she began, thinking she had to get these lines down, had to let him *know* there were lines. But then his chuckle came again, warm, rough...like callused hands on her skin.

"You got a hell of a blush there, Princess. Pretty as a spring day."

She heard his heels thump as he brought his feet down and she looked at him again, knowing she probably shouldn't, and if she had been a nun and she had been wearing socks, they would have melted clear off her feet when he grinned at her.

"We need to keep this...impersonal," she managed to say, her voice strained. "Professional. We have to, Gunner, or I'm not going to be able to work with you."

He thought about asking her why. Maybe it was as simple as the sheer enjoyment of rattling her high-brow sensibilities now and again, but he thought "impersonal" could get pretty damn frustrating after a while.

"Sure," he said easily, not meaning it for a minute. He rubbed his jaw again and went on as though they'd never gotten sidetracked. "What I'm thinking is this. The man exists, but Christian Benami isn't his name. So we'll let Igor try to find out what his name *is*, but that could take forever, so we'll pay a little visit to Harvey Baum and get the good judge to give us a compliance order in the meantime."

"For a blood type." Tessa groaned. Judge Baum was iffy under the best of circumstances. He had a reputation for being lenient on criminals. The inside word was that he could be bought, but no one had ever been able to prove it.

"Maybe we ought to try skipping around Baum entirely," she

suggested. "Could we go directly to Benami and ask him to give us some blood?"

Gunner made an incredulous sound. "As in, 'Right over here, sir, would you kindly step into this gas chamber'?"

Tessa stiffened at his sarcasm even as she knew he was right.

"I've got this nagging, rotten feeling that Benami's going to slide right through our hands like a snake," he murmured. "He's already disappeared once, from somewhere. If we go to see him, we'd be tipping him off that we're looking into him."

"Well-spoken for a man who didn't even think Benami was guilty as of yesterday," Tessa said pointedly.

"Oh, I thought it. I just wanted you to be damn sure of why *you* thought it. Trying to convince me sure put your ducks in a row, didn't it?"

Tessa shrugged. It had, she thought, and she hadn't thought about Matt too much at all.

That bothered her.

"Still mad?" he asked. He gave her that crooked grin again and she wondered how anyone, anywhere, could ever stay angry with this man.

"No. Just mildly miffed. It would have been worse if I'd had to buy you that beer."

Gunner nodded, opened the desk drawer again, and peeled several Life Savers off the roll this time. He thrust the whole handful into his mouth.

"Come on, let's go see Benami and give it a shot. So what if we tip him off? Maybe it'll shake him up, make him make a mistake. Besides, I feel like getting mean with somebody, and you're too sweet and cute."

Tessa felt her heart hitch. "*Impersonal,* Gunner. We've got to keep this relationship impersonal."

He gave her a long, measuring look that made everything inside her roll over again. "We can try."

"Park here," Tessa said suddenly. They crept around Logan Circle through heavy traffic, trying to move back toward center city. Philadelphia's one-way streets were a maze that could daunt even the cabbies who worked them. "In the Four Seasons garage," she directed. "I want to try something."

Gunner shot a look at her. "Do you have any idea what that's going to *cost?*" No, he thought, it had never even occurred to her. "No need to stick a pea under *your* mattress."

But when he reached it, he turned into the garage. The department would reimburse him.

"Four blocks," she said as they made their way back to the sidewalk, glancing at her watch.

He realized what she was getting at. "Closer to five," he corrected.

"Okay." They both stopped and drew in their breaths.

"On your mark, get set, go," said Tessa.

They turned south.

Gunner appreciated the fact that she didn't run, though they hadn't discussed it. Benami couldn't have made the trip at a jog in evening clothes, not without attracting a great deal of attention. He might have taken a cab, but if he had, they would find out about it. And if he had calmly taxied his way to the Four Seasons only once, then he had probably killed Daphne before he even got there. The account given by over one hundred witnesses suggested that that was probably what had happened, if he had killed her at all.

But Tessa seemed to be thinking that Benami had been in and out of that party, Gunner realized. It still didn't preclude a cab or two, but as he watched her face, he knew she was thinking about that, and that he was following her mind with a fair bit of rapport.

His eyes were still on her, his gaze angled across at her, when they reached the first intersection. He felt rather than saw a body approach him from the curb. After six years in the department, three of them in Homicide, the hairs on his nape stirred instinctively.

Then he saw that the approaching body belonged to a girl of Haitian, or maybe Dominican descent. She was barely seventeen. She held a wilted flower out to him.

"For you, handsome man."

Gunner saw a basket stuffed with more drooping flowers behind her. "Well, that's nice, honey. Good merchandising, too."

"Gunner!" Tessa cried out from behind him. He looked back to see her sort of jogging in place. "We're *timing* this," she reminded him impatiently.

He reached for his wallet, giving the girl a bill.

"Thank you, sir, thank you," she gushed.

Gunner started moving again. Then he stopped once more.

"I don't *believe* this!" Tessa cried.

This time he passed the flower on to an elderly woman pushing a walker along ahead of her. "For you, beautiful lady," he said. The woman reared back, looked suspiciously at the flower, then she smiled slowly.

Gunner jogged on again.

"At least you could have been original." Tessa panted, catching up with him a second time.

"Doesn't matter. Made her day."

Actually, Tessa thought, it had probably made *both* women's days. She found herself smiling. He might be arrogant, but he certainly had a way about him.

In spite of herself, she thought again of how he had deliberately kept her off balance all of yesterday. And half of today. Talk about a seesaw, she thought. One of these hours she was going to have to decide how she felt about being paired with John Gunner, whether she was alarmed by it or was enjoying it.

They had reached the Benami town house. They stopped, and Tessa got irritated all over again. For all the smoking he had undoubtedly done until this very morning, *she* was the one who was winded.

They both looked at their watches at the same time.

"Eight minutes and roughly thirty-six seconds," Gunner said.

"So say seven minutes, maybe seven and a half, if Benami didn't stop to flirt. Twice. With one woman old enough to be his grandmother, and another young enough to be his daughter."

Gunner shot a brow up and laughed. "*Flirt?* Princess, that wasn't flirting. When you see it, you'll know it."

Her belly rolled again.

She lowered her voice, looking back over her shoulder at Christian's home. "I've got a hunch," she said quietly.

"I gathered as much."

"I'm just wondering if he didn't try to kill Daphne before he went to the party, but she mounted a pretty significant defense. So maybe he managed to drug her and tie her, made his appearance at the hotel, slipped out, went back, killed her after she was groggy, then returned to the Ball. Maybe nobody even noticed he was gone."

"How many people were at this bash?"

"Over two hundred and fifty. If he circulated consistently the whole time he was there, he could have pulled it off. That's quite a crowd. If someone wasn't talking to him, they would just assume he was chatting with someone else."

"And you've got firsthand experience with these shindigs."

Tessa hesitated, then she nodded. Gunner didn't sound judgmental, and he didn't choose that particular moment to call her "Princess" again.

"If you're right, *somebody* ought to have noticed him missing," he said.

"I hope so."

"We only have statements from a hundred or so of the two-fifty."

"And nobody's taken statements from the help yet. And *they've* got eyes in the backs of their heads."

"Okay, we'll move onto them tomorrow." He hesitated. "In the meantime, why *not* just take a cab? Why do you think he didn't?" He had his own theories, and wanted to see if they'd match hers.

"He would have, if he'd only needed to make the one trip. More than one, and he was risking too much. For sure we'd raise a brow if we found out he'd been taking taxies back and forth all night. And we can trace that sort of thing. It's a lot harder to trace a five-block stroll in either direction."

"Yeah," Gunner said. "So let's go mess with him a little."

Benami was hostile. It wasn't particularly obvious at first, more like something tainted and sour sifting through the first cracks in his carefully polished veneer.

"Coffee?" he offered as he allowed them into the foyer. "Or maybe...I don't know what else I have around here. It's been... difficult."

My foot, Tessa thought instantly. She caught Gunner's eye and knew they were both hearing the man's words again. *What else I have around here.* Not we, but I. And Daphne hadn't even been dead for ninety-six hours yet.

"Coffee would be fine," Tessa said softly, settling into the old, tried-and-true, good-cop routine. She sat gently on the corner of a settee in the parlor that Benami rushed them into.

Gunner paced.

No, she thought, watching him, her pulse quickening in spite of herself. He didn't pace exactly. He...prowled. He made his way around the room while Benami went to get the coffee. Once he stopped beside a low, cherry-wood table and picked up a figurine sitting atop it.

"Dresden," Tessa murmured.

"Yeah?" He shot her a look and put it back. "I guess it didn't come free with a ten dollar purchase."

Tessa felt her mouth curling into a smile again, then Benami came back into the room with two mugs and a coffee pot. Yes, Tessa thought, the veneer was cracking.

"I'm not clear on what you want with me," Benami said, pouring. He smoothed a hand over his blond hair as he sat. It was styled to lay back from his forehead, short and neat. He was a handsome man, almost too pretty, Tessa thought. He had Adonis looks, though he seemed soft. He definitely wasn't as rough or as muscular and appealing as Gunner.

She got off that line of thinking fast.

"I already told you how I found her," Benami said.

"You found her hanging," Gunner said coldly. "Suicide."

Benami didn't quite flinch. Then he flinched too much.

"That's right."

"Wrong," Gunner snapped.

"I beg your pardon?"

"Your wife was murdered, Mr. Benami. She didn't kick that chair away all by herself."

Tessa thought that the man's sudden pallor was more or less genuine.

"I don't—" he began.

"Understand? Sure you do," Gunner said shortly. "It wasn't her idea. She wasn't despairing, despondent, depressed, and she didn't take her own life."

"Christian," Tessa said softly. "We need a sample of your blood. We need to get to the bottom of this."

"My blood?" He looked dumbfounded. "Why?"

"Because whoever urged your wife up to that chandelier left a little piece of himself behind," Gunner said, and there was no hint of the man who had given the old lady the flower. "Interesting, huh? Care to push your sleeves up a little, chum?"

"Am I a *suspect?*" Benami nearly shouted.

"You're a spouse, so you're a suspect," Gunner answered coldly.

"We'd just like to rule you out," Tessa said quickly. "You'd be amazed at how often family members turn out to be responsible for a victim's murder. It's standard procedure for us to start looking at the people closest to Daphne first. Then we'll work backward from there, as we gradually rule people out."

"I see," Benami said curtly. "You'll have to forgive me. I'm still reeling from the...from knowing that...she didn't—"

"You'll give us the blood?" Gunner interrupted impatiently.

Benami's face hardened. "I will not."

"Why?" Gunner began moving in on the man, closing the distance between them. "Hiding something?"

His face was hard now, chiseled, his eyes like flecks of gray stone, Tessa realized. Benami had seated himself in the chair closest to the hearth. As Gunner drew closer, he shot to his feet.

"This is an invasion of my privacy," he said harshly. "It's harassment. It's a heinous breech of etiquette in my time of grief. I—"

Tessa interrupted this time, letting her features settle into a mild scowl. "Don't you *want* to help us figure out who did this to Daphne? I should think—"

"Get out," Benami snarled.

Tessa stood up slowly. Gunner took another step closer to the man. Benami fought for a moment to hold his ground, but he was intimidated. He took a quick step back until his legs came up against the chair behind him.

"I don't have to take this!"

"Sure you do," Gunner answered. "You're a scumbag."

"This is brutality—"

"I haven't hit you yet," Gunner said menacingly.

"I'll have your badge, Officer."

"Detective. That's *Detective* Gunner, scumbag. I worked hard for that promotion."

Tessa suspected he had gotten the promotion the same way he seemed to do everything. He had probably done it without planning or effort. She really couldn't tell yet if his lazy indifference was real or forced. She wondered just how much granite was underneath that crooked grin of his.

She found out soon enough, in a way she'd never anticipated.

"We can do this one of two ways," Gunner said. "You can voluntarily come with us to a medical facility of our choice, and let a pretty little nurse take a few drops of blood out of your finger there. Or you can cause all this fuss—which, by the way, *really* makes me wonder why you're fussing—and you can tick me off, in which case I'll haul your skinny butt into the nearest court and get a compliance order. One way or the other, you're going to end up with a pricked finger, and *I'm* going to get my blood."

Benami only shook his head.

"Why, Christian?" Tessa pleaded, and answered herself. *Because he's a scumbag.* She almost laughed aloud. "It would be so much easier if you'd just—"

"Get out of here," Benami snarled.

"Gunner's right, you know. We'll *have* to get the compliance order if only to continue with our investigation in a neat and orderly fashion."

"I said *get out.* I'm in mourning. Get out of here. Before I—"

"Hang us from a chandelier?" Gunner suggested harshly.

"Get out," Benami said again.

Gunner gave him a mock salute. "See you in court."

They were nearly back to the door when Benami stopped them again. His voice was oily and too quiet.

"Tell me something, Tessa. When *your* husband went down, did the police harass you? Did they ask *you* for blood? Did they make you relive it over and over again, how his *eyes* looked after he was dead? How did they look, by the way? Were they open the way Daphne's were?"

Tessa froze. She fought it, didn't want to succumb to the likes of this monster. She knew she was *smarter* than that, and yet she couldn't help it. She thought of how Matt had looked at her, how he had looked *for* her, his eyes searching and wild, as he had died.

A small, involuntary cry escaped her throat, then she gasped more loudly.

Gunner had been nearly out the door. He spun back, cutting in front of her, and grabbed Benami by the front of his sweater. And the expression on his face now was nothing at all like the one that had been there when he had merely been playing with the man, bouncing counterpoint tough-cop insults off Tessa's niceties.

His expression was deadly.

"Gunner!" she cried out instinctively. She clutched his arm in panic. His muscles were like steel beneath his jacket. "Gunner, for God's sake," she yelled, panicked. "Don't hurt him. It's not worth it!"

It seemed to take forever for him to release his grip on the man. He opened his fingers deliberately and slowly.

"Better get yourself a lawyer, pal."

"I will. You'll pay for this, Detective." Benami smoothed his sweater down.

Tessa wasn't even sure if Gunner had heard him. He was already out the door again. She watched him go then she looked back wildly at Benami. Her heart hitched and this time something cold scooted through her entire body.

He was smiling.

"That was cruel," she gasped.

"So is what you're doing to me."

"No." She shook her head, gently at first, then more frantically. "I would have given *anything*—blood, my *arm*—if I'd thought it would help convict the man who shot Matt."

Benami only shrugged.

She turned and ran after Gunner. He was nearly a full block ahead of her by the time she reached the street, but he veered suddenly and started coming back toward her. When he saw her, something strange happened to his face. Relief, shame, simmering anger...it was all of those things, and no single one.

"It took me ten steps to realize that you weren't with me," he muttered, "that you were still back there, alone with him."

"That was *stupid*," she hissed.

"Sure was."

"I don't mean—no, not leaving me there. Grabbing him! Gunner, for God's sake!"

His eyes narrowed. Her breath hitched. *She* took a quick step backward when he looked that way.

"Yeah? Well, you didn't see your face when he said that to you." But he had, Gunner thought, oh, yeah, he had. He had seen the memories in her eyes, and for a minute there, for one lousy, god-awful minute, she had looked again the way she had looked at Matt Bryant's funeral.

And for one second, one god-awful second, he had felt like killing the bastard who had done that to her. Something still hurt in the area of his chest. Something that shook him up more than a little.

"I'm not some hothouse flower, Gunner!" she cried. "I can't work with you if you keep treating me like a...a child! *I am not going to fall apart!* I've had a year to fall apart now, and I haven't done it!"

"You were in the *Fifth*," he snapped, still reeling. "They don't have guys like Benami in the Fifth."

She was shaking. Badly. "I was in the Fifth for nine months! Not my entire career! You can't do this to me, Gunner. Please. Don't do this to me."

His eyes cleared. The relief and the shame of leaving her ebbed. Now there was only anger.

"Tell you what, Princess. I might not trail a pedigree behind me as long as the state of California. I might not know Mr. Dresden from Mr. Uniroyal, but I know right from wrong. And I'll be damned if I'm going to stand around with my hands in my pockets while somebody hurts a woman I like and respect. Pedigree or not, I wasn't raised that way. So if you can't take it, then head on back to the Fifth right now and leave me the hell alone."

He turned and stalked up the street again. Tessa watched him for a full heartbeat before she realized her legs were unsteady.

Never, she thought, never had a man stood up for her that way. Not Matt, who had always treated her as an equal, who'd always been so impressed with her mind. Matt had been smart, cunning, but gentle. Her refined father had never threatened anyone on her behalf, nor her aristocratic brother.

No one. She sat down hard on the curb and put her forehead to her knees.

It took her a few minutes to realize that Gunner had come back, that he was standing beside her again. She looked up at him slowly. He scrubbed a hand over his beard, definitely darker now for all the hours that had somehow passed since they'd met at the unit office that morning. He looked rough and dangerous.

"I warned you," he said finally. "I told you I was liable to get ugly without my nicotine."

"So you did."

"So can I have a cigarette now?"

"Not a chance."

He cracked a small grin and gave her a hand, pulling her to her feet again. "I stand corrected."

"About what?"

"You *are* tough. Tell you what. *You* can handle our bleeding-heart judge."

She started walking beside him. "Can I drive, too?"

This time he grinned fully. "Not a chance."

Chapter 5

They went back to the office to try to arrange a Saturday visit with Judge Baum. They didn't even make it down the hall to their desk before their captain stopped them.

"In here," Kennery said shortly, blocking their way, thrusting a thumb over his shoulder. "Now."

Tessa knew that tone.

Her heart sank, then her face got hot. She knew it, but it had never, *ever*, been directed at her. She'd been with the department for five years now. The first two she had been on the streets, trying to earn respect—or even disrespect—for something, anything, that had nothing to do with her name. Then she'd worked under Roger Kennery in Homicide for two more years, until she'd been exiled.

She'd heard him rant and rave at others, but never at her. She was conscientious. She crossed her *T*s and dotted her *I*s, and that was that. Until John Gunner had come along.

She shot him a helpless, furious look.

"Easy, Princess," he said in an undertone. "His bark's worse than his bite. Trust me."

"And you would know, right?" she whispered hotly.

Gunner grinned and stepped back to let her enter Kennery's office first. Kennery went to his desk.

He was a huge man, at least six foot five, and he was shaped like a barrel. His chair squeaked when he lowered his girth into it, as though complaining of the strain.

Gunner roamed and Tessa took a chair across from the desk.

"You know," Kennery began, "when I paired you two, I thought it was a really smart move." He looked pointedly at Gunner. "I thought you'd be real good for our princess here."

Our princess. God, how she hated that label. And funny how it didn't irritate her half as much when Gunner said it.

Gunner nodded.

"And you." Kennery swiveled his big head again to look accusingly at Tessa this time. "I thought *you* might keep *him* in line."

"God couldn't keep him in line," she snapped impulsively, and Gunner grinned wider.

"Come on, Cap," he said, finally coming back to the desk to sit on the edge of it. "You paired us because I was between partners. Again."

Kennery narrowed his eyes on him. "And I thought it was a brilliant arrangement. Guess I don't have to tell you how much I hate being wrong. A couple of days into this partnership, and I'm already getting calls about you two. And I was dragged into this office on a Saturday specifically to take such a call."

Tessa stared down at her clasped hands. She was going to kill Gunner for this. Slowly. With enjoyment.

Kennery's chair squeaked again. Tessa looked up quickly to find that he was leaning back now, his hands clasped behind his head.

"Badgering witnesses is lousy protocol, and I won't have it in my unit. Now that I've reprimanded you like I promised that jerk I would, fill me in. I take it that Benami's a suspect."

Tessa blinked.

"Damn straight he is," Gunner said.

"What jerk?" Tessa asked.

"Basil English the Fourth," Kennery said shortly.

Tessa groaned.

"Who's that?" Gunner asked.

"The best criminal attorney in the city. After my father," Tessa murmured. "And Dad's firm doesn't do criminal work anymore since Jesse—my brother—took the D.A. post."

"*La-ti-da,*" muttered Gunner.

Her gaze slashed air as her eyes came around to him again. "I'm warning you, Gunner—"

"Easy, children," Kennery chided. He leaned forward again to clasp his beefy hands on the desk in front of him. "The long and short of it is as follows. Christian Benami will not give you the blood you asked for. I take it the autopsy showed that the killer left something of himself behind?"

Both Gunner and Tessa nodded.

Kennery rubbed a hand over his crew cut. "Well, if you pursue trying to match it to Benami, English says he'll hit the city with a harassment suit."

Gunner was out of his chair like a shot. "The bastard's a *suspect!*"

"Why?" Kennery asked evenly.

Tessa filled him in on Benami's lack of a paper trail. "Could be Witness Protection," Kennery said pointedly, as Tess had. "We're seeing an awful lot of that these days. For every odd occurrence, there's at least one possible innocent answer. What else have you got?"

Tessa dropped her eyes again.

"What else?" Kennery demanded again suspiciously.

"Nothing," Tessa and Gunner answered together.

Kennery sat back slowly. "Let me get this straight. You beat up on a witness because he has no *paper trail?*"

"Gunner didn't beat him up! I mean, he never actually struck him." Tessa took a breath. "And he's right. Benami is a suspect, and since when do suspects get to threaten harassment suits?"

"When they've just come into more money than God," Kennery said shortly.

"If he was innocent, Captain, he'd give us that blood," Tessa insisted.

"Sure he would," Kennery agreed mildly.

"We need to get a compliance order, and if he sues, well then, too damn bad," she said faintly.

Gunner raised a brow at her. "That's telling him, Princess."

"Stop *princessing* me!"

"Baum's not going to give you a compliance order," Kennery said. "And Baum's on our bench this month."

"We've got to try," Gunner snapped. "What do you want us to do? Back off and let the jerk walk?"

"Nope," Kennery said. "But I sure would be grateful if you'd keep your hands to yourself from here on in."

Gunner's jaw hardened.

"It was my fault," Tessa said softly. Both their gazes swiveled to her. "Benami was...taunting me. I didn't handle it as well as I could have. Gunner was just doing the White Knight routine." She looked at him almost dazedly. That still overwhelmed her a little.

Then she realized that, for perhaps the first time since she had known him, Gunner seemed speechless.

"Yeah, well, hands off from now on," Kennery muttered. He picked up the phone, spoke briefly and slammed it down again. "Baum'll see you in his chambers in an hour. Keep me posted on this one," Kennery said. "I want every little detail. It's a potential time bomb. If it's going to blow the department off its foundations, I want to know about it ahead of time."

Gunner went to the door. "We need twenty-four-hour duty on this one, Cap," he mentioned.

Tessa paled.

"*Now* what's the problem?" Kennery asked, watching her closely.

"I...nothing." She shook her head. Twenty-four-hour duty meant that they could, would and should be armed at all times. She darted a look at Gunner. "Do you really think that's necessary?"

"Benami is a sleazeball," he snapped. "I don't trust him."

Tessa sighed. He was certainly that.

She was not afraid of gunfire. She was *not*. Not so long as she, too, was armed, ready and able to *do* something this time. She had aced her marksmanship courses at the Academy.

Both Kennery and Gunner were still watching her too closely.

"I'm fine," she snapped, and left the office. She was halfway down the hall again before Gunner caught up with her.

"You want a hot dog while we wait for Baum?" he asked too idly. "My treat."

She groaned and shot him a look out of the corner of her eye. "The one you talked me into yesterday kept me up half the night." Of course it had had nothing to do with the sometimes-titillating thoughts of John Gunner that had plagued her.

Those thoughts were not getting any less tangled. She combed her hand through her hair nervously.

"Suit yourself, Princess." He fell silent and waited until they were in the elevator to go on. "Just for the record, I can fight my own battles."

She blinked at him. "I beg your pardon?"

"I didn't ask you to take the rap for me in there. Right from the start I guess you ought to know that I take my own flak. I don't drag anyone else down with me, partner or not."

The elevator doors opened. Gunner stepped out. It took Tessa a moment to follow.

"You know, Gunner," she called after him, "you ought to do something about that machismo problem!"

He pushed through the lobby door in search of his hot dog, turning around at the last moment to look back at her.

"There's no problem, Princess. My machismo is fine."

Baum wouldn't give them the compliance order. Nor was he happy to have been pulled away from his golf game to see them. He sat behind his desk and glared at Gunner.

"You have no probable cause," he said flatly.

Gunner planted his palms on the judge's desk. "The hell we don't. Benami doesn't exist. He's using an alias. His wife didn't commit suicide and as far as we know, he was the last one to see her alive. She had blood under her fingernails. I want to know if it's Christian Benami's."

"It could not possibly be Mr. Benami's," Judge Baum said. "Please remove your hands from my desk. I'm not a thug you can intimidate, Detective, and if you continue this behavior, I'll fine you."

Gunner hesitated a moment too long before jerking away.

"Your Honor, we have no irrefutable proof that it's *not* Benami's blood," Tessa argued. "And you have to admit that his lack of a background is suspicious. He bears looking into."

Baum's gaze moved to her. It changed from hostile to guarded. She was a Hadley, after all.

"What's your point, Detective?"

"Benami could have been in and out of that party without anyone being the wiser."

"You've got over a hundred statements in this file. He's got an alibi."

"Not really. It's not airtight. There are holes all through it."

"All the same, if I gave you a compliance order, that *would* be harassment. I can't risk a lawsuit over pure conjecture. Bring me something else. Bring me something incriminating, and I'll co-operate with you. As it is, you've got no grounds for this request."

Tessa shot a quick look at Gunner. A little nerve was beginning to tick hard and fast at his jaw. He thrust a finger at the judge.

"You're impeding this investigation."

Tessa gasped.

"Watch yourself, Detective," Baum warned.

"The man's a snake," Gunner snapped. "And I can guarantee you that if he slides out of our grasp, I'm going to make damn sure that why and how become a matter of public record. He's already disappeared from somewhere once."

"Prove that," Baum said tightly. "Prove it and I'll—"

"We could have that bastard nailed by nightfall," Gunner said, interrupting him. "A blood match could hold him over for trial, and by then the DNA will come in."

"He'd get bail," Baum snapped. "He could still disappear even after you got a blood match."

"Maybe, but at least I wouldn't be standing around and patting him on the back, smiling and watching him go."

Baum stood up. "We're finished here."

"No. We're finished when Christian Benami—or whoever the hell he is—is behind bars. We could close this case yesterday with your cooperation, just a little cooperation."

"I'm going to choose to believe you're not threatening me, Detective, if you'll just leave promptly."

Tessa felt something stiffen inside her. They all knew there was only one reason that Baum would make such a choice. *She* was present.

Gunner's machismo was not going to take this well at all.

Tessa stood quickly. "Thank you. You can rest assured that we'll be back."

Baum's gaze was unreadable as he turned his attention back to her. "Of course, I hope you are. I hope you can give me *something* with which to convict this man, assuming he is indeed Mrs. Benami's killer. At the moment, that just seems like a long shot."

Gunner vented a particularly descriptive expletive. Tessa flinched.

She left the office ahead of him, not looking back, only hoping against hope that he would follow her and not antagonize the judge any further. She heard Baum's office door slam behind her. She wondered if Gunner had done it, or if it had been Baum.

When he caught up with her, one look at Gunner's face told her the answer.

"Have a cigarette," she said shortly. "Just smoke a cigarette, would you, please?"

He shot her a look as he lengthened his stride. "No."

"No? I'm giving you carte blanche, Gunner. The deal's off."

"I've gotten this far. I'm not going to wimp out now."

"Then get some of those patches, that gum, *something*, Gunner. Nicotine's an addiction. And let me be the first to tell you, your withdrawal is foul."

He stopped suddenly, turning toward her. Tessa took a wary, instinctive step backward at his expression. Her spine hit the wall. "What?"

He planted a hand against the plaster on either side of her head. "I'll tell you what's foul, Princess. *Politics* are foul. The haves getting away with murder while the have-nots just watch—*that's* foul. And I'd be just as angry about it if I had a full load of pollution in my system. It's *wrong*, damn it."

"I see," she said quietly.

"What's that supposed to mean?" he growled.

It meant, she thought, that suddenly she understood him. He was nothing more—and nothing less—than an idealist. He really *was* a white knight—albeit with armor that was just a little tarnished. He had a staunch and unwavering sense of right and wrong.

Like her.

The difference, of course, was that she had been raised in a world where you handled it politely. Gunner, on the other hand, was strong willed, unabashed and unapologetic.

And definitely, incurably macho. She took a deep, careful breath.

"It means," she said softly, "that where there's power, there's always someone around who's willing to abuse it to get more."

"All right," he said just as quietly, but he made no move to step away from her.

He was close enough that she could feel his breath on her face. Close enough that she could feel the heat of him. Close enough that she could *smell* him, that woodsy cologne again, something virile, something strong. His broad chest was inches from her nose.

She tried for another breath and couldn't quite get air this time.

"It means..." she began again, and noticed that her voice was a high-pitched squeak. She cleared her throat. "It means that we got from Baum exactly what we expected to get from him. It means that we'll just have to work a little harder to show him up."

Gunner realized he wasn't really hearing her. He wasn't thinking about Baum any longer. He was noticing the way her black hair curled behind her ear. And that tiny little diamond there. Classy. Understated. Pure Tessa Hadley-Bryant.

He caught a whiff of her again—that faintly floral aura. It filled his head and did odd things to his senses.

"We'll just bring him his proof so he *has* to cooperate with us," Tessa said. "Move back, Gunner. I can't breathe."

"Want a beer?"

"What?" she asked dazedly.

"A beer, Princess. It's the middle-class answer to champagne." Or eighteen-year-old Scotch, he thought. "It's after four o'clock, we've run all over the city—half of it on foot—and I'm thirsty and willing to trade one vice for another."

"A beer," she repeated. No, she thought, that's over the line. It was too close, too cozy, too...something. Her heart started picking up its pace a little. Oh, God, he smelled good. "Do I have to buy it?"

"Nope. You won. My treat." His voice was suddenly as intimate as a touch.

"I...sure," she heard herself answer. "Okay."

He straightened away from the wall and crooked an elbow around her neck in a purely friendly embrace, a gesture of sheer camaraderie, and pulled her down the hall.

Tessa was all the way to the elevator, matching his stride, before she realized that her lines had definitely been crossed. And they had an audience.

Three city employees—*female* city employees—were standing

outside one of the bail-bond rooms, watching them. They stared until Tessa and Gunner stepped into the elevator.

Before the doors slid closed again, Tessa saw them put their heads together, whispering.

Gunner took her to a sports bar on Filbert, just down the street from City Hall. It was jammed with people watching the last of an NFL playoff game, and not one of the patrons seemed to be as bloodthirsty or as avid as the three women who had been standing outside the bail-bond office, watching Gunner hug his new partner.

They would talk, Tessa thought resignedly. This was certainly a day of firsts. She had never been taken down by her boss before, and she had never been the point of salacious gossip before, either. Gossip, certainly, but not the kind that was going to come about because of *this*.

It was all Gunner's fault.

"Sit tight and hold the fort," he told her when they found an empty booth. "To tell you the truth, Princess, you look a little worse for the wear."

"Thanks so much."

He went to the bar. She watched him, propping her chin on her hand with far more insouciance than she felt.

They were both tired, she thought. It had been a long day. She *did* feel haggard and limp. But on Gunner, the wear and tear just looked...rugged. Something still simmered inside him, she realized, a certain indefinable energy. She knew it could erupt at any moment and drive him on for hours more.

His jeans—clean and stiff that morning—were a little rumpled now. They still clung. When he turned back from the bar with two frosted mugs, there was a trace of catsup on one thigh from that ghastly hot dog he'd eaten.

He wore it well.

He slid the mugs onto the table and peeled out of his leather jacket, his dark hair ruffling along the collar of it, then settling again. He tossed the jacket into the booth and sat down, grinning at her, then he lifted one of the mugs in a toast.

"To Day One."

"Day Two." She corrected him automatically, being a stickler

for details. "We were assigned to each other yesterday, if that's
what you're talking about."

"Yeah, but yesterday was just a how-do-you-do day." He took
a swig and licked the foam from his lip. His tongue was fast, sure,
agile.

Her heart stalled.

She had to get a grip, Tessa thought wildly. She had to stop
noticing these things. But her stomach seemed to curl and she
found herself watching, mesmerized, to see if he would do it again.

"What?" he asked. "Do I have catsup on my chin or something?"

"Uh, no," she croaked. "It's nothing."

"You didn't toast."

"Oh." She looked down at her beer. "I don't drink."

"*Ever?*" It occurred to him that he didn't think he'd ever
known a woman who didn't. The ladies he knew could pretty
much keep pace with the boys. To be fair, though, the vast ma-
jority of them had been buddies rather than lovers.

And he had no idea why he was thinking of lovers at the moment.

"Well, sometimes," Tessa was saying. "I think I had my
monthly quota last night." The wine had ended up being three
glasses.

"Is this a Hadley-type thing?"

She stiffened. "No. It's a me thing."

"Why?" he asked bluntly.

"I worry myself when I get tipsy." She couldn't control her
emotions when she got tipsy. Not in the past year.

"*Tipsy?*" he repeated, then that half grin came back. "Yeah?
What do you do? Should I start plying you with liquor here?"

"It depends on what you want from me." Then she heard herself, and she blushed to the roots of her hair. "I mean—"

Gunner's burst of laughter interrupted her. It was delighted.
"No way, Princess, you said it fine the first time. Tell you what.
Your virtue's safe with me."

She felt unaccountably stung. Pride, she thought. Just irrational
female pride. No woman in the whole department was safe from
John Gunner. Except, apparently, the delicate Hadley princess with
her law degree and her trust fund and her ins to every political
office in the city.

Yes, it stung.

"For the record, I've never had to get a woman drunk in my life," Gunner avowed, still grinning.

"Machismo again?"

"Could be." Then he thought about it. "No. Actually I just don't like sloppy loving."

His voice had changed, she noticed. Was she crazy, or had it really gotten huskier, deeper? Was it really stirring gooseflesh over her skin?

She had to stop this.

"I'll never take anything from you under the influence that you wouldn't give me sober," he said.

"I...oh. That's...remarkably...gallant of you." Her heart was beating a fast tattoo against the inside of her chest. She grabbed her beer and drank deeply from it after all.

One of his brows went up. "Does that mean you're feeling safer now?"

"It means I'm thinking that this isn't very impersonal." It had been a mistake to come here with him, she realized.

He leaned back against the leather seat lazily. About as lazily as a caged lion, she thought. "Sorry. I guess I just forgot we're supposed to be impersonal."

"Your mood's improved." She tried valiantly to change the subject.

"Not really." He drank again. "How's your *mood* at the moment?"

"Fine," she answered, watching him warily.

"Good. Because I want to hit you with something." He eyed her beer. "Better take another swig of that after all, Tess."

This time her heart whaled against her chest. What was he up to? She had been partnered with him through all of two days, and already she knew it could be anything, anything at all.

"I want that proof," he said.

"Proof?" she echoed dumbly.

"*Baum* wants proof. So I'm going to find it. I'm going to nail this jerk."

"*We* will," she said correcting him.

He smiled slowly. "Good. I'm glad you feel that way. Does that mean you'll break into his house with me?"

Chapter 6

"Break in," Tessa repeated slowly. She stared at him, hoping against hope that she hadn't heard him right.

Of course she had.

Gunner pounded a fist on the table. "That scum's stalling, Tess. He's got his fancy, high-priced lawyer, and Baum's probably all cozy in his pocket, so he'll hold us off with his bluster long enough to collect the lady's life insurance and then—" He broke off, snapping his fingers. "Poof. By the time the DNA comes back, by the time we find proof of an alias, there won't be anybody to test, anybody to force to comply, because Benami'll be gone."

She couldn't argue with that possibility, but she shook her head. "The insurance company won't pay out right away since we've put Daphne on the books as murder. Gunner, those companies *never* pay up until they absolutely have to."

"They'll pay," he said stubbornly. "They'll have to pay if we can't charge Benami with her death pretty soon. Are you going to sit there and try to tell me that Benami's not going to be on the phone to them every second, pressing them to get on with it?"

"We can tell Citizen Life that he's a suspect."

"Harassment." Gunner bit out the word. He finished his beer in one irate swallow.

She was starting to understand how he had gotten the rest of his reputation, the part that didn't have anything at all to do with his charm and his sexual prowess.

"No," she said flatly. "I won't be a part of this."

"Why not?"

He looked as indignant as a boy whose home run had just broken a window, and he couldn't figure out why no one was congratulating him. Impossibly she found herself fighting a smile.

"Those were damn good reasons I just gave you," he said.

"But you're overlooking one very important point. We're officers of the law. Justice has *rules,* Gunner. And I, for one, have always believed that there's a right way and a wrong way to do things, and taking the wrong way is always a conscious choice. Taking the wrong way will catch up with you. Always."

"The end justifies the means here, Princess."

"It does *not!* Gunner, what's the point? Even if you break in, anything you get under the circumstances wouldn't be admissible!"

"Doesn't matter," he muttered stubbornly.

"You're out of your mind!"

"It's a gray area," he persisted.

Tessa felt a headache coming on. She wondered if she could be somehow implicated by association even if she didn't go in there with him.

She clasped her hands together tightly in front of her. "No," she repeated. "No way."

"Look," Gunner argued, "the place is still marginally considered a crime scene. We don't actually need a judge's cooperation or a search warrant to go in there, so we're not doing anything blatantly illegal."

"Not if we make an appointment and do it on the up-and-up."

"Won't work. That gives Benami a chance to tidy up first. And if we *don't* make an appointment, if we just bang down his door, then he can scream harassment again."

"The crime scene tape has been removed," Tessa said. She was desperate. It was her last good argument. "Benami's been permitted to reenter the town house. He's been living there. Therefore, anything you find will be considered tainted. The chain of evidence is broken."

"Broken or not, there's *something* in that house. Something incriminating. There's got to be."

She closed her eyes and took a careful breath. When she looked at him again, his expression had the formidable threat of a very big thundercloud.

"Don't you think Baum's going to ask where and how we got this 'something'?" she asked, striving for calm. "Besides, the district officers who got there first already went through the place once. They didn't find anything."

"They didn't know what we know."

He had an answer for everything. Tessa stood and snatched her purse from the booth. "I'm going home."

"Is that how we're going to settle disputes, partner?" Gunner charged. "Just get up and walk out?"

He was actually mad because she wouldn't go along with this crazy scheme. She looked at him wildly. "Don't get ugly, Gunner."

"This isn't ugly."

"Angry, then."

"Yeah, I'm angry. It's been a long day and we've been turned back at every damn corner."

"So we need to think about this. We need to think of another way. We need to go to our respective homes and sleep on it."

"Are you always this calm and reasonable and genteel?" he snapped.

Tessa flinched in spite of herself. Then her jaw hardened. "No," she said harshly. "Believe it or not, sometimes I actually scream. Like when my husband is dropped at my feet."

She turned on her heel. She was outside before he caught up with her. He was still struggling into his coat.

"I'm sorry," he said gruffly. "I never even thought about Matt when I said that."

"Then don't apologize."

"What?" He was baffled.

"Look, Gunner," she said tightly as she began walking. "About the only thing I've really liked about you in two whole days is that you don't coddle me. Much. Matt was shot. He went down in front of me. Okay. It was bad, *horrible,* but life goes on. I'm a cop, and I'm a good one, and I've put it behind me. You don't have to watch every little thing you say to me. Don't start apologizing for something you didn't mean. You were right the first time. You didn't think about Matt. That's the way it should be. I'm not ticked off about that. I'm mad because you're mule-headed and stubborn and irresponsible.''

"Are you finished?"

"Yes."

"Good. Where are you going?" She was moving at a fast clip, he thought. She strode angrily on the pavement. A cold fog was beginning to roll into the city.

"I told you. Home."

"The car's back in the city lot on Thirteenth," he reminded her. And they were already at The Gallery on Tenth Street.

"I'm going to stop the first cab I see."

"No, you're not."

"Yes, I am."

He grabbed her arm, spinning her back to face him. It only made her madder that his eyes were amused.

"Are we having a fight?" she demanded suddenly.

"Sure sounds like it."

"Okay, then."

He watched, curious and confused, as she took a deep breath. What was she doing? He tried his damnedest not to notice the way her breasts rose and fell even beneath her bulky wool jacket. He tried his best not to remember what she looked like without that jacket. He was still trying when she hauled off with her fist and punched him squarely in the gut.

"I win," she said calmly, and then she began running.

It took him a moment to recover from his surprise. But he was big, he was fast, and he was strong. In the next heartbeat he caught up with her again, and Tessa found herself airborne.

She cried out as he scooped her off her feet, looping an arm around his neck out of a pure instinct to hold on. "Put me down!"

"I'm driving you home."

"No! You're acting like a—a *Neanderthal,* Gunner! This is ridiculous!"

"I haven't grabbed you by the hair yet, so don't give me ideas."

"Gunner, I mean it!" She tried to kick. He tightened his hold.

"Listen, Princess, we harassed the hell out of Benami today, and you're not walking down Filbert by yourself in the dark and a bunch of fog, hoping for a cab to come along."

"Okay. All right!" she gasped. "Just put me down. At least... just put me down."

Her voice was less forceful than panicked now. He noticed it and looked down at her sharply.

Her palms had gone damp and her heart was hurtling. Not once, not in nearly a year now, had a man touched her, Tessa realized, at least not a man to whom she wasn't related. And she didn't like her reaction.

It didn't matter that Gunner did it in temper, in amusement, out of some frustration. It didn't matter at all that there was nothing sexual about it. It didn't matter because his shoulders were so hard under her arm, swaying a little with each of his steps, and that was so *male.* His right arm was beneath her back and the side of that hand unintentionally skimmed her breast as his arm came up around her ribs. His left arm was tucked beneath her knees and that hand rested on her thigh, nearly on her bottom. He held her against his chest and his torso, and she was aware of the hardness of him again —*no flab*— and this wasn't impersonal, not at all.

Suddenly she felt aware and alive. It was a sensation that speared through her without warning. And she hadn't felt it for anyone, with anyone, in so very long. Suddenly the solitude she dragged around herself all year seemed miserable, suffocating, too heavy to bear.

"Please!" she almost wailed. "Gunner, *put me down now!*"

He looked down at her. Her face had paled. She was wild-eyed. Gunner swore. He set her carefully on her feet again. He wouldn't apologize this time. Damn it, he couldn't even be sure what he was supposed to apologize for!

A cab whipped around the corner of Tenth. He stepped angrily into the street and waved it down.

"Go on then," he said tightly when it had stopped. "Go home."

"Yes, I...thank you." Still, she stood on the curb, thinking there was something else she really ought to say. She was trembling. Her thoughts were jangled, sharp, chaotic, and her pulse was still scrambling. Her face felt flushed.

"Go *home*, Tess," Gunner said again, opening the door for her. She nodded and scrambled into the taxi.

Gunner watched as the taillights got smaller and finally blended in with the other traffic. He wished mightily for a cigarette.

* * *

He was marginally calmer by the time he'd finally collected their car and turned it toward the south part of the city. Calm and troubled. Anger had given way to a nagging feeling of concern.

He hit the brakes as he passed a 7-Eleven store on Twelfth Street. The bet had been that he wouldn't smoke in her presence, he thought. He parked and went inside, bought a pack of cigarettes, then stood out front on the sidewalk, scowling down at them in his hand.

He'd have to smoke it right here, he thought. If he did it in the car, she'd probably smell it tomorrow.

So what?

Damn it, she wasn't his *jailer*. And tomorrow was Sunday anyway. Maybe they would both give it a day off.

Then again, maybe they wouldn't.

He didn't know how long it was going to take for this nicotine craving to go away. He'd never tried to quit before. But something told him that the hours he already had under his belt were going to make a difference. That if he smoked tonight, or tomorrow, then Monday was going to be as much of a pure hell as today had been.

He swore and tossed the cigarettes into a trash can. It had nothing—absolutely nothing—to do with her opinion of him. It was just common sense.

He went back for another hot dog and a pack of gum, then he finally returned to the car and sat for a while, watching winos and good upstanding citizens move in and out of the store. So she didn't think they ought to break into Benami's house, he thought. No big deal. He'd had enough of those kinds of disagreements with partners before. So why was his gut in knots?

Because he wasn't sure this partnership was going to work out after all.

He felt as if it were an instinctive, worrisome thing moving under his skin, pulling his nerves tight. Tessa Hadley-Bryant was his fourth partner—in Homicide, at any rate. And not one of those relationships had felt this way.

This wasn't impersonal. Somehow, it hadn't been from the start.

He'd argued with his other partners plenty. But not like this. Was it a male-female thing? All his other partners had been men. Did that have something to do with it?

And what in the hell was *it?*

She was damn good-looking, he thought, just the kind of woman he liked. Soft, not overdone. He knew better than to fool around with anyone who worked for the city, and he wouldn't. No, he never would. But he'd have to be dead not to notice her eyes, the way they flashed and smiled. Maybe that was just skewing his thinking somehow, altering his brain processes.

Hell, she *blushed*. And it turned him inside out.

She made him feel protective. Too protective. Maybe that was it. She wasn't frail, fragile, not at all—God, she could jump back at him faster than he could expect it. And he liked that. But something about her made everything male inside him rise to shield her, to smooth the way for her. Something male, and okay, macho, he thought.

He'd been out of line with Benami, grabbing him that way. And he knew himself well enough to guess that he probably wouldn't have laid a hand on the man under any other circumstances. He was pretty inured to scum by now.

Rapport notwithstanding, there was no way this partnership was going to work, he thought again, not by her rules. Not by his own.

He couldn't function this way. Whether she liked it or not, there was something vaguely and unrelentingly personal about their interchanges. He felt it, and she did, too. Maybe he could work around it, but not if she got that panicked look in her eyes every time he inadvertently moved too close. He couldn't measure every word he said, every gesture he made. He would go out of his mind.

She'd told him that he shouldn't tiptoe around her, then she'd lost it when he didn't. So if he didn't tiptoe, didn't keep back from those invisible boundaries of hers, they wouldn't be able to work together at all.

God, that look in her eyes when he had picked her up! He closed his own against the memory of it. She had been...aware. Of him. As a man. And that had gone through him as if it were lightning.

Well, Angela had warned him. And Angie was one smart cookie.

Gunner finally started the car. Then, impulsively, he made an illegal U-turn and headed east instead of south.

By the time the taxi dropped her off in Elfreth's Alley, Tessa was much calmer. She'd been out of line. She'd overreacted, she realized, still embarrassed.

She paid the driver and went inside, and Maxwell was especially out of sorts. It had been a very long day. She stepped over him and went to the kitchen to feed him, then she found herself talking to him again.

"I wasn't wrong about breaking in. I didn't overreact about that," she murmured. The cat ignored her, chowing down. "Any sane person would have argued with him about that, Max. He's nuts. He takes too many chances. I can see that now."

She rocked back on her heels, her spine against the wall, moving the cat food can from hand to hand until the smell got to her. Then she stood abruptly and hurled it into the recycling basket.

There was still the rest of that bottle of wine from last night. Opened, not finished.

What was she doing? she thought halfway through pouring herself a glass. She really didn't drink. Hardly. But the cabernet was warm and soothing when she took a sip, loosening a bit of the tension that still gripped her just under her skin.

"I overreacted when he touched me," she told Maxwell, who was cleaning himself and purring now. She sipped again, closed her eyes. "It was just..." *I'm widowed,* she thought for the second time that day, *but I'm not dead.* And it was a thought that had never once occurred to her in virtually twelve months now.

The problem was, there was no way to keep things impersonal with a man like John Gunner.

The *biggest* problem was that she didn't even know how to deal with a man like John Gunner. She'd never met anyone like him. He ran through life with no constraints, she thought, sipping again. He was full of feelings, and he acted on them right off the cuff, without thought for the possible repercussions. He barely knew her, yet he'd been ready to punch Benami's lights out this afternoon because of what he'd said to her. There was no restraint there, she thought.

What in the world was she going to do about this? About him? She couldn't be attracted to him...and she was, in a purely physical, leaping, instantaneous way that made her no different from any other woman in the department. She'd known it as soon as he'd picked her up. Even before that, she admitted.

He was all simmering, unadulterated sex appeal, and it made young girls gush and old ladies blush. He didn't mean any of it, of course. Not seriously. Of that, she was fairly certain. He hadn't stayed married when he'd had the chance, had he? By his own admission, he wasn't a committed sort of man. He was dangerous, one of life's quintessential bad boys, obviously free with his loving and his touches. She might have been able to disdain that, except he had a macho heart of gold.

She wished Matt could tell her what to do about him. If Matt were alive, would he suggest that she might want to think about asking for a different partner? Then she had another, horrible thought. If Matt were alive, was it possible she would *still* be attracted to that cocky, animal magnetism in Gunner?

Yes, she thought, shaken, she would be. Because it had nothing to do with morals, with common sense, with decency and all the rules she had grown up believing in. It was elemental. Gunner's laid-back charm was something that simply *was,* but the mature, the sensible, the moral people of the world acknowledged it and walked around it.

At the moment, after today, she wondered if she had a mature, sensible, moral bone in her body.

She made her way upstairs quickly. She left her wine on the dresser and stepped into the bathroom. She started to fill the tub, then she thought better of it. She was tired, so bone-deep tired. It was a good feeling, one she had missed badly these past twelve months. But there was also the very real possibility that it might have her falling asleep in the bathtub.

If she drowned, Gunner would be convinced that Benami had had something to do with it. He'd probably kill the man, no questions asked. She laughed breathlessly, then sobered. He really did need to learn control.

She turned the shower on and washed quickly. She was just towel-drying her hair when the doorbell rang. Her heart skipped, stalled, then started again too fast. *Gunner.* She was sure against all reason that it was him.

She flew into her bedroom and rummaged through her drawers for underwear, for clothing, more panicked about the situation than it warranted. The resounding chimes started up again, impatiently.

What if it *wasn't* Gunner? What if it was Benami?

She slammed the drawer shut and grabbed her robe off the

bathroom door instead, hurrying. Then she remembered that she was on twenty-four-hour duty now.

She ran to her night stand for her gun, loading it with fumbling fingers. *Calm down.* She slammed the magazine into place and crept back down the stairs. When she reached the front door, she moved to the side of it and put her back flush to the wall.

"Who's there?" she demanded.

"Your apologetic partner. Open up."

Tessa breathed again. Her knees went weak. Her belly fluttered. She almost dropped her gun.

She moved in front of the door again and flung it open. "Gunner, what are you—"

"Good girl." He glanced down at the gun in her hand and nodded.

"What are you doing here?" *Lines,* she thought. She didn't want him here, at her home. She had never intended that this should happen. She had *promised* herself that it wouldn't. And oh, God, the lines were crazy, all messed up, scattered all over the place, making no sense anymore at all.

How had this happened in two *days?*

"What do you want?" she gasped. "It's late and—"

He stepped past her into the entryway. "What are we going to do about this?" he said, interrupting her.

"I...don't know." The air went out of her. She didn't even pretend that she didn't know what he was talking about.

"This impersonal business of yours is garbage, Tess. It's not feasible. It's not possible."

"Maybe not," she whispered.

"So," he muttered.

"So we'll talk," she managed to say reasonably, but her heart thrummed. "Would you like a cup of coffee?"

"At this late hour?"

Tessa flushed. It was barely past seven.

Gunner finally grinned.

The tension drained out of his face, and his smile was crooked, endearing. He moved past her down the hallway, looking around as he did.

The inside of her brownstone was more or less what he'd expected. There was a sunken living room off to his right. He noticed hardwood floors and an Oriental rug, dark wood, plants and white

walls. There were a few quiet prints. It all looked like money. He
hesitated, his gaze taking accurate stock of everything in the spare
moments she gave him.

It struck him that he noticed nothing personal whatsoever in the
room. He wondered if that was a rich-girl thing, or a result of her
tragedy, if she had emotionally cleaned house afterward and
thrown out all the boxes.

He glanced into a dining room as he passed it and found another
place of understated elegance. There was a breakfast nook in the
kitchen. This was predominantly white, too, with touches of sunny
yellow that flared when she threw on the overhead light. Lots of
plants here, he saw.

"Is instant okay?" She set her gun carefully on the counter.

"What, no cappuccino, no espresso maker?"

She glared at him.

"That's better, Princess."

"What's better?" she asked warily.

"That look like you're thinking about flaying me alive. I can
deal with that better than—" He broke off abruptly.

Better than vulnerability, he thought uncomfortably. Better than
the softness that made him jump to protect. Better than the brilliant
smiles and that quick little way she tucked her hair behind her ear.

He sat down at the table, and that was when he finally realized
that she was only wearing a robe. It was a silky thing that seemed
to whisper when she moved. Short, midthigh, belted, some kind
of exotic print on a background of royal blue. It slid over her skin,
and unless he was badly mistaken, she was not wearing a bra.

Her hair was wet, tousled. He realized that she must have just
gotten out of the shower. She had very incredible legs. He'd registered that she was reasonably tall. It went without saying that
she would also have long, slender legs. Didn't it? Sure it did. It
usually did, with most tall women.

But this wasn't most women.

He cursed himself up one side and down the other for barging
in on her tonight, for putting himself through more of something
he was already having a tough time handling.

"Gunner?"

He snapped his eyes back to her face. It was the damnedest
thing. His mouth felt dry. Oh, yeah, big mistake. It had definitely
been a mistake to come here.

"What?" he asked hoarsely.

"I asked if you wanted cream or sugar."

"Uh, no. Black. Black's fine."

"There you go." She put a mug on the kitchen table and sat down carefully across from him.

"Thanks." Then something bit his ankle and he came up again like a shot, shaking his foot, staring down disbelievingly. There was something large and hairy wrapped around his ankle. "What the *hell?*"

"Maxwell!" Tessa leaped to her feet again. "Oh, God, Gunner, I'm so sorry."

She pried the animal off. He went unwillingly. He got his claws into Gunner's jeans and refused to retract them, hissing and spitting as Tessa pulled him away.

"He's never done this!" She finally got him free. She carried him to the kitchen door and threw him unceremoniously onto the back porch. "Bad kitty," she snapped.

"Bad *kitty?* Sweetheart, that thing ought to be classified as a lethal weapon." Gunner sat again, feeling even more shaken. He did not like cats. He was a dog man. A man's man. He was—

Tessa faced him and flushed, and it was charming.

"I'm so sorry," she said again. "I told him he'd never meet you." She was rattled. "Maybe he was miffed."

Gunner raised a slow brow. "So what does he do when you have a date?"

"I don't...I never...I haven't..."

No, he thought, she probably hadn't.

He wasn't surprised and was sorry he had asked. It only reminded him how fragile she really was, though she'd take his head off if he said so. But a woman who still didn't date wasn't ready for...well, he thought, much of anything.

"How did he take to Matt?" he asked bluntly, remembering that she'd specifically jumped all over him for touching that subject too cautiously. So he grabbed it, trying to steady the boat.

"He never knew Matt," she said on a sigh, but her voice *was* steadier. "I rescued him from the pound right after...after Matt died. The house was empty and quiet. Too empty and quiet. But Maxwell has never livened things up quite like this before." Then again, she realized, he rarely ever met strangers.

She sat across from Gunner again, sipping her own coffee. "You wanted to talk," she said carefully, changing the subject.

He looked at her. He'd had every intention of telling her that he thought they should put in for reassignment. Now, right away, with no hard feelings. It just wasn't working. It was what he had come over here to tell her.

"What the hell are we going to do about this?" he asked instead.

"Do?" Her voice was cautious.

He noticed that she didn't hem and haw about what "this" was. He liked her even more for it.

"I think it's best if we just ignore it," she continued on a burst of breath. "It isn't feasible."

Feasible? A hell of a way to describe someone ringing your chimes, he thought. "Honey, this isn't a business deal."

"But it is—in a way. It should be."

"Too late."

She paled a little, but she was stubborn. "Of course it isn't. We haven't...haven't..."

He couldn't resist. "Made mad, passionate love in the back of our city car? I guarantee you that if we had, you wouldn't be sitting here discussing it in terms like 'feasible.'"

Color flew into her face. And it still fascinated him.

"Nor will we," she said tightly. "Do it or discuss it."

"Of course not."

Was that amusement in his eyes? Damn him, was he laughing at her? "Lines, Gunner," she said through clenched teeth. "That's all it takes. Just a little self-discipline and restraint. We just need lines. You stay on your side. I'll stay on mine. Just kindly refrain from picking me up on busy city streets—" *from touching me, please don't touch me* "—and we'll get along fine."

This time he laughed aloud. He couldn't help it. "Sure. We can give it a shot."

"Good," she said stiffly.

"Good," he agreed, grinning. "In the meantime, while we're saluting these little lines, we have some unfinished business to attend to."

"What?" she asked warily. But she knew. Of course, she knew.

"I can't break into Benami's place without your help."

Chapter 7

Tessa groaned.

"Or at least I can't do it as safely as I could with your cooperation," he said.

"Why not?"

"Because you're the one with all the connections. We need to find out when he's going to be out of the house, when he's got some sort of social engagement. We've got to find out what kind of alarm system he has on the place."

"Gunner, I don't like this 'we' business. This is your baby."

He watched her guilelessly. "Please?"

The simple word shot something warm and weakening down to her toes. "I *could* flay you, Gunner, I really could."

"And?"

"It's wrong. It's *illegal.*"

"It's necessary. I want this guy."

"What if we get caught? You're on probation, Gunner, aren't you? For that last car you lost? The one that got towed away? You'd probably get thrown out of the department if Kennery caught wind of this."

"If it means Benami doesn't have a chance to disappear again, I'll run the risk."

She stared at him. He was serious. The ramifications to his own life weren't important. Right and wrong was important. If Benami had killed Daphne, and if Benami got away with it because of a probably crooked judge and the money to buy a good attorney, then that would be very, very wrong.

She let out her breath carefully. "I won't go in there with you."

"We'll discuss that part later."

"No, Gunner, *no*. We won't discuss it at all. I'll find out when he's going to be out of the house. I'll even find out what kind of security Daphne has on the place. But I will *not* break in with you."

"I really need a lookout, Princess."

She covered her face with her hands. "Oh, my God." She peered at him through her fingers. "And don't say 'please' again. Don't you dare."

"Just think about it."

"Do you honestly think for a minute that I'm going to be able to do anything else?"

He grinned crookedly. "I hope not."

"You're incorrigible."

"You owe me something for the mortal wound your damn cat just gave me."

"Maybe Maxwell is just a good judge of character. And you're breathing, Gunner. Until I see you collapsed on my floor, that won't hold water."

He drained his coffee and got to his feet. "What about tomorrow?"

"What about it?"

"We should start trying to track down the help at that party and see what they have to say about Benami's comings and goings."

Tessa stood as well, hugging herself, suddenly self conscious in her robe. "It beats the devil out of breaking into a man's home, I guess."

"Well, we'll work on our plans for that, too."

He had never taken his coat off. He thrust his hands into his pockets and wandered down the hall again. When he was outside, halfway down the front walk to the cobblestone alley, she shouted after him.

"Gunner!"

He turned around, walking backward to grin at her. "What, Princess?"

"Do you always get your way?"

"I try my damnedest."

Tessa was sleeping deeply, dreaming disjointed dreams, when the telephone jarred her awake the next morning. They weren't the same nightmares that had haunted her in the months after Matt had died. Not quite. This time she was in a funhouse, with too much glass, too many reflections, and bullets were spitting, cracking, flying. Glass sprayed, razor-sharp and lethal, and she ducked and shielded her face and screamed. She was trapped in there.

But Gunner was in one of the passageways.

She caught glimpses of him in the mirrors, his gun drawn. His voice echoed eerily, shouting to her that he would protect her. But she didn't need his protection. She had her own gun this time. She looked down at it in her hand.

It was a hot dog.

She sat bolt upright and gasped. The phone kept jangling.

"Hello," she croaked, finally fumbling for the phone.

"'Morning, Princess."

Gunner. Again. Already.

She slumped back against the headboard, then she cracked one eye to check the bedside clock. She would be reasonable about this.

"Do you know what time it is?"

"Sure. Seven-thirty."

"Gunner, it's Sunday."

There was a short silence. "What, do you go to church or something?"

"I was planning on sleeping in," she answered tightly.

"Not today. We've got work to do. I'm calling to tell you that I'll be there in half an hour." With any luck, he thought, by calling ahead this time he would give her enough warning that she wouldn't be wearing a short blue silk robe with the hint of nothing underneath.

He could handle this. Damn it, he could.

"No!" Tessa protested.

"No?" Gunner repeated. "How come?"

Last night had been one thing, she thought frantically. She couldn't, *wouldn't* let it establish a precedent. She had *told* him they needed lines! But suddenly she felt like a tumbleweed, being bounced along by a strong wind, and there was nothing at all she could do to stop her momentum.

"I'll meet you at the office," she said, resigning herself to being awake at seven-thirty on a Sunday.

"Not cool, Princess. Our desk isn't the place to talk about what we have to talk about."

She remembered his decision to break into Benami's town house. She remembered her tacit agreement to help him. It flooded in on her, leaving her cold, then hot and itchy with nerves. She didn't answer.

"Come on, Princess, you don't strike me as the type who'd welsh on her word."

"Maybe if it was given under duress, I would," she grumbled.

"That wasn't duress. It was just gentle persuasion."

She wondered what classified as duress, then.

"Half an hour," he repeated. This time he hung up before she could argue.

Tessa leaped out of bed. He was coming here. Again.

She dressed fast and ran a brush through her hair, refusing to put makeup on, not even a little, just because he was coming over. Then she raced downstairs into the kitchen. She flung open the refrigerator. She'd been so excited about being reassigned to Homicide that she hadn't been to the market in days.

The refrigerator yawned back at her, virtually empty. There was a small slab of Gouda cheese and half a tin of water biscuits. There was a leftover Caesar salad—probably limp by now—and three bottles of mineral water. Nothing at all that would interest a man like John Gunner, she realized.

She pushed the door shut again and hurried into the living room to use the phone there. The gourmet market around the corner made sandwiches.

"I need some sort of breakfast sandwiches," she demanded as soon as someone answered. "Whatever they have at fast-food places."

"Are you serious?"

She thought of Gunner and his hot dogs. "Very. Anything with cholesterol. Lots and lots of cholesterol. On second thought, maybe you should throw in some sausage instead of the bacon. He'd like that. Bring me two of them. No—three! And hash browns." It would be a real macho, Neanderthal treat.

"Got you covered."

She'd barely hung up when the doorbell rang. Half an hour, my foot, she thought, going to the door.

She realized that he'd probably called her from the car. But at least he had called this time. Then she pulled open the door, and her thoughts staggered.

How could he always look so *good?*

His cologne was fresh and it immediately filled her senses. She stepped back to let him inside, and he gave her that crooked grin as he passed her. No T-shirt today, she noticed as he shrugged out of his jacket and dropped it on the newel post. He wore a blue polo shirt. The neck was unbuttoned. At the V below his throat, she could see a few dark chest hairs. They matched the soft, dark down on his forearms. His jeans hugged his body. And in spite of herself, she thought of how hard and unapologetically masculine he had felt last night when he'd held her, and something in her belly curled.

She needed coffee. She needed it badly.

"What's for breakfast?" he asked.

Maybe worse than her attraction to him was the way she was already coming to anticipate him, she thought sinkingly, following him into the kitchen. "It's on its way."

"On its *way?*"

"That's right. I called to have something delivered."

He helped himself to a coffee mug, filled it with water and stuck it in the microwave. He grinned. "Delivered, huh? Damned if I couldn't get used to living this way."

"Don't," she said quickly. "We're not starting a precedent here."

"Whatever you say, Princess."

The doorbell rang again. She hurried back to collect the food and pay for it.

The market had done itself proud, and Gunner was pleased. The breakfast sandwiches dripped with cheese and an ungodly amount of grease, she thought. Gunner ate two of them. His stomach must be cast iron, Tessa decided.

It sure had felt that way, she thought, being tucked against him last night when he had carried her up Filbert.

"So," Gunner said, finally wiping his mouth and leaning back in his chair. "Let's straighten out the mechanics of getting into that house first. Then we'll go track down the help from the party."

Tessa nodded slowly, resignedly.

"The first thing we need to do is find out when Benami is going out, to where, and for how long."

Tessa chewed her lip. "Well, this is the time of year for charity balls." She couldn't believe she was actually doing this. "There's got to be something coming up. I guess I could call my mother."

She sighed and got to her feet. Gunner watched her go, enjoying her walk, then he felt a twinge of remorse at the tension in it now.

He had done that to her.

It would probably be better, kinder, if he didn't take her with him, he realized, and wondered if that was his urge to protect her talking, or just fear of an unhappy God striking him with a thunderbolt for dragging a sweet-faced angel down into sin and crime. He got up to make another cup of coffee, and that was when he noticed the cat outside on the porch railing.

Maxwell glared in at him malevolently. Gunner glared back.

"The mayor's having a fund-raiser. Tonight."

Tessa's voice startled him. He quickly turned back to her. "Perfect."

"I called Millicent Craig. She's the mayor's right-hand man, or woman, as the case might be. Christian is on the guest list."

"Better yet." Gunner nodded. "What about the security?"

"I'm waiting for a call back on that." Even as she spoke, the phone rang again.

She was gone longer this time. Gunner went back to eyeing Maxwell. Impulsively he wrenched open the door and jumped at the animal, shouting, trying to startle him.

Maxwell didn't move a muscle except to yawn.

"Damn fleabag," he muttered.

"Gunner, you've really got to work on your aggression."

He looked over his shoulder at her, vaguely embarrassed. "It's the principle of the thing."

"You have those?"

"A few. What did you find out?"

"The windows are wired and there are motion sensors on both doors."

"You're sure?"

"Reasonably. It's a town house, I know the woman who lives next door, and she says the builder put the same system in all of them. I called and pretended that I was thinking of changing what I have on this place, asking for a recommendation." At eight-thirty on a Sunday morning, she thought. Anita had probably thought that she'd lost her mind.

"Okay. Good," Gunner answered.

"It doesn't *feel* good, Gunner!" she cried suddenly. "It feels sneaky and underhanded and wrong."

He wanted to touch her. He wanted to hug her, to smooth her ruffled feathers, to hold her and tuck her hair behind her ear. With any other woman he would have done just that, impulsively and without a thought.

Lines.

He kept his distance. "Don't wimp out on me quite yet, Princess. The worst is yet to come."

She paled a little. "What if Benami actually catches us in the act? What if we get past the security, and Benami comes home unexpectedly?"

"We, huh?" His grin widened.

"Figure of speech."

"Mmm."

"Well, what if he does?"

"We'll talk about it when and if the time comes."

She stared at him incredulously. "I'm not going in there unless I have some sort of game plan mapped out ahead of time, Gunner. And it had better cover *every* eventuality."

He shrugged. "Okay. I'll have one by the time we get there."

She watched him warily. "Promise? Are you good for your word?"

"Oh, yeah, Princess. Always."

Tessa realized she believed him.

Six hours, fifteen waitresses, three bartenders and seven bus boys later, Tessa was almost starting to agree that extreme measures might be required to nail Benami. Almost, but not quite. Unfortunately, not one single person had noticed Christian leaving the Heart Association Ball.

They sat in their car outside the apartment of the last person they had interviewed. Tessa leaned her head back against the seat wearily.

"Are we wrong?" she asked quietly. "Did Benami *not* kill her? Is it *possible?*"

Gunner only grunted. "He's just good," he said finally. "Very, very good."

"So how'd he do it?" she wondered aloud.

"Like you said. He just made sure none of the help was watching." He paused. "We were asking for a lot from those people, Tess. Two hundred and fifty guests, and we asked them about a man they know only from a photograph we showed them."

She nodded wearily.

"Some of them didn't recognize him or even remember seeing him at all," he reminded her, "but we know he was there."

"Yes," she agreed quietly.

"We'll just have to go on to those other hundred and fifty guests who haven't been questioned yet. Tomorrow. Right now, we've got a little breaking and entering to see about."

Her heart sank. "I've been thinking about that. I really don't want to do it, Gunner. There's got to be another way."

"Okay."

She whipped around in her seat to look at him. *"Okay?"*

"I've been thinking about it, too. I'll go in alone."

"I don't want you to do it, either!"

"That's *not* okay."

She swore. He cocked a brow at her in mild surprise. "And all this time I've had you on a pedestal."

It seemed safest to ignore that. "Christian has to have slipped up *somewhere,*" she said suddenly, vehemently.

Gunner started the car again. "That's what I'm counting on."

"Let's swing by and check Igor first. I'll think about...the other." *Breaking in.* She could barely even say it, she realized.

Igor had nothing new to tell them.

When they were standing outside the Administration Building, Tessa hugged herself. "I guess you're not going to let me walk home now, either," she muttered.

"Sure I am."

Her jaw dropped. God, he kept her off balance.

"Today you're armed," he explained.

And that simply, her heart swelled. It was such a matter-of-fact vote of confidence. And it was given with no questions asked. She nodded slowly.

Gunner waited.

"So what about tonight?" she asked finally.

"I'll do it on my own," he said again. And something inside him squirmed.

It really made the most sense for them to do it together. He would have insisted on the cooperation of any of his three earlier partners. He *did* want backup, another pair of ears, eyes, another mind absorbing impressions. And if he should get caught, he'd sure prefer it to be two against one, two armed detectives against Benami's madness.

He *was* protecting her again. These lines, he thought, weren't amounting to diddly after all, at least not where it counted.

"No," Tess said quietly. "If he comes home in the...in the process of this, I'd rather it be two against one."

Gunner smiled very slowly, hearing his own thoughts.

"What?" she demanded when she saw his grin. In that moment, he looked more arrogant, more cocky, more self-confident than ever.

"Good point," he agreed.

She hesitated, then nodded. "Okay. So how...how exactly would this be accomplished? All that security—"

"The sensors are easy. It's the wires that are tricky. Assuming there are no wires on the doors, all we have to do is slide underneath the beams. They rarely cover the air below three feet, two at the least."

"Do I want to know how you know this?"

"I had a reckless and misspent youth."

"You're a cop. You can't possibly have a record."

"Maybe I was too smart to get caught at anything." His gray eyes laughed. She couldn't be sure if he was serious or not.

She sighed. "I was kind of hoping you'd tell me that you'd done a stint in the Burglary Unit. Or maybe that you'd had a case once where motion sensors came into play."

"Nope. Sorry," he said baldly.

"What if they *do* cover below two feet?"

"Hope's all we've got here, sweetheart. I just hope they don't."

"Then there are the wires on the doors to consider," she said pointedly.

"That's not what you said earlier." His voice turned sharp. "You said 'the windows are wired and there are motion sensors on both doors.' Those were your exact words."

She thought they probably had been. She was beginning to realize that he had a mind like a steel trap.

"Gunner, I don't want to attempt this based on assumptions," she said too loudly.

"Shh." He looked around. "We need a little circumspection here, Princess. We're more or less standing on a street corner, in front of Administration, no less."

Her skin flamed. "Which just goes to show I'm not cut out for this stuff."

"I told you. It's your call. If you don't want to come with me, then don't."

She saw something tick at his jaw again. She took a deep breath. "Okay. So we break open the door—"

"The back door," Gunner amended. "And *I* break it. This is one of those things like driving, Princess. I do the dirty work."

She'd agree to *that* without a fight. "So what if you slide under the sensors, then we find out that they're lower than you thought, or that the door *was* wired. What then?"

He grinned. "We run like hell."

She had the strongest urge to slug him. She turned her back on him and began walking instead.

"Call me when you have your ducks in a row, Gunner."

"They're lined up, Tess. Hell, they're saluting."

She stopped and looked back at him wildly. To her way of thinking, they were definitely still flapping all over the pond.

"The sensors are the biggest thing," he said, closing the distance between them again. "So I'll go under first. That way if I set anything off, you can get out of there pronto before the police come. No need to drag your career down the tubes along with mine."

Her career? She was thinking more along the lines of what it would do to her brother's reputation, to her father's and her uncle's, if she were caught.

She shuddered. "What if the alarm is the silent kind?" she

asked. "I forgot to ask that. I'm not any good at this sort of thing, Gunner."

"It probably is. But there's got to be a box either inside the front door, or inside both doors, something that can deactivate the system. They all have some such thing, in case the owner messes up and trips his own alarm."

"There are codes, though, Gunner! You can't just cruise in and turn the damn thing off! You have to put in a *code*."

He lifted a brow at her frustration. "Exactly. I'll find the box and check it as soon as I'm inside. If it's blinking, then I tripped it. I'll try to untrip it. Even if I can't, we should have plenty of time to get out of there. The alarm rings at the security company. The company calls the homeowner to see if it was a mistake. If there's no answer, *then* they call the cops. Besides, homeowners aren't crafty or creative by nature. The codes are almost always somebody's birthday, or their anniversary, or their social security number. I'll punch in every number pertinent to Daphne that I can think of. If it stops blinking we're fine. If not, we go."

It was, she thought, the most comfort she was going to get.

"What time is this thing supposed to start tonight?" Gunner asked.

"Eight o'clock," she whispered.

"So I'll pick you up at eight."

He left her and moved back into the building to return to the annexed parking garage. Tessa watched him and hugged herself again.

She was actually going to do this, she realized.

She was out of her mind.

Or maybe, she thought, maybe he was starting to rub off on her, and in a lot of ways, that was even worse.

Chapter 8

At a quarter to eight, Tessa sat on the edge of her bed, her hands clasped tightly between her knees. Once she looked up and caught sight of her reflection in the dresser mirror.

She didn't know whether to laugh or to cry.

She wondered if she was overdoing this. She'd dressed all in black—jeans, a turtleneck, even boots. She wore no jewelry—gold and diamonds caught light. She'd found a pair of leather riding gloves that she hadn't used in years, dark brown though not black, and they were clenched tightly in the single fist she made with her hands.

Her eyes fell to Matt's picture on the dresser.

"I have to do this," she told him breathlessly. And if he were here, she was pretty sure he'd understand.

"I can't let him go in there by himself," she explained. "He's my partner." And there was a sanctity about that, a deep and profound responsibility. It didn't always matter whether you agreed totally with what the other guy was doing or not, she thought. If you disagreed often enough, then you got reassigned, the way Gunner's other three partners had eventually done. Because when push came to shove, you had to be there for your partner. You had to cover him.

You had to keep him alive.

She swallowed dryly. If Matt were Gunner's partner, she knew that he would probably go into Benami's home with him once he realized that he couldn't talk him out of it. That wasn't the part that disturbed her.

What she simply couldn't get out of her mind was the fact that Matt would never, ever choose to break in himself. No matter what. He would let Benami walk and curse the system, but he wouldn't break his beloved law. Just as he would not have nearly come to blows with Benami yesterday, no matter what Benami had said to her.

Matt had always gone by the book. As she did. And it had gotten him killed.

She thought shakily that if Gunner had stepped through that restaurant door that night, right into the middle of a mugging, his own gun would have been in his hand before his wife, his girlfriend, his date—whatever—had even hit the street. Matt had approached the perp carefully, placatingly, his hands outstretched, trying to reason with him.

Crack, bang, roar. Three steps and he had been down, just as she'd stepped outside.

Tessa made a small sound in her throat. Why, dear God, was she sitting here and comparing the two of them?

Because she felt safer doing this with Gunner—this wild, irresponsible thing—than she had walking into the mugging that night with Matt. And that was heinous. It was surely some kind of betrayal, she thought. Somehow it felt so very *wrong.*

Her heart spasmed. She looked at Matt's picture again.

"I'm sorry," she whispered. "I don't...it doesn't negate what we shared."

Then the doorbell rang downstairs. It was time.

Gunner grinned approvingly when she opened the door. His gaze coasted down her legs, moved slowly upward again, then finally settled on her eyes.

"You could make a new career out of this, Princess."

In spite of herself, Tessa's heart swelled. She told herself that she didn't want his approval because she had dressed appropriately for a break-in. *Good God.* She told herself that the approval of a man like John Gunner should be dubious at best. And something melted inside her and she felt herself smiling back at him.

They walked to the car and when they got inside, she noticed a small, black leather pouch on the floor in front of the passenger seat. "What's that?"

"Tools of the trade."

She'd had to ask. She did *not* ask where they'd come from.

He pulled into traffic much more circumspectly than usual. She noticed that he, too, was dressed all in black. It gave him a delicious, devilish air. He wore a dark, long-sleeved T-shirt, untucked, and his hair was pulled back into a short ponytail—to keep it out of the way, she imagined. She got the strong feeling that he relished the job at hand and that dressing the part was half the fun.

The closer they got to Benami's place, the more her heart hurtled. When they turned around at Logan Circle and started south, and it boomed, leaped, hammered. She took a deep, steadying breath.

"What about when—if—we get inside?" she asked. "What's your plan?"

"We stay together," he said promptly. "That's the whole idea of taking you with me in the first place. Two against one. We don't want to get separated, just in case."

Still, Tessa tried for bravado. "We could cover more ground more quickly if we split up."

"No."

She saw that nerve at his jaw tick a little, warning her off the subject. She let her breath out slowly. "Okay. Fine by me."

He grinned. "I think that's the quickest you've ever given in, Princess."

They parked a block away, at the mouth of the alley. When Gunner put the Philadelphia Police Department cardboard in the window, she laughed nervously at the irony of it. This time he grinned sheepishly.

It was full dark.

They moved back up the alley on foot. There was no one else around. The night was cloudy. There was no moon. Tessa kept close to the back of a large, sprawling, brick home, probably circa 1880. Before the turn of the century, it had been someone's city mansion.

Benami's place was dark. There was a small, rear stoop just big enough for two people to stand on. Four concrete steps led up it.

Off to the side, chained to the ornate, wrought-iron railing, were two garbage cans.

The rest of the area was bare concrete, maybe six feet wide to the alley. Light spilled from the rear windows of the adjacent town house, the one belonging to her friend Anita. The homes were three floors, and it seemed to Tessa that every single rear room over there was illuminated. Golden-white light spilled out onto that side of the alley.

Gunner had the pouch in his hands.

"Where's your gun?" he asked.

"Right here." She'd holstered it under her sweater. She hadn't worn a coat. Her nerves were too wired to let her feel the chill, and it would only get in her way. It could slow her down if she had to climb, run...

Oh, God.

"Give it to me," Gunner said.

"What? Why?" Her heart skipped again.

"Because if you have to make a run for it, I don't want you armed. If you get caught darting up Eighteenth Street like your tail's on fire, it'll be easier for you to explain if you're not waving a gun."

She began shaking. She gave him her weapon.

"I'll give it back to you as soon as we're inside."

"*If* we get inside."

"We will." He checked the safety and shoved her revolver into the waist of his jeans, beneath his own T-shirt, then he went to work on the door.

She didn't want to watch him, wanted to keep her eyes open for anyone approaching up the alley, or a change in the light from next door that would tell her that someone was standing in front of one of those windows. But she was fascinated. There *was* something dangerous about him now, something wild and titillating. He ran a gloved hand expertly along the door frame, his gray eyes narrowed and intent, the quintessential bad boy doing plenty wrong. Her heart rate picked up again, but not with fear this time. In that moment, he was the kind of forbidden male who made good girls the world over swoon in their tracks. His face was strong, ungodly handsome, for once unsmiling.

"The sensors!" she hissed as he finally set to work on the lock.

"They'll be on the inside."

He had more little picks in that pouch than she wanted to know about.

A moment later there was an almost inaudible click.

"All right," he whispered. He hunkered down.

"Won't the sensors pick up the motion of the door opening?" she demanded in an undertone.

"The good ones are made to overlook that. They're density sensitive. The density of a body is different from that of a door. Or something like that. I think."

"You *think?*"

"We'll find out soon enough. Let's go."

There was no chance for her to argue further. Gunner was flat on his belly, sliding over the threshold, sliding the door open slowly with his momentum.

Tessa held her breath, but no sirens went off.

She did *not* want to be standing out here without him, without even her gun.

Her heart started skittering in panic again. She dropped down quickly after him, onto her tummy, moving as he had done. A few moments later, she came nose to heel with his boots. She felt ridiculous. And then her heart exploded.

Gunner swore.

"What? *What?*"

"It's blinking," he answered.

"It's blinking? What's blinking? The *alarm's* blinking?"

"Yeah. When was Daphne's birthday?"

"Her birthday?"

"You're repeating yourself, Tess."

"How am I supposed to know when her birthday was?" she hissed. "You were supposed to know this before we got here!"

"I did. I thought I'd memorized it. I forgot."

"You *forgot?*" She scrambled to her feet beside him and started turning in little, panicked circles, looking around wildly. "Oh, my God. Oh, dear God."

"Chill out, Princess. I'm just playing with you. A little levity to loosen you up."

That was when she realized that she'd been hearing little tapping sounds all along. Gunner was working at the number pad on the alarm system.

She was going to kill him.

"Gotcha," he said finally. The little red light at the top of it went out. "With seven seconds to spare."

"Seven seconds," she repeated hollowly, dazed. "You don't know that, Gunner. You can't see your watch. It's too dark. What if—"

"I was counting in my head."

"In your head? While you were putting *another* set of numbers into that thing?"

He turned away from the alarm to look around as well. They were in a small mudroom. "Yeah. Turned out she used her mother's birthday."

She'd been right, Tessa realized. He had a mind like a steel trap.

It was vaguely—though not much—comforting. She forced herself to breathe again as she looked around as well.

"Now what?" she whispered.

"What did he do that night?"

"Pardon me?"

"Walk me through how you think it happened."

"Right." *Breathe in, out,* she instructed herself. *Relax.* "The dining room."

"The scene of the crime. Before that."

"Her bedroom. No, no, he would have lured her downstairs on some pretext."

"Yeah, probably."

"He would have had a gun, or maybe a knife, would have tried to coerce her up onto that dining room chair."

"So we're looking for a weapon." He was already moving out of the mudroom, into an adjacent laundry room. "If you were a gun, where would you be?" He skimmed all the usual clandestine places. In the washer and the dryer. Beneath the basin sink and in the drain. The tools came out again for that job. He looked in the cupboards and checked to make sure the sheet vinyl flooring was firmly fastened in all the corners. He tapped the walls for hidden safes.

"Nothing," he muttered quietly, stepping across the small hall into the kitchen. "Go on."

Tessa took another deep breath and followed him as he methodically did all the same things in that room that he had done in the laundry room. Almost without thinking about it, she began helping him.

"Daphne fought," she said. "Hard and well. He hadn't been expecting so much of a fight. He had to immobilize her. He tied her hands."

Gunner opened the refrigerator and moved fast to hit the little button that would keep the light out. "Hold this," he said.

Tessa reached over his shoulder to press her gloved finger against the light button while he rummaged, opening Tupperware and various containers and peering inside. There was no way to do it without touching him. Her arms just weren't that long.

Oh, God.

She had no choice but to lean into his back. He was crouched, and her thighs were flush against his shoulders. Every time he moved, reached, shifted, he rubbed against her, shooting little frissons of sensation down her limbs.

She choked. If she laughed, it would be a crazy sound, ringing off the walls.

This was absurd. It was impossible. They were *breaking in*. She was doing something that could forever wreck her career, that could bring her family no end of bad press. And here she was getting fidgety and warm inside over her partner in crime, with all her thoughts centered on the way his body felt pressed against her legs.

"What?" she asked hoarsely. He was saying something. God help her, he was talking to her and she hadn't heard a word he'd said.

"I asked you where he got the rope to tie her hands. When he went to look for it, she could have fled, gotten away."

"He already had some attached to the chandelier, ready and waiting for her. When she saw that, she knew what he intended. That was when she went wild."

"Right. But Angie said that the fibers on her hands were different from those at her throat."

Tessa thought about that. Then she went on, fast, excitedly. "It wasn't a gun. He used a *knife* to coerce her, Gunner. He had that on him, so he was able to cut the rope away from the chandelier, the one that he'd originally planned to hang her with. He used it on her arms instead."

Even in the darkness, she could see him grinning when he

straightened away from the refrigerator. She let the button go in the split second it took him to close the door again. She stepped back, putting space between them just as quickly.

"Yeah," he agreed, turning again to work on the freezer. "But if he just tied her arms, she still could have run."

She had to hold the freezer light out, too. Tessa gritted her teeth and leaned into him again.

"He tied her *to* something," she said. "To something big, heavy, immovable."

"The table'd be my guess."

"Yes," she whispered. "Mine, too."

"While she was tied to the table, he went to get another rope." Gunner took over the scenario they were creating. "It was the *second* rope that actually hung her. And it turned out to be different in composition from the first one. He probably got the sedatives then, too."

"By now it's probably close to seven-thirty," Tessa whispered.

"Right," Gunner agreed.

"And if he's *too* late getting to the party, that's something people would notice."

"So he's running out of time. Better to revamp his game plan."

"Drug her—"

"Secure the ties—"

"Appear at the party—"

"And at about eight-fifteen, after making damn sure everybody knows he's there, Benami slips out again." Gunner paused. "No knives in the freezer. Let's try the living room furniture and that thing holding the tea set in the parlor."

Tessa stepped back quickly again to let him move. She realized that he had a second sack pushed into the waist of his jeans. This one was empty. He shook it out, and before he left the kitchen, he went to examine some knives stuck in a wood block on the counter. There was a paring knife small enough to handle easily, with a lethal blade that could have cut through rope, or have intimidated someone far braver than Daphne. He dropped it into the sack.

"Gunner, he'll notice it's missing! We can't—"

"He misplaced it," he said mildly and finally left the kitchen. Tessa moved fast to keep close to him.

"So he leaves the party again," Gunner resumed, nosing

through the parlor, lifting various odds and ends and peering into drawers. "He hotfoots it back here. No cabs. That's too risky, like we agreed before. He probably took one there the first time, though, because he was running late."

"We'll check," Tessa agreed.

"So at about eight-thirty, given that we figure it took him about seven minutes to make the trip on foot, Daphne would be good and groggy. She would have had the sedatives in her for about an hour by then."

"And *that* was when he hanged her," Tessa said. "Angela said she'd ingested the drugs roughly an hour and a half before she died."

"Yeah."

Nothing seemed to jump out at them in either the parlor or the living room. Gunner took a small plastic bag and a razor blade from his wallet. He finally proceeded into the dining room. This time he didn't rummage around, looking for a weapon. He went directly to the table.

"Give this thing a shove, Princess."

She understood immediately what he was getting at. She went to the table. It was huge, heavy mahogany and would probably seat at least twelve. By leaning her hips against it and using her legs for leverage, she was just able to budge it.

If Daphne had been tied to one of the legs, with her arms behind her, growing increasingly groggy, there was no way she would be able to drag this table anywhere, Tessa thought. She would have been helpless, agonizingly aware of what was going to happen to her when her husband came back. She wouldn't have been able to do anything about it.

Fury pounded through Tessa.

"Easy there, Princess," Gunner cautioned.

She realized she had given the table an extra push, scooting it a good four inches in her anger. She flushed and tried pulling it back toward her, looping her wrists around a leg. It was harder that way. Both she and Gunner had to work together to bring the table back to its original position.

No, Daphne would not have been able to move it, no matter how desperate she was.

Gunner went down to his knees, working around each leg. He took the razor and scraped at the carpet in each place, pushing minuscule and invisible particles into the plastic bag, then he folded it and put it back in his wallet.

"With any luck, no one's vacuumed in here these past few days," he muttered.

"Gunner, how are we ever going to get this analyzed?" she whispered helplessly. "What are we supposed to tell Forensics about how we got it?"

He shrugged. "One of the district cops who took the call is a friend of mine."

"So?" she hissed.

"So he got it when he was here the first time around."

"So what's he been doing sitting on it these past few days?"

"He didn't. He gave it to me. I misplaced it."

"Chain of evidence," she snapped. "What could have happened to it while it was missing? Oh, Gunner, I just don't know about this."

"I put it in my locker and forgot about it. I know where it was the whole time."

She smiled a little. "Boy, are you going to catch hell."

"Yeah." When he straightened, she saw that he was grinning, too.

"And Basil English the Fourth is going to make mincemeat of you on the stand, assuming we even get that far," she said.

"Well, I'll work on it, come up with something better. I just thought of that off the top of my head." He looked around the dining room and went to check the breakfront. "Okay, we're done here. Let's check their bedroom."

They started for the stairs. They were on the second floor landing when they heard noise at the front door.

Tessa panicked. In a single heartbeat, all the blood she possessed seemed to sluice right down to her toes. Her heart kept it there, exploding from a few staccato beats into something so fast that no blood could possibly come back into it.

"Oh, my God!" she yelped. *Keys.* She heard the distant but distinct metallic jingle of keys. "Gunner! It's *him!*"

Gunner was gone. She reached for him and flailed at air.

She caught sight of his shadow moving down the hall and she took off after him, her legs wobbling with terror. He stopped dead in the doorway of the first bedroom they came to, and she plowed into him from behind, skittering backward a few steps.

"Do something!" she cried quietly. "Gunner, *do* something!"

He let out a long stream of invectives that more or less indicated he was trying.

The bedroom was the master. Definitely not a good place to hide, Tessa thought wildly. But it was too late. She heard the door open downstairs. Footsteps come into the entryway. "What's he doing?" she moaned in a whisper, barely audible.

"Do you want to ask him?" Gunner snapped in an undertone.

She was going to kill him. "You never gave me my gun back!"

He finally clapped a hand over her mouth to shut her up.

Just in time. The footsteps were coming up the stairs now. Tessa knew she would have screamed. Instead, with Gunner's palm flush over her mouth, over her nostrils, she could scarcely breathe.

No more time. They darted together into the bedroom, across it to the master bath, bumping into each other, fumbling in the darkness. Tessa beat at Gunner's hand to get him to take it away from her face.

The shower curtain was heavy, some kind of dark, satiny material, with a somewhat lighter liner. Each side of the curtain itself was drawn back into a tie on either side of the tub. Gunner and Tessa dove in. She wondered wildly if they made any noise. Surely they had, some swish, some rustle. *Where was Christian?*

She answered herself a moment later. He was in the master bedroom. She could hear him moving around in there through the open bathroom door.

Gunner pressed a hand against her shoulder and motioned to the bottom of the tub. *Down, he wants me to get down, maybe Christian can see our shadows through the liner, if he comes in here I am purely going to die.* She eased down and squirmed to the back behind the heavier, outer curtain.

In the next moment, Gunner was literally on top of her.

It took every bit of her will not to make a sound. Her heart was hammering hard enough to leave her chest. She was kneeling, but leaning back at an unnatural angle, her spine pressed to the porcelain. And Gunner faced into her, a knee wedged down on either side of her hips. His arms were tight against her shoulders as he braced his weight. There was no way he could give her her gun now, no way they could even move.

Her heart galloped harder, almost painfully, even as terror swept through her as if it were numbing ice. And impossibly, in spite of that, awareness suddenly shot through her again. It was hot, liquid, stealing her breath. Christian would almost certainly find them. And all she could think of was Gunner on top of her.

His scent. That woodsy aura, clean and sharp, somehow green. It was like a silent forest just before dawn before the birds came alive, she thought. He was too close to her. There was no escaping it.

His legs. Splayed around her, over her, his hips straddling hers, pressing against her intimately, like tangled lovers. If they had been unclothed it would have taken no more than a shifting of his weight to slide inside her.

Don't think about it.

His weight was solid, strong, bearing into her, making her turn her face to the side to inhale, and then her cheek was flush against his chest and she could hear his heart beating.

It was steady. How could it be *steady?*

Then she felt him rub his cheek over her hair.

He was trying to calm her. On some level, she knew that. He was just being Gunner. He was easing her terror the only way he could under the circumstances, with a silent touch, but it started a strange ache inside her again, a poignant hunger for something *more,* something different than what he intended.

Sound came from just outside the shower curtain. Benami was in the bathroom. The medicine cabinet opened and closed.

She turned her head, burying her mouth against Gunner's chest to keep from crying out. Her arms came up hard around his waist, almost of their own volition, holding him, holding on.

She was trembling. Gunner felt the little tremors scoot through her body, and it hurt something inside him because he had dragged her into this. Then Benami left the bathroom again and he realized her shudders had changed. They weren't panicked any longer. They were deeper than that. Her breath hitched, and it didn't sound terrified any longer.

For a moment, they stayed very still.

He felt her take in air, dragging it greedily into her lungs. He felt her breasts push against his chest with the effort. It was as though she was absorbing the nearness of him, taking him in greedily with the air.

Ah, hell.

He closed his eyes and cursed silently for Benami to get on

with it. *Get what you came back for and get the hell out of the bedroom. Now, fast, before I lose it.*

Too late.

He could tell himself that he didn't really want this woman for all the reasons that were becoming a litany to him by now. That *she* didn't want *him*. He could tell himself that she wasn't ready, that he wasn't serious enough for her, didn't know *how* to be serious about a woman. But his face was still in her hair—*flowers, springtime, soft and easy*—and his body wanted her. He wanted her with sudden, pounding urgency, and his body took the cue and ran with it.

He felt himself hardening against her. She was so close. She assaulted all of his senses. A subdued groan escaped him. With the way they were sitting, those sweet, blushing, ladylike lines of hers were about to get blown clear to hell, and what would she do about that?

What she did was *wriggle*. His head swam. His heart pounded.

Tessa heard his heartbeat change. Not steady anymore, she thought. No, it was wild now, and it wasn't because Benami had come closer—had he? No, she couldn't hear him out there anymore, couldn't be sure *where* he was now, but she knew the man had nothing to do with why Gunner's heartbeat had changed. She knew it with every instinct she possessed, with instincts as old as womankind. She knew it and craved, knew it and wanted, knew it and ached.

She felt him growing hard against her. It was delicious, intimate...crazy.

Her own heart started to thunder again. She looked up at him pleadingly and could barely see his face in the darkness. *Tell me it's me, Gunner, tell me this wouldn't happen with any woman you got trapped in a bathtub with.*

But of course, it would have. He was John Gunner.

"I think he's gone," Gunner said in a husky whisper. "I haven't heard him in a while."

"Gone," she managed to reply vacantly.

"I'm going to get up now."

"Good." *Bad, don't go, stay here, touch me, I don't care why.* What was she doing? What was she *thinking?*

Unbidden came thoughts of Matt, images clearer than they had been for months now, his face, his eyes, and the sense of guilt that swept through her now was so much more painful than it had been when she had stared at his picture earlier tonight. She shoved Gunner hard and frantically.

He eased his weight backward until he could crouch, then stand. He watched her almost warily for a second. His breath was still coming too fast, too harshly. It filled the small enclosure, making her own throat close. It could have been any woman trapped beneath him, she told herself again. Any woman. And the same thing would have happened.

Gunner felt amazed, rocked, a little bit scared. Okay, so she was pretty and classy and sweet. Blue-blooded and off limits. But how the hell could he turn him on like that under *these* circumstances?

It was the air of the forbidden, he decided. That was all. That was why he had reacted in such a place, in a way he never had and never would have reacted before. Sure, he loved women, but he loved himself more.

Finally, silently, he eased the curtain open. He motioned to Tessa to stay put for a moment. He stepped out of the tub.

Tessa waited in agony. Because of what had happened, because of what might still happen if he was wrong, if Benami was still out there.

Dear God, she hadn't even heard the man leave!

Gunner stuck his head back into the shower. "Okay," he whispered. "Coast is clear."

"He's downstairs," she said in an undertone.

"No. I don't think so. I think he left again while we were... never mind."

Tessa crept out of the tub. Gunner opened the medicine cabinet quickly and quietly.

"I want to get out of here, Gunner. *Please.*"

"Soon," he said quietly.

She watched him take a single pill from each of the little bottles he found in the medicine cabinet. He dropped them into the sack, too. He went back into the bedroom, and she hurried after him. One of the dresser drawers was still open. Benami had come back for something in that drawer, Tessa thought. Gunner went to it and rummaged through it. After a moment he held up a money clip. He had come back for cash.

Gunner finished with a quick, superficial search of the bedroom. After a moment, though she was still shaky, she began to help him to hurry things along, to make their hunt as comprehensive as possible. Of all the rooms in the house, this was the most likely to contain something the man might have hidden. *Everyone* hid things in their bedrooms.

They looked under the mattress, in the closet, in every drawer. Gunner went back into the bathroom and took a quick peek into the toilet tank. He glanced back at Tessa and shook his head. Nothing. He motioned to the hallway, to the stairs.

They left the bedroom and crept down. Benami was no longer on the ground floor, either.

Tessa didn't start shaking—*really* shaking—until they got outside again. Then the adrenaline rushed out of her. She leaned weakly against the wall of Benami's house.

"Oh, my God," she said tremulously, then something else dawned on her. "All that for *nothing!*"

Gunner began walking without her. "Not quite nothing," he said when she hurried to catch up. "We got the knife—"

"But Angela Byerly never said anything about her having been cut anywhere! We don't even know if that's the one he used to coerce her!"

They reached the car.

"Even if he just poked her with it, there could still be skin cells on it or something," Gunner insisted. "Anyway, hell, I didn't expect to find the other rope laying there on his bed, for God's sake." And then he fell silent.

He was going to talk about it, she realized, about what had happened in that tub. Was he *embarrassed?* No way, she thought, not John Gunner.

She wasn't going to mention it, he realized. He wondered if it was class or fear that kept her reticent now. Impersonal, he thought. Yeah, right.

They reached her brownstone. "See you in the morning," he said shortly. "Thanks for helping me out."

He sounded so stiff, so formal. Everything had changed. Tessa felt like crying.

She held herself together until she got inside. She wandered vacantly into the living room, then the bones went out of her legs and she collapsed on the sofa, trembling.

She wondered what they were supposed to do now, and she wasn't thinking about the case at all.

Chapter 9

Gunner didn't wake her with a phone call the next morning.

Of course he wouldn't call, Tessa thought, waking groggily to the thin, strident sound of the bedside alarm. She wasn't willing to consider that it was the first semiconscious thought she had—measuring the silent telephone against the fact that it was Monday. It was a regular workday, and she'd see him at the office in less than an hour. So why should he call?

She sat up, and that was when she had her second semiconscious thought. She realized that she hadn't dreamed last night.

She'd expected to. Last night of all nights. And not entirely because of what had happened with Gunner. Today was December31.

For the first time in a long time, she didn't particularly want to get out of bed. The thrill of having her job back didn't help today. It had been a year ago tonight that Matt had gone down, and she knew it was going to be a long day, a bad day—and that wasn't even considering how she would feel tonight.

She finally forced herself to get up. She showered frenetically, as though trying to wash the sin of their crime off her skin and the memories of the bathtub out of her mind. The image made her grimace, then laugh a little. She was in a better mood until she found herself taking inordinate care with her appearance, looking long and hard to find just the right thing to wear.

Something that would look professional, she thought. Something neat, impersonal, not provocative. As though it had been something about her personally that had brought on his reaction in the tub last night.

It could have been any woman in there with him, she reminded herself harshly. Still, she didn't want to do anything that might, just *might,* turn Gunner's reputedly hungry sights directly on her. Of course, she didn't.

She chose navy tights and flats, plaid, wool walking shorts, and a cable-knit sweater over a neat, white blouse. Gold studs in her ears instead of diamonds. Just a little blush, and even less perfume. Perfect.

She walked to work, her steps growing slower the closer she got to the Administration building.

Gunner was already at their shared desk. This time he was actually sitting behind it rather than on it. She wasn't prepared for the way the sight of him hit her. He looked the same as he did every other day, a little bit rough, straight out of the shower, the ends of his hair still wet. He smelled the way he always did, that woodsy scent—only this time it hit her from all the way across the room. He'd run a hand through his hair once too often so that it was a little more disheveled than usual. He wore a blue chambray shirt, and jeans again. The sleeves of the shirt were rolled half up his forearms and the neck was unbuttoned.

It could have been any woman, she told herself again.

She cleared her throat and crossed to their desk. He looked up fast, briefly, his smoke-gray eyes unreadable, his face set in a mild frown.

"'Morning," he said politely.

"Same to you." She inched around him carefully to the coffee machine. "Want a cup?" She noticed that he didn't have one on the desk yet.

"Please."

The next voice she heard was Kennery's, bellowing good morning.

She looked quickly over her shoulder and saw their captain directly approaching their desk. Her heart thumped. She kept her back to them deliberately.

"Christian Benami just called," Kennery said. "Better yet, make that his attorney. I just had the honor of speaking with The Great Basil himself. Again. For the second time in two days. How about that?"

"Yeah?" Gunner asked idly. "What's he screaming about this time?"

"He says somebody broke into Benami's place last night."

"No kidding."

"Damnedest thing," Kennery added. "He said nothing was stolen."

"Maybe he's wrong then. Maybe nobody broke in after all."

"Well, that's what Benami decided at the time. He had a fundraiser to go to last night, that thing for the mayor. But he forgot to take some prescription medication. So he came home to get it, and he found that his alarm system was disengaged."

Tessa's heart thundered. Of course, Benami would have noticed that.

"He probably forgot to turn it on," Gunner said helpfully.

"Well, he thought *that*, too, at first. That in his profound grief, he'd just overlooked it."

Gunner grunted. "Must be some grief. I guess it got better after he went to the party."

"Hmm. Anyway, he had a look-see around during the brief time he was home. Nothing was disturbed. He checked some cash he had in the house. It was there. None of the heirloom silver was missing. So he went back to the party, figuring he'd just screwed up the alarm. Then he got to thinking about it overnight, and it seems he distinctly remembers setting it."

"Hell of a memory," Gunner murmured. "What with his grief and all."

Kennery was noncommittal. Tessa didn't dare look at them again.

"Well, The Renowned Basil says to make damn sure it wasn't any of my people who went in there. Basil says that goes above and beyond harassment."

"I'd say so," Gunner agreed. "He's sure nothing was taken?"

"Mr. Benami will look again, but at this juncture, he says not. So what do *you* think, Detective?"

Tessa jumped as she realized that Kennery was talking to her. She couldn't lie worth a damn.

She made herself extra busy with the coffee, stirring easily a ton of sugar into her own. "It's unfortunate," she replied. And, she thought, Christian either had not used that particular knife on Daphne, or he didn't want to call attention to it. Either it was so incidental that he *hadn't* noticed it missing, or he was laying low.

"Well," Kennery said, "I just thought you two ought to know about this development. It being your case and all. Of course, nobody left any prints. The officers from Benami's district were over there this morning. Just in case something turns out to be missing, Benami wanted to file a report. But they didn't find a single print, nothing."

"Smart crook," Gunner said. "No prints, and he got past the alarm, too."

Tessa fought the urge to send him an incredulous look. He was really overdoing it.

He finally changed the subject. "Listen, Cap, can we bring in a little extra manpower on this? How's the budget this month?"

"Bad. Broke. When isn't it?"

"When we've got a hundred and fifty people from that Heart Association Ball still left to interview," Gunner answered. "It'll take Tessa and I clear to Easter to wade through all of them on our own."

"I take it you've got something else to follow up on?"

"You take it right."

They did? This time Tessa did look at him. It was the first she'd heard of it.

"Give me the list," Kennery said. "One fifty, you said? Keep twenty-five for yourselves."

The captain left. "Ask for the moon," Gunner muttered when he was gone, "and at least you might end up with a few stars."

"All those smarts," Tessa murmured, "and such eloquence, too. I'm impressed, Gunner."

She finally came back to their desk, putting their coffee down, sitting neatly on the edge. She was trying hard for the rapport they had begun to develop. Then Gunner finally looked at her, really looked at her, meeting her eyes.

Something chilly washed through her. His gaze was finally impersonal. So why wasn't she relieved?

For the first time she realized that they were alone. The unit office was abandoned. It wasn't quite eight o'clock yet, and it was New Year's Eve to boot.

"About last night," they said together.

Tessa flushed and looked down into her cup. "Go ahead," she whispered. "You first."

He didn't answer.

She finally looked up at him again. He was leaning back in the chair now, looking up at the light fixtures, his hands hooked behind his head.

What the hell was he supposed to say? Gunner wondered angrily. That he was *sorry?* As if he'd had any sort of control over the matter at all! She had *wriggled,* damn it, and she had *breathed,* and if he'd gotten turned on then it had been as much her doing as his own.

Say something, Tessa pleaded silently. *Tell me it was me, something about me personally, that made you feel that way.* She suddenly knew that if he said that, then she could deal with it. It would scare her, certainly, but she knew, too, that it would at least make her feel flattered, not just as if she were any port in a storm. For the first time it occurred to her to wonder why he hadn't gone to the *other* end of the tub last night. Because moving there would have been too noisy? Because there hadn't been time?

Gunner said nothing. Tess shot off the desk. "Never mind," she muttered. "We'll forget it. Put it behind us, on the other side of those lines."

"Right," he said tersely.

She scrambled to change the subject. She didn't want to consider how hurt she was. "What did you do with the...the stuff?"

"What stuff?" He looked at her sharply.

"From last night."

"Oh. It's all with Angela. We're covered."

"We are?"

"Yeah." He seemed relieved to have business to talk about. "Turns out the first guys on the scene took all of it and gave it to her. She's still filtering things over to Forensics as her people get through with it, so she'll send the knife and the carpet shavings along. She's had it from the get-go, but Ed Thackery had to make sure the knife didn't match any wounds on Daphne's body. As for the carpet shavings, they just got inadvertently placed with her as well."

"She must like you a lot, Gunner, to go out on a limb for you like that." *Did you ever get aroused in a bathtub with her?*

"I told you, we go back a long way."

"So what now? These people?" She picked up the remainder of the guest list. Her hands were tense, fumbling.

"Eventually. After I dropped you off last night, I got to thinking that I'd like to talk to Gale on this."

That was what he had been thinking about? Tessa very nearly flinched. Then she finally, really heard what he'd said.

"Gale?" Her heart lurched. "Gale Storm?" She'd pretty much avoided the department shrink for nine months now.

"Yeah." A bit of genuine emotion finally touched Gunner's face. It was surprise. "What's wrong with that?"

"I...nothing."

"I'd just like to get a read on what we can expect from a psychopath like Benami. I need to get a handle on this dude. I've got carpet dirt and a knife, a guest list and that's it. And the clock's ticking."

I, she thought dismally. Everything was "I" this morning. The word "we" seemed to have dropped from his vocabulary. She was amazed at how much it bothered her. And it wasn't purely a professional reaction. She felt...abandoned, bereft.

"Fine," she said shortly. "Let's go find Gale."

She got off the desk, took two steps and stopped. For a moment, her head overruled the dubious goings-on in her heart.

"Psychopath?" she repeated. "When did we decide that Benami was a psychopath?" That put a slightly different spin on things than assuming he'd just offed his wife for the money.

Gunner stood as well. "Same reason I gave you on Friday. They apparently had a decent marriage. She was a looker. He had access to her money whether she was dead or alive. So why not just keep her alive?" That really had been nagging him from the start.

"Maybe there's someone else," Tessa said suddenly. "Maybe he's involved with someone else and he married Daphne for her money, planning to knock her off after a reasonable period of time. Maybe the whole time he's been waiting to collect his inheritance and go back to his true love."

Gunner looked at her again for a moment, but his expression was still unreadable. "There's a thought. We'll have to check into that, too." He started for the door.

"One other thing," he said when he reached it. He held it open for her and gave her a wide berth. "Only a psychopath would have left us alone in the bathtub last night."

Tessa almost stumbled. "What are you saying?"

"He knew we were in there."

He was halfway down the hall already. She chased after him. "You can't know that."

"I thought it last night. Now I know it."

"Why?"

"Because he noticed the alarm was disengaged. And he didn't do diddly about it. He didn't even reactive it. He just took some pills, messed with his cash and took off again."

Tessa thought about it, feeling a little squeamish. "Why?" she asked again. "Why would he do that?"

Gunner stopped at the elevator and punched the button. "Because he's a psychopath. Which brings us back to why I want to see Gale." The elevator arrived and they stepped inside. They each went to an opposite side of the car. Carefully. Deliberately.

"I had a case a few years back," he explained. "That guy who was knocking off homosexual sailors down at the naval shipyard. Remember that?"

She did. She'd heard through the grapevine that Gunner had had nothing but circumstantial evidence. So he'd taken to tailing him on his own time, finally catching him in the act.

"You got that guy." It wasn't a question.

"Sure did. He's in a mental hospital. If he ever gets out, he goes straight to prison for life, no chance of parole. Anyway, what I remember most about him was that he was a raving lunatic. Really. It wasn't just a trumped-up defense thing. He pulled some crazy stunts while I was investigating him. Benami reminds me of him in a way. Arrogant. *Real* egocentric. A sense of superiority, like he can do no wrong, can't possibly be caught. He really believes that this garbage about harassment is going to hold sway long enough for him to wriggle off the hook. And because he's so sure of himself, he's taking chances on playing with us. He's making a game of it. That's all he was doing with us last night, Tess. I'd wager a hundred to one that he didn't need any medication. He came home for something else, then he realized that we were in the tub. Hell, maybe he even heard us, I don't know. You were bleating like a calf there for a few seconds."

Bleating? "I did *not* bleat!"

"Whatever, my point is, we weren't anywhere else, so we were probably in the bathtub, so he thought he'd hang out in the bathroom for a little while. And play with us." They got out on the third floor.

Tessa nodded. "Which is why he didn't mention the knife being missing."

He shot her an appraising look. "Bingo. *We* know we've got it, *he* knows we've got it. By not mentioning it to Basil English and Kennery, it's our little secret. A gauntlet thrown."

Tessa shuddered. They had reached Gale's office. She was a little startled to realize that she'd gotten this far without being tripped up, ripped up, by memories.

She actively disliked Dr. Storm and hadn't set foot in this particular hallway in nine months. She knew it was irrational. She'd poured her heart out to the psychologist during those first few weeks after Matt had been killed, before she'd learned to be cautious about what she said. And Gale had used all that against her.

Just as the thought was completed, the doctor opened the door to her inner office.

Gale smiled at Gunner first. The reflex was genuine and warm. The psychologist was a tall, raw-boned, horse-faced woman to Tessa's uncharitable way of thinking, and she positively glowed when Gunner took her outstretched hand.

Tessa wondered irritably how Gunner would have reacted in a bathtub with *her*.

"Tessa," Gale said, finally looking over at her. "Good to see you again. I'd heard you were back."

"Finally," Tessa agreed tightly.

"Well, come on in. Sit down. Coffee?"

They both accepted, and Gale poured from the machine behind her desk. Gunner didn't waste any more time on niceties. Tessa noticed, almost in spite of herself, that he really wasn't his usual charming self this morning.

"Did you have a chance to look over that file I sent ahead while I was waiting for Tessa?" he asked.

"I made it a point," Gale answered.

Oh, God, was she gushing? Please don't let her gush, Tessa thought.

"Ask away," Gale said. "I'll tell you whatever you want to know."

She *was* gushing.

"Motive," Gunner said shortly, either unaware or immune.

"Mmm. Well, the money has something to do with it, obviously. But I'm not sure that it's central to what's going on here. Possibly it's just an added fringe benefit."

"How so?" Tessa asked.

"The lack of a paper trail keeps jumping back at me. It's entirely possible that this is a man who's done this sort of thing before. And if it's repetitive behavior, then I'm going to take the chance and say he's doing it for the thrill."

Tessa bit her lip hard. She wasn't sure if her resentment for the woman was coloring her opinion, but she thought that this was hardly an earth-shattering revelation. She had been operating on pretty much the same hunch when she'd consulted Igor.

"If this is the case," Gale said, "then I want to say that he'll probably exhibit some other obsessive tendencies. Such a personality might be inclined to have kept something that either belonged to Daphne, or more likely an object that was involved in her murder."

"Like that other damn rope that's conspicuously missing," Gunner muttered. "Or maybe the weapon he used to coerce her with."

"Exactly like that," Gale agreed. "Something that will bring back a rush of memories, intimate memories of the moment his wife died."

Tessa made a strangled sound. They both looked over at her sharply.

"That's...sick," she said quietly. "It's *evil.*"

"You knew her, didn't you?" Gale asked.

Tessa stiffened. Was the doctor going to try to make something of that? Part of her knew she was being paranoid—on today of all days—but another part of her decided to nip the possibility right in the bud.

"Vaguely," she answered shortly. "We hadn't had much contact since high school."

Gale nodded, then she looked at Gunner again. "What else do you want to know?"

"For discussion's sake, let's just say he kept the weapon. A knife," Gunner began. "*Where* would he be likely to keep it?"

"Probably not at his home," Gale said promptly. "Or if he did, it would be in plain sight."

Gunner finally looked at her. Tessa met his eyes, and knew they were thinking the same thing. *Bingo.*

"Am I missing something here?" Gale said suddenly, looking between them.

"Nope," Gunner answered. "My partner and I are just thinking." Together. With one mind. Ah, hell.

"Where else, if not at home?" Tessa persisted.

"Somewhere he'd have reasonable access to it. If he's the type of personality that I think he is, then he's of superior intelligence and cunning. I mean that literally. He probably has a very high IQ. He could be a genius at chess, at computer games, fantasy games, anything like that. That's why I say any incriminating evidence may not be in his home. That's too easy. In fact, I'll go so far as to say that he has it in a place where it would take an *equally* creative and cunning mind to find it. He'd treat it like a game."

Tessa's heart thumped. That fit pretty well with Gunner's estimation of Benami's behavior last night.

"Let's say a creative and cunning mind found it," Gunner said.

Tessa couldn't help herself. She gave a little snort. He was certainly patting his own back over their break-in last night. She also knew he was talking about the knife now. She'd been thinking more along the lines of the missing rope.

"How would Benami be inclined to react to such a scenario?" Gunner asked.

"It would be part of the game." Gale looked a little pale. "If I'm right about him, then this is a supremely dangerous man. If...a detective possessed such a thing, I think our killer would take it as upping the ante, so to speak. Increasing the stakes of the game. Anything would go."

"I see," Tessa said quietly.

Gale's eyes flashed to her. "You're prepared for this to get ugly?" she asked just as softly.

Tessa's jaw hardened. "I'll do whatever I have to do to see this monster behind bars." God help her, but she couldn't get that image of Daphne out of her mind...tied to the table leg, *knowing,* helpless and aware, unable to save herself, unable to do anything but think about what was going to happen to her when Christian came home. If it had happened that way—and she was sure that it had—then it was one of the most psychologically cruel murders she'd come across in her time in Homicide.

Gunner stood. He shook Gale's hand again, thanking her with that crooked Gunner-like grin. Tessa got to her feet more slowly.

"You coming?" he asked her when he got back to the anteroom door and she didn't follow.

"In a minute." She looked at Gale again. It was, she decided, time to start laying some old demons to rest. Her heart stuttered, then steadied. "I want to talk to Gale a moment," she explained. "It's...personal."

Tessa thought he closed the door a little harder than he had to. She finally looked back at the doctor again.

"I've held this past year against you, you know." There. It was out. Tessa felt immensely better already.

Gale smiled. "I know. Please believe me when I tell you I'd rather have you resent me than get hurt, or hurt someone else."

Tessa acknowledged that with a brief nod.

"How long..." She trailed off. *Don't get into it with her!* The voice of her self-preservation fairly howled at her to be cautious with this woman. She went on anyway. She badly needed to know.

"How long might a person be expected to...I don't know, be haunted by the sort of memories of what happened that night with Matt?"

"You're still grappling with it?" Gale asked sharply. "With the dreams?"

That provoked her into saying what she might not have said otherwise. "Just the opposite, as a matter of fact." *Especially these past few days.* She remembered how, on Friday night, right after being paired with Gunner, she had stood in her bedroom and hadn't even been able to conjure Matt's face for a moment.

"I see." Gale nodded. "Well, it could be just as simple as the fact that you finally have something to sink your teeth into again work-wise."

"Then why didn't you let me do that sooner?" Tessa demanded.

The doctor sighed. "I had nothing to do with how long you were reassigned, Tessa. I just thought you needed some time before you went back to Homicide. It was your captain and your chief inspector who determined that it ended up being—what? Nine months?''

Tessa sighed. She knew that, of course. "So what about my memories?" she asked again. "Or lack thereof, as the case might be?"

"Is this a recent development?" Gale asked.

Yes, since John Gunner.

No, she thought. That wasn't entirely true. Of course it wasn't. Her memories had been sketchy for the past month or so. It was just that now, lately, Matt was barely in her mind at all, unless she deliberately looked at his picture, unless she tried to remember him and called him there.

Especially today. Even today.

"The bottom line is that every case differs," Gale said. "I know that probably doesn't help much, but it's true. Some people only begin to forget, to *really* forget, when they fall in love again. Provided that doesn't happen immediately in a sort of rebound reflex, provided they have ample time to grieve first."

Tessa paled.

"I take it that's not what you wanted to hear," Gale said quietly.

Tessa cursed the woman's intuition. She wanted to shout that her lack of turmoil had nothing to do with Gunner. But who had actually said anything about Gunner? Nobody had even mentioned Gunner's name.

She pressed her fingers to her temples. It was just that little devilish gremlin inside her, she realized, the gremlin that ached and trembled when Gunner touched her, when he picked her up in a fit of pique, when he pinned her to the bottom of a damn bathtub. And now it was in there warbling loud and clear in its mischievous gremlin voice and she didn't like what it was saying at all.

She certainly did *not* love the man. That was ridiculous. She barely knew him. She just liked him a little more than she'd thought she would. If she could just avoid touching him again, she could probably avoid thinking about him too much at all.

He had nothing to do with the way she was forgetting Matt. *Nothing.*

She made a quick move for the door. "Thank you," she managed to say. "You've helped."

Gunner was waiting for her out in the hallway, pacing in that caged-animal way he had. Her stomach rolled over when she saw him.

"Everything okay?" he asked with more warmth than he'd demonstrated all morning.

"Great. Fine. Wonderful," she growled and stalked past him. "Don't touch me, Gunner. Just don't...touch me...again."

Chapter 10

Tessa went to the elevator and punched the Up button with enough force to knock out a heavyweight champion. Now what the hell was this all about? Gunner wondered.

Women. Oh, sure, he loved them, from his crotchety old grandmother on down to his youngest niece, through the various women he had dated. Maybe he'd never met one he'd be lost without, but the bottom line was that he still appreciated them thoroughly. He liked their smells, their nuances, their softness. He thoroughly enjoyed the whole feminine mystique in all its many shapes and forms.

And if he lived to be ninety—probably a hundred now without the cigarettes, he thought—he knew that he would never understand them.

Women marched to their own drummers, he thought, hurrying to catch up with Tess too late. The elevator doors slid closed in his face. He turned and went to another, less-used one down an adjacent corridor.

Women got caught up in these obscure emotions, he thought, leaving the men of the world behind while they scooted up to some ozone layer only they could find. There was probably a sign up there, he thought darkly as he rode up to the Homicide floor again. *No Men Allowed. No one sane, sensible, practical, minus hormones, may pass these portals.*

Suddenly he was mad.

When he got out of the elevator, he jogged down the hall, around the corner, rushing to meet the one she had taken. Being in the center of the building, he figured that it had probably had to stop several more times than his own. He was right. When the doors opened, Tessa was inside.

He slammed a hand against the door to keep it open and blocked her way. He couldn't have said if there was anyone else in the elevator. He never looked.

"What the hell was that about?" he demanded.

Tessa blushed to the roots of her hair.

She'd had just enough time on the ride up to become horrified by what she had said to him. She couldn't *believe* she had said it. There he had been, stalking around in the hallway, and she had just talked to Gale, so she had opened her mouth and—out it had popped.

She was going to die of embarrassment.

"I'm sorry," she said hoarsely. "It had nothing to do with you, actually." *It didn't.* Of course it didn't.

"Well, where did it *come* from?" he asked, mystified. "I haven't touched you all morning. I— " And then he broke off, giving some serious thought of his own to dying on the spot.

Last night, he thought. She must have told Gale Storm about last night. It was all that made sense.

"Ah, jeez, Tess, for God's sake!"

Tessa backed up instinctively until her spine hit the rear of the elevator car. "Gunner, look—"

"You *told* her."

Tessa looked at him blankly. "Told her what? What are you talking about?"

"What are *you* talking about?"

"What I said to you downstairs. And I said I was sorry!" She was starting to get angry, too.

"Downstairs?" he repeated. His head was spinning. It was that ozone layer, he thought. He had definitely just been admitted to the ozone layer.

"What exactly were you talking to Gale about?" he asked slowly, carefully.

"I told you. It was personal."

"What kind of personal?"

Yes, she was getting angry. Temper scooted through her. "By sheer definition, Gunner, personal implies that I'm not going to tell you about it."

He took a deep breath. Take the bull by the horns, he thought. One way or another, they were going to have to settle this, because he couldn't stand skittering around her the way he'd been all morning.

"Was it last night?" he demanded. "Were you talking about what happened last night? Because I've got to tell you, Tess, if you broadcast that I got hard in a bathtub hiding from a perp, there's a strong chance it might be the last thing you say in this lifetime."

Her eyes had widened slowly. Her jaw dropped. "You thought I told her *that?*"

"Well, what in the hell *did* you tell her?" he raged, frustrated.

"I was talking about Matt!"

"Matt?"

"*Matt.*"

He stared at her dumbly. He felt like a fool. Then he got mad again. "So what does he have to do with me not touching you? You specifically told me not to touch you. And the only time I really did that was last night."

She blushed again. He decided he was on to something here.

"Let's hear it, Tess," he warned. "Spit it out!"

"No."

"It had something to do with me, or you wouldn't have come out of there blasting with both barrels."

She finally managed to scoot past him. "I'm going to end this conversation, Gunner. Here. Now. Before it gets any more stupid. Any *crazier!* This has nothing to do with the bathtub!"

She started up the hall to their office, then she stopped dead. *Oh, God.*

Heads poked out of every single doorway, watching them, listening to them, staring. She realized how loud their voices must have gotten. She whipped back to look at him again.

"Gunner," she said helplessly.

"Let me get that guest list," he said hoarsely, "and we're out of here."

Tessa bolted back to the elevator. This time she pounded at the Down button again and again. She felt their eyes, hot and curious and probing, all over her back.

How much had they heard? She couldn't *believe* this was happening to her neat, orderly, sane life!

Gunner reached their desk and snatched the remainder of the guest list off it. How much had they heard? He didn't care for himself so much—hell, they talked about him all the time, and he guessed he could even weather the bathtub business if he had to. But Tessa was so ladylike, so classy, and depending on how much they'd heard, this was going to flay her reputation all to hell.

The elevator had just opened when he caught up with her again. They both moved inside at the same time. Tessa sagged against the wall and closed her eyes.

"Oh, God," she whispered.

"It'll blow over."

"Probably not."

No, he thought. Probably not. They were two of the most talked about people in the unit. Him for his reported liaisons and exploding city cars, and her with her trust fund and law degree and pretty manners.

"Sorry," he muttered. "I shouldn't have started that...there. Should have waited for a better time."

"Yes," she whispered.

"Hey, don't leave me standing here holding this guilt bag all by myself," he snapped, his temper heating up all over again. "You're not all that lily-white yourself."

"I said I was *sorry,* Gunner," she said miserably. "What do you want from me?"

He fell silent, leaving that one alone. He thought it had been pretty obvious last night.

Tessa broke the silence when they reached the parking annex. She couldn't stand it anymore. "I can't believe you thought that I'd tell her *that.*"

"Maybe it's been on my mind," he snapped, unlocking the car doors. "Maybe it's been bugging me all damn morning."

She slid into the car. Her heart hitched, partly with hope, partly with dread. "I thought you were just grumpy because of the nicotine withdrawal."

"That's getting better." Sure, he thought angrily. Bang your thumb with a hammer, and your headache goes away.

"Why?"

He looked at her as he started the car and began making the descent to the street. "Why what?"

"Why has it been on your mind?"

He gaped at her. "Why do you *think?* For God's sake, Tess, what do you think I am?"

"I don't know yet," she admitted honestly.

He swore colorfully and narrowly missed a parked car in his temper. "I'll *tell* you what I am. I'm normal, human. Just your average, all-American, red-blooded male. And when a fine-looking woman who smells great goes *wriggling* around underneath me, then yeah, I react. So shoot me."

Her heart stalled completely. *A fine-looking woman who smells great?* "I didn't wriggle," she retorted, her throat feeling strangled.

"Trust me, you wriggled."

"I did *not.*"

"Oh, yeah, you damn well did."

"I don't remember that."

"I do."

Her heart finally started beating again. It went wild.

"So it was me?" she whispered almost to herself. "It was something about...*me* that...that set...that off?"

He looked at her disbelievingly. "Tess, you might have missed this, but there was nobody else in that tub."

"But...it would have happened whoever I was," she said helplessly.

He parked the car so suddenly, veering to the curb so sharply that she was thrown against the door. "Gunner, you're acting like a madman!" she cried.

"Is that what you think?" he asked with lethal calm.

"Yes! What if somebody had been behind us in the right lane? You didn't even check your mirrors!"

He had to clench his hands to keep himself from grabbing her and shaking her. *Don't touch me, Gunner,* she had said. *Just don't touch me again.*

Okay, he thought. Fine.

"It would *not* have happened whoever you were," he said in

measured tones. "Hell, given the circumstances—" He broke off. He couldn't even *think* of where his mind had been while Benami had been in the bathroom, as opposed to where it ought to have been.

"Oh," Tessa said in a very small voice.

"For the record, I'm not a—a raging bull," he said furiously. "I know where to put it and when."

She felt her skin flame. She didn't want to let *those* images get into her head at all.

"And a killer's bathtub is not 'where,'" he argued, his voice a tight growl. "It is not 'when.' Got that?"

"Got it," she whispered, and decided she was going to wait until she was alone to sort this out.

She was so inordinately *glad.* Glad and scared and amazed.

"Good," he said shortly. "Can we forget it now?"

"Yes, please." *Not in a million years.*

"And in the future, kindly keep your wriggling to a minimum." She blushed again and covered her face with her hands.

"Because I can handle this. I can handle these not-quite-impersonal lines you want just fine. I can be as cool as they come. If that's what you want, then, honey, you've got yourself an ice-cold cucumber. No off-color jokes, no nothing."

"Gunner, cucumbers aren't—"

"It's a pretty damn good partnership we've got here in spite of all this other malarkey." He interrupted her harshly. "Together, we just might be able to nail this bastard. So stop wriggling and stop breathing and let's get on with it."

She lowered her hands disbelievingly. "Stop *breathing?* Gunner, what are you talking about?" He opened his mouth to answer and she cut him off fast. "No, on second thought, I don't...I don't want to know. Just drive."

He drove.

They'd gotten to the first address on their list before he realized that he still didn't have any idea how he tied in with whatever she had told Gale Storm about Matt.

It was three-thirty before they got back to the unit office. Tessa felt brain-dead from trying to assimilate everything told to them by twenty-five different people, and her feet hurt on top of it. But this time they had something—sort of.

It was starting to become apparent that no one remembered seeing Christian Benami at the Heart Association Ball between the times of eight-fifteen and nine o'clock. Of course, a lot of people couldn't recall exactly *what* time they'd seen him, she reminded herself as Gunner drove back to the parking garage.

"I'll feel more sure when I can *see* it," Tessa murmured aloud. "I want to make a graph. A slot for each hour between seven and midnight. And then I'm going to put down every name of every guest who knows when they saw him. I'll put each name in the appropriate slot."

"Yeah," Gunner agreed. "Good idea."

"We *think* a pattern's emerging here," she said. "This way we can really be sure. We can see it in black-and-white."

"All right. We'll stop by the Req office on our way upstairs and get whatever supplies we need."

They finally reached their desk to find the Homicide Office silent and deserted.

"I don't believe this," Tessa murmured, looking around.

"Funny how on certain days of the year, everybody suddenly has to work out on the streets," Gunner agreed. "New Year's Eve, Christmas Eve, the Wednesday before Thanksgiving."

That was when something vaguely uncomfortable shifted in Tessa's stomach. The way she looked and smelled notwithstanding, John Gunner must certainly want to be somewhere else right now than this office with her.

"Why don't you go?" she suggested suddenly. "I can draw lines on this cardboard and sift through the guests' statements on my own. It's really a one-person job."

Gunner shot a glance at the wall clock. "Nah, I've got hours yet. It'll go quicker if we both work at it."

What were his plans? she wondered. And, in spite of herself, she tried to imagine who they were with.

"Here, give me that cardboard and let me tack it to the wall."

Tessa handed it over. She sat Indian-style on top of the desk, the file in her lap, turning over one statement after another, reading off the name and the time that each person recalled seeing Christian. She was just as glad not to be alone, she realized uncomfortably.

Some of the reports had already come in from the other detectives Kennery had assigned to the job. She added those lists to their own. Close to two hundred and twenty people had been covered by now. It took them nearly an hour and a half, but a pattern definitely began to emerge.

Of the two-twenty, almost a hundred either couldn't remember noticing Christian or didn't know what time they had. Close to a hundred more remembered him making a donation on his and Daphne's behalf at ten o'clock.

There were a flurry of names in the seven-thirty time slot. Apparently Christian had made it a point to greet a good many people when he had arrived.

"Establishing an alibi," Tessa murmured.

"Yep. But he would have needed a clone to have done that at eight-thirty." Not one person, not one single guest, could remember seeing him when the main course had been served. The people at his assigned table could state only that he had definitely been there for dessert, but none of them had found this too unusual. It had been a powerful, political group. People mingled, wandered, visited the bar, sat briefly at other tables. And Benami had been at his own at some point.

Tessa reached for the phone.

"What are you up to?" Gunner asked.

Tessa tucked the phone against her shoulder and dug into her purse for her address book. "I was thinking of trying to get in touch with some of Daphne and Christian's acquaintances. I want to find out if there's any evidence of Christian having a girlfriend squirreled away somewhere."

"We already covered Daphne's friends on Friday," Gunner said slowly. "They said the marriage seemed perfect. Approaching from that angle isn't going to get us anywhere."

"I just want to find out if Christian had any friends of his own," she answered stubbornly. "If so, maybe *they'd* know if the marriage wasn't perfect."

His eyes narrowed. "You're going to call these people on New Year's Eve?"

"No time like the present."

"What's going on here?"

She flashed him a quick, neutral look. "What do you mean?"

"It's New Year's Eve," he said again.

"Yes, Gunner, we've established that."

"So how come you're not running home to get all spit-shined?"

"Have I mentioned yet how crude you can be when you try?"

He ignored that. "How come?"

She sighed and hung the phone up again. The first number had been busy anyway.

"Because I'm not going anywhere," she said finally.

He stared at her a moment more, then he shook his head. "Cut me a break."

"I just did." She looked down pointedly at her address book and began flipping pages. "I told you what you wanted to know so you'd stop bugging me."

"Do you mean to tell me," he said slowly, "that there's no hoity-toity gala somewhere in this very large city that you're expected to attend tonight?"

She looked at him again, exasperated. "Of course there is." *Leave it alone, Gunner,* she thought. *Please just leave it alone.*

"But you're not going."

"No."

"Why not?"

Of course he wouldn't leave it alone. Tessa rubbed her hands over her face. What difference did it make? she thought wearily. She might as well tell him. He'd figure it out soon enough anyway, or he'd just keep badgering her until she did.

"My parents are having a party at their home," she said finally, without inflection. "Champagne and caviar and enough dead animals on women's shoulders to make even the most liberal wince. The conversation will be as cold and dull as watching snow melt. I can guarantee you that it will do nothing whatsoever toward keeping my mind off things. Therefore, I've come to the conclusion that I'm better off working. Satisfied? Will you leave me alone now?"

"No. What do you want to keep your mind off?"

Tessa took a deep breath. "It was a year ago tonight that Matt was killed," she blurted helplessly. "Now, please, leave me alone. Let me work. I know how to handle this."

Gunner swore ripely.

He felt like a dunce. He had just been thinking about that the other day—on Friday, as a matter of fact, when Kennery had assigned him to her just in time for her to face this dubious anniversary right in the face. And then he had forgotten about it. Even when she had mentioned Matt Bryant this morning, he hadn't remembered.

He started to apologize and thought better of it. "So come home with me," he said instead.

Tessa felt her heart suck up into her throat as though someone had just siphoned it there with a heavy-duty vacuum.

"Home?" She squeaked around her heart. "With you?"

He pushed away from the wall he'd been leaning against. This probably wasn't a good idea. Hell, he *knew* it wasn't a good idea. Not after last night. Not after the turmoil the bathtub had caused them. It had taken them most of the day to really get back onto a nice, even, businesslike keel, and he'd be the first to admit that the keel felt precarious. It had wobbled every time he'd noticed her, the way she moved, the way she blushed, the perfume she wore.

He had promised her that he could handle this almost-impersonal business, and he could. But he was beginning to think that he was going to have to keep a good arm's length from her to pull it off.

They just didn't belong together, he told himself yet again. Forget his rule about women who worked for the city. Even without that, she was too serious, and he never got tangled up with women like her, no matter how good she looked. She was the marrying kind—a forever type of woman. And he was definitely *not* a marrying man. It was best just to keep his distance, then his body couldn't put ideas into his head that his head knew he was better off without.

She'd say no, anyway, of course. Those lines of hers, he thought. And that would be fine.

"Where?" she asked.

"Where?" He looked at her, dumbfounded.

"Home with you where?" she clarified. "Are you giving a party?"

"A party?" he repeated. "Uh, no. I didn't mean my...uh, my apartment. I meant my folks' place. Down in South Philly. The Mummer's Parade. You know, all that hoopla. People start warming up tonight, for the parade tomorrow." He rubbed his jaw, then clamped it shut. He was babbling like a fool.

Tessa thought about it with a little bit of longing. She was a

Philadelphian by birth. She'd watched the Mummer's Parade on television every New Year's Day of her life. And of course she'd heard of the all-night carnival atmosphere that preceded it. But she'd never taken part in it.

No memories there, she thought. It sounded like fun. Then she shook her head.

"Thanks, but no," she said quietly.

Gunner breathed again, not sure if he was relieved or not. "Yeah, I guess it's not your kind of thing."

"It's not that."

"It's not?" He felt damn off balance here.

"No. I'd just be in the way."

"Of what?"

"You know, hanging around with you and your date."

"What date?"

The moment it was out, he realized that he was sounding more and more like a moron as the seconds ticked by. He felt a little bit panicky, and a lot like he wanted her to say, "Okay, sure, let's go."

Not cool at all.

Except if she didn't go, she'd work. And hurt. And he wanted to protect her from that.

Oh, hell. He tunneled his fingers through his hair, aggravated.

"I'm not following you, Gunner," she was saying carefully. "You're confusing me."

At least it was catching. "This is a free-for-all, Princess," he said finally. "No pairing off allowed."

"Oh."

He finally reached for his coat. "The doors start opening in about an hour, and I need to take a shower and shave, so I'm out of here. You coming or what?"

"What would I...uh, wear?" she asked tentatively.

And that was the moment, the exact moment, when she realized how very much she did not want to be alone tonight. It was when she knew just how frightened she really was. Because going to his parents' house with him was not impersonal. It was, in many ways, even more intimate than what had happened last night. It was *family*. It was his stomping grounds, his home turf. It meant stepping into his private world.

And she was willing to do that. She was willing to do almost anything to avoid being alone tonight. Fear rolled in her gut again. What if she stayed home by herself and she found that once again, even tonight, she could barely remember Matt's face?

She cried softly without even realizing it. She pressed her knuckles to her mouth.

Gunner looked at her sharply and felt as though someone had kicked him.

Tessa pushed to her feet. "Yes," she said suddenly. "I'll come."

"You will?"

Please, God, don't let him change his mind. "Please?"

"Yeah," he said hoarsely. "Sure. I invited you, didn't I?" He swung out the door. "Jeans," he said. "Do you even own one single pair of plain, old blue jeans?"

"Of course," she answered indignantly.

"Then wear them and a warm coat. Not fur," he cautioned quickly. "Along about midnight, somebody'd be apt to try to shoot you."

Tessa heard herself laugh. Already she felt better, steadier, stronger.

"Thank you, Gunner."

"Don't mention it." His voice croaked. His gut churned.

It was going to be a long night.

Chapter 11

No dates. No pairing off. That was the South Street party credo, and for the first time in a long time, Gunner did more than take it for granted. Given what something as simple as a bathtub could do to him where this woman was concerned, he was profoundly grateful.

They stopped at Tessa's place first. She went upstairs to shower and change, and Gunner prowled her kitchen, keeping one wary eye out for the cat.

He would have invited anyone—anyone at all—home with him tonight, he told himself, if he had witnessed them sitting at that desk the way she had, with that sad-puppy look. But he wondered if maybe he wasn't just asking too much of himself here, by taking her home.

Asking too much of himself was something that Gunner rarely did anymore. As long as he steered clear of it, he couldn't disappoint anyone. Not even himself. Nothing was on the line.

There was plenty on the line tonight. He had to stay away from her. Hands off. For her sake. For his own.

''Ready,'' Tessa said from the doorway. He looked around at her sharply. It was rare that a person could sneak up on him, but she managed to do it time and again—at least when he found himself here, in this room in her home.

He wondered if there was a correlation there anywhere and decided he didn't want to think about it.

"Well, good," he answered. He thought his voice sounded a little raw. It was well past time to get a grip on himself here.

"Do we need to stop at your place?" she asked as they went back to the car.

Gunner shook his head. "We're running late. I keep a change of clothes at my folks' place. I'll do everything I need to do once we get there."

Tessa didn't know if she was relieved or disappointed. She realized she was curious to know where he lived after all—now that all those lines she had tried to establish really had been scattered now like so many spilled matchsticks.

His parents lived in one of the Irish pockets of South Philadelphia. The street was already packed with cars and people when they got there. They parked and Tessa stood on the sidewalk for a moment, looking around, absorbing all the sights and sounds.

All the *people.*

It was barely seven o'clock, but already every stoop, every porch, was so crowded with lawn chairs and the like that there was no room for anyone to move—except for narrow paths left open at the center, leading the way to gaping front doors. It couldn't even be thirty degrees outside tonight, Tessa thought, but door upon door stood wide open and welcoming, heaters working hard just to spill their warmth outdoors. Every home was brightly lit, some still with Christmas lights, others simply awash with lamplight.

"The electric company must love this," she murmured. They'd make a small fortune in the south part of the city tonight.

Gunner laughed.

He led her up a stoop. She realized then that the people seated outside were almost all elderly. Canes and walkers were pushed back against the railings, out of the way. Voices rose in welcome as Gunner leaned over to kiss an old woman's wrinkled cheek.

He scooped up a little girl and settled her on his shoulders as she squealed. He took an old man's hand and pumped it hard, slapped another man on the shoulder, grinned warmly at a toothless old woman who smiled widely. Tessa wondered, amazed, why the cigarette dangling from her mouth didn't fall out.

"Hey, Mrs. P., breathe some of that my way." Gunner laughed and leaned close to inhale her secondhand smoke. He shot a look back at Tess. "You never said anything about other folks' smog," he said pointedly.

"No," she agreed bemusedly.

"You finally quit those damn cancer sticks, John?" one of the men called out.

"Had to. Got myself a real mean partner," he answered, thrusting a thumb at Tessa. "She won't let me smoke."

"'Bout time somebody kept you in line, John," the first old woman said.

"Come on, Gram, you keep talking like that, you're gonna ruin my angelic reputation."

Tessa's head swiveled back and forth as the conversation bandied about. Gunner was different here, she thought...and yet he was the same. He was just a little looser, sexier, warmer...and just as teasing and irreverent. He never quite lost the devil-may-care gleam in his eyes as they kept working their way toward the front door. When he encountered another old woman trying to make her way onto the porch, he grabbed her and kissed her soundly.

"That's in case I miss you at midnight," he told her.

The woman blushed and adoringly watched him pass. Tessa followed him, feeling eyes on the back of her head.

"You finally get yourself a real lady, John?" someone asked.

Tessa blushed.

Gunner thought about it. A lady, certainly, but the "get yourself" part was a pretty fair stretch of the imagination.

"She your date, John?" another man called, as though reading his mind.

"No dates allowed, Ernie. They made that rule because of that year you tried to bring three of them."

He'd stepped around that nicely, Tessa thought, following him into the hall. Her heart didn't know whether to swell with gratitude or shrink with...with what?

Don't think about it...about anything. Just enjoy.

The kitchen was at the front of the house. Even so, it took them a long time to get there. The hallway was crammed with bodies. When they finally reached the kitchen, one glance around told

Tessa that this was *the* most lived-in room of the Gunner household. It was big, chaotic. The table was laden with food and a big punch bowl, but there were magazines and unopened mail, kitchen utensils, a toy robot and various other odds and ends strewn all over the counters.

It gave her an ache that she couldn't quite understand. It was so...homey. Though she had promised herself she wasn't going to think too much about anything, her thoughts wandered to what would be going on at her parents' home up in Chestnut Hill right about now.

The caterers would be rushing around. Her mother, Isobel, would be overseeing things—the florist, the musicians, all the last-minute details. Her father would still be upstairs with his brandy, dawdling just enough to make her mother fret. And her brother, Jesse, would arrive at any moment, early enough to kill two birds with one stone. He would stay at the party just long enough that it could be said he'd attended, and he'd arrive well in advance so it could be said that he'd paid a family visit as well.

Tessa realized suddenly that she hadn't called any of them to let them know she wouldn't be coming tonight. As soon as things calmed down, she thought, she'd have to ask Gunner if she could use the phone.

''John!'' Voices rang out, and Tessa's thoughts jolted back from Chestnut Hill to South Philly. She finally looked around at the crowd, and then she saw Angela Byerly.

''Be right back, Tess,'' Gunner called. He deposited the little girl he'd been carrying back on her feet. ''I'm going to run upstairs and grab a shower.''

Tessa's eyes remained on Angela, and something inside her shrank. What was *she* doing here? Gunner had said no dates! He'd said it at the office, and again outside.

Someone pushed a glass of punch at her. She took it and drank deeply, grateful to have something to do with her hands.

''I'm Antoinette Gunner,'' the woman who handed her the drink introduced herself.

''Thank you,'' she said, holding up the punch. Then a little thump of surprise hit her in the chest. ''Gunner?''

The woman gave a halfway sort of grin. In that moment, there was no doubting the blood relationship between her and John.

''I'm his mother.'' Antoinette sighed. ''I *tried* teaching him manners. I really did. But I think maybe you'll be better off if you just circulate and take care of introducing yourself. We tend to be an informal bunch around here.''

The woman moved off again. She had the muscled, agile grace of a dancer. Her hair was black rain, spilling to her waist in a ponytail. Huge gold hoops swung from her ears. Traces of silver shocked her temples.

''She's a gypsy.''

Tessa jumped and looked at Angela Byerly. The medical examiner had come to stand against the wall beside her. It took everything she had not to blurt, ''What are *you* doing here?''

''I beg your pardon?'' Tessa asked instead, startled.

''Antoinette. Although actually, everyone just calls her Tonie. She's second-generation Hungarian. She worked with the circus for years. High-wire and trapeze.''

''Wow.'' Tessa realized she was more impressed than she would have been with any high-profile politico she might have met at her parents' party.

She sipped more of the punch. It was delicious. It tasted like cherries, but not quite. There was something almost nutty in there, too, but she couldn't quite place it. It had a very gentle bite.

''I want to thank you for your help with the Benami thing,'' she said cautiously, not sure if she should mention it but inbred manners won out.

Angela looked genuinely surprised. ''Help? Oh, that.'' She laughed again. ''I owed John a big one. Maybe now we're even.''

Tessa wondered what classified as a ''big one.'' She was dying to know, and too polite to ask.

''A bunch of years ago, I had a problem with...with this guy,'' Angela explained without prompting. ''John dissuaded him for me.''

''Dissuaded him,'' Tessa repeated.

''He laid in wait for him in my bushes one night. Charlie—that was his name—came by to harass me again. I don't know what happened exactly, and I honestly don't want to know. I saw Charlie once right after that, and he had a broken arm. He never bothered me again.''

''I see,'' Tessa said. She shivered a little, remembering what he had nearly done to Benami. *''I might not know Mr. Dresden from Mr. Uniroyal, but I know right from wrong. And I'll be damned*

*if I'm going to stand around with my hands in my pockets while
somebody hurts a woman I like..."*

"You're good friends," Tessa observed carefully after a moment.

"We grew up together. Excuse me." And then Angela was
gone again, Tessa got the feeling that she'd realized she'd said
more than she'd intended to.

Tessa went to refill her punch glass and felt Gunner behind her
before she saw him. She sensed the warmth of him first, then she
caught a whiff of a forest at dawn. His hand came down on her
shoulder, hard, strong, but oddly gentle. He rubbed his thumb
briefly over her collarbone.

Something silvery and quick seemed to scoot through her.

"You doing all right?" he asked quietly.

"Yes." Her voice was too breathy, she realized. Someday,
someday soon, she was really going to have to decide how she
felt about this man.

She turned around and he scowled at the glass she held. "How
much of that have you had?" he asked.

"It's my second glass. Why?"

"You said you didn't drink."

"There's liquor in this?" She honestly couldn't taste it.

"Sure there is." About seven different kinds, he thought, if his
memory served him correctly. He took the glass from her hand
and set it down on the table. "Come on, let's go."

"Where?"

"We'll cruise the neighborhood. That's what this is all about."

He led the way through the crowd to the front door again. Tessa
started after him, then she felt someone tug on her elbow. It was
Tonie Gunner. She pushed a large thermos into Tessa's hands.

"Here, you'll need this."

"I will?"

"Now don't let them drink all of it, you hear? Tell them it's
yours and to get their butts on down to my house if they want
more."

"Oh. Okay. Sure." Tessa tucked the thermos under her arm.

She finally caught up with Gunner again on the street. He was
waiting for her.

They turned north and started walking. She noticed that he kept his hands thrust deeply into his jacket pockets. He also kept a good foot of space between them.

She wondered what it said about his Don Juan reputation that he was spending one of the most romantic nights of the year alone. It could mean anything, she realized. It could mean that his reputation was inaccurate, she thought with a startled thump of her heart. Or it could mean that every other night of his year was so crammed with female companionship, it was a relief and a refreshing change of pace for him to go solo once in a while.

Probably the latter.

What was it he had said that first day when they had been talking about love? Maybe I'm just not capable of it. *"Maybe love's just too confined, too stringent for my tastes."* Certainly if there was a steady woman in Gunner's life, she wouldn't be very happy about him spending New Year's Eve by himself.

And why was she even thinking about this? Tessa chided herself. She had promised herself that she wouldn't get bogged down in heavy thoughts, not about herself, not about him, not about anything.

As they proceeded down the street, it became less difficult for her to remain distracted. "This is *wonderful!*" she exclaimed after a moment.

Gunner finally grinned. "Yeah. It's definitely unique."

A tall, skinny man on stilts was coming up the middle of the street toward them. He was draped in some glittery, silver material and it trailed along behind him. Children raced after him and pretended to try to step on it, giggling. He was strumming a banjo, and every once in a while he turned and shook it at them menacingly, which only elicited more giggles.

Tessa had to step out of the way quickly to let a short, fat man pass them. He was dressed in a diaper, nothing else. He had a bottle of Scotch in one hand and didn't seem to feel the cold. She turned around to walk backward for a moment, watching him.

A moment later a younger man with a heavy beard stopped them. He greeted Gunner and pointed to the thermos that Tessa carried.

"Is that Tonie's punch?"

"Yes," she answered, surprised. "It is."

He grabbed it from her and swigged.

"I believe I'm supposed to tell you that if you'd like more, you're supposed to get your...ah, butt to her house,'' she explained.

The man grinned. ''That's the direction I'm headed in right now.'' He gave the thermos back to her. Tessa wiped the mouth on her sleeve and took a mouthful herself.

''Where'd you get that?'' Gunner demanded.

''Your mother gave it to me when we were leaving.''

He decided he'd better keep an eye on it. Though it might be amusing to see what happened if she got...what had she called it? Tipsy. But not tonight, he thought. Definitely not tonight. Not with the damn bathtub still fresh in his mind. He had a promise to keep. *I can handle this not-quite-personal business just fine.* Sure he could. As long as she didn't get drunk and start wriggling and breathing.

''Come on,'' he said suddenly. ''Let's stop in here.''

He swerved up the nearest walkway. Tessa finally understood what he'd said earlier about the doors opening. This one was agape, too. Gunner once again went through the mandatory handshaking, hugging and kissing with everyone on the porch. Tessa killed the time with the thermos.

They went into another kitchen, and someone gave Gunner a can of beer.

''Hey, is that Tonie's punch?'' someone called out to her.

''Yes, and you're supposed to go to her house if you want more of it.'' She handed the thermos over again to the man who had asked about it.

Someone was playing the harmonica outside the open back door. After a while, they left that way. Gunner danced with a little girl in the alley for a moment. Tessa kept her eyes carefully averted. She was *not* going to notice the way he moved. She stared up the street for a moment, then she slid her eyes his way. He had a natural rhythm even when he was clowning around.

They made their way up to a cross street, stopping again in the next open doorway. Someone grabbed Tessa and tried to dance with her when they made it into yet another kitchen.

''I can't!'' she gasped. ''I don't know how to do that.''

''So I'll teach you.'' The man smiled at her. He was tall and good-looking, blond, with a glass full of partially melted ice in his hand.

Before Tessa could respond, the man slung an arm over her shoulder and dragged her closer.

"She's with me," Gunner growled from behind them. He took her other elbow and steered her unceremoniously outside again.

"Gunner, that was rude!" she cried.

"Was it?" he asked tersely.

"Why did you *do* that? I was going to learn to dance."

Yeah, Gunner thought, why?

"He's only interested in one thing—and it's *not* dancing," he muttered after a moment.

"The guy I was going to dance with?" She saw that nerve start ticking at his jaw again.

"Yeah, the guy you were dancing with. His name's Ben Flannagan. Anything in a skirt," he muttered angrily.

It occurred to her that given Gunner's reputation, that was a little like the pot calling the teakettle black. "I'm wearing jeans," she informed him reasonably.

"Anything that moves then." He corrected himself. "Anything at all. He's not picky."

"Thanks for the compliment." Tessa sighed. "Gunner, I really can take care of myself."

Yeah, he thought, she probably could. She'd taken care of herself just fine with him so far, hadn't she? Until she had wriggled.

He knew in that moment that she *hadn't* known she was wriggling last night. She'd done it so damn innocently, so naturally, so sweetly. Which only made it more potent, more arousing, more devastating than with a woman who was practiced in the art of seduction. Sensation—maybe even an urge or two—had touched her, and she'd reacted to it simply and unconsciously.

He wondered if it would have happened with any man who was laying on top of her in there, and wished he could get the whole damn incident out of his mind.

Tessa let out another gasp. He looked up to see that a whole string band was coming up the street toward them now. Tessa laughed and stopped to watch them pass.

"They're warming up for the morning parade," Gunner explained, stopping as well. "They'll go at it all night. I've always wondered why they don't fall flat on their faces on New Year's Day."

He watched her rapt expression, her fascination and wonder, as her eyes followed the band. Something shifted inside him. Something warm. Something good. Something *new*.

He'd never seen New Year's Eve in quite this way before.

She laughed. "Come on, Gunner." She grabbed his hand suddenly.

"What?" He pulled back out of sheer wariness.

"Let's dance." She pointed. Fifty or so people trailed along behind the string band now, doing a rowdy approximation of the Mummer's Strut.

"You want to *dance?* For God's sake, Tess, five minutes ago you were saying you couldn't."

"That was with him," she said simply.

He almost choked. Then his heart shifted again.

He followed her into the crowd. He didn't hear the people laughing, singing, calling out. For a single, strange moment, there was only her voice. Everything else seemed to fade, leaving only the clear ring of Tessa Hadley-Bryant's laughter, her eyes lit brightly, her grin one of pure pleasure. Too damn much beer, he thought. Time to switch back to coffee.

"Like this," he called out to her. He pumped his arms up and down. She imitated him and laughed again, then she added an impromptu, twirling step all her own.

"Watch out, Princess." He laughed with her. "They'll have you recruited by dawn."

Someone bumped into her. She spun around again, startled.

"Hey, John," the man said. "Is that your mom's punch?"

Tessa clutched the thermos to her chest. "Yes. And just take your butt to her house if you want some. This is *mine.*"

Gunner's jaw dropped. And then he understood.

"Let me see that," he growled.

She tried to hold it away from him. He snagged it anyway. It was empty. "Oh, hell, Tess."

"I hardly got *any,*" she complained. "They went and drank it all up on me."

"They did, huh?"

"Yes." She looked around vacantly. "Where's your house?" She laughed again. "I want to take my butt back there and get some more for myself."

Gunner closed his eyes and reminded himself that he was a man of his word. She was a charming drunk.

"This way," he said, taking her arm carefully, just so, turning her and pointing.

"Thank you, Gunner."

"You're welcome."

"I lost my bearings."

"No doubt." What the hell did Mom put in that stuff? He tried to remember. Tia Maria, he thought. Amaretto. Bourbon? God, was there bourbon in there, too?

"This is the best thing that ever happened to me," Tessa breathed, her gaze moving avidly again, trying to take in everything at once.

He slanted one eye in her direction. She really was something else.

They reached his parents' house again. He hoped like hell that his mother's punch was gone by now. He glanced at his watch. It was after eleven.

Tessa laughed at something again, her laughter musical, and he had a change of heart. He hoped there was some punch left. He thought maybe he could stand a good shot of it himself.

Chapter 12

Gunner kept one unobtrusive eye on Tessa as she sat on the floor, her back against the wall, smiling bemusedly. All the kitchen chairs were taken. After a moment, a man in a hot pink suit and a polka-dot tie came to squeeze into the space beside her.

Minkie Perez seemed thrilled to make her acquaintance, and Gunner decided immediately that it was going to be a short-lived relationship. Minkie was as slick as they came, Gunner thought irritably. The man could sell sand in the desert. He settled for used cars, for appearances' sake, anyway. Gunner knew he also dabbled in fencing stolen goods. Gunner managed to justify ignoring that by occasionally using the man as an informant. It was damn hard to bust someone you'd grown up with. He brought Minkie in mostly when he needed information that could only be found on the uglier side of the street.

Gunner looked at his watch. It was after eleven-thirty.

"Left field is getting crowded," Angela said from beside him.

Gunner looked at her sharply. "What?"

"You told me I was way out in left field when I mentioned on Saturday that there was something going on between you two," she reminded him, her gaze moving between him and Tessa. "Minkie must believe you, though. Brave man."

Gunner made a sound that could only be called a growl.

Angela was unable to stop a grin, but it faded fast into worry. "You haven't taken your eyes off the lady all night."

"I'm worried about her."

Both Angela's brows went up at that. "We're not cannibals, John."

"I don't mean that," Gunner snapped. "I just realized earlier today that this is the anniversary of the night her husband was shot. You remember reading all that in the papers last year?"

"Oh," Angela answered. *"Oh."*

"Yeah," Gunner muttered. "Oh."

"Well, that still doesn't explain why she's scarcely taken *her* eyes off *you*."

His heart did something sudden and strange. It moved in a way he'd never quite experienced before.

"You're wrong," he answered tersely.

"Nope."

"Drop it, Angie."

"I just don't want to see you hurt. She's got problems and she comes from a different world. She'll break your heart."

"I don't have one," he reminded her shortly. "Look, I want to get her some more punch. Go find something better to do than bug me."

He zeroed in on the last of the potent red stuff in the bowl. The more he thought about it, the more he decided that getting her "tipsy" probably wasn't a half-bad idea. She needed to relax, take her mind off things.

Suddenly he realized that no matter what the rule might be about pairing off, it *never* held sway at midnight. That was asking too much. In about fifteen minutes, people would start drifting. They would start trying to make sure that they were beside the person they wanted to be with at the stroke of twelve.

And when midnight came, no matter how cool Tessa been all night, no matter how distracted she'd been by this amazing new world he'd shown her, she was going to hurt. She'd look around at people groping for the body closest to them. She'd look around at embraces simple and urgent, friendly and passionate, tentative and hopeful and determined. And in that moment, if at no other time tonight, Gunner was reasonably sure that her husband's poignant absence was going to swamp her.

It was not her first New Year's without Matt Bryant, he reminded himself. But last year at this time, she would still have been stunned, pain raining through her like broken glass, unwilling and unable to assimilate the rolling over of one year into the next. This year would be different.

He reached down impulsively and caught her hand, hauling her to her feet. Tessa scrambled not to lose her balance.

"Gunner, what are you doing?" she cried.

He realized he didn't even have a clue. More punch, he remembered. He'd been planning to ply her with more of the punch. With any luck, she'd pass out and miss midnight entirely.

"Here," he said, dragging her over to the table.

"Oh, I don't think so." She shook her head. "I think I've had enough."

Probably. "Yeah, but it's New Year's," he insisted, filling another glass for her. He had no idea where her other one had gotten to. *There you go, Angie,* he thought. *If I hadn't taken my eyes off her, I'd know where it was.* He was absurdly proud of that point.

"No, Gunner, really," Tessa said, shaking her head. "I feel dizzy."

He stood helplessly with the glass in his hand. After a moment, he tossed it back himself. He felt the bourbon or whatever it was shoot into his blood and clear his head.

"Come on," he said suddenly.

"Where?" Tessa scowled at him. He was acting strange, she thought. Or maybe it was just her perception. Everything was slightly off-kilter. She had to close one eye periodically to let the room straighten itself out. She wasn't drunk. She *never* got drunk. But she'd had enough to think maybe she ought to stop now.

She looked up at the clock on the wall. It was almost midnight. Something inside her squirmed.

Gunner wrenched her arm suddenly, pulling her into the hallway.

"What are you *doing?*" she cried again. "Gunner, you really have to learn to stop acting so impulsively." She remembered that during one of these past, long nights, she had decided that that was his biggest problem. But it was refreshing, she thought now, fighting the urge to laugh. It was like the backlash of wind in your face on a roller coaster ride.

He nearly had her to the stairs. "I'm going to show you your room," he answered, his jaw tight.

"My *room?*" She pulled back against his grip.

"Yeah. That way when you've had enough, you can just go to sleep." And if he dragged this out long enough, she'd still be up here at the stroke of midnight, he thought. Alone. Without fifty to a hundred people cuddling up to each other right in front of her eyes.

"Gunner, I can't stay here all night! You never said anything about all night!"

"Well, what did you think I was going to do?" he snapped. "Stay here until dawn and then come back for the parade at ten?"

"I don't—I didn't—" They were halfway up the stairs. She thought frantically. "I don't have a toothbrush!"

He glanced back over his shoulder at her. "So use your finger. Or I'll run out to the nearest drugstore and buy you one, for God's sake."

"They're not open now."

He swore. He could not believe they were arguing about a damn toothbrush.

"I can take a cab home," she said. "You don't have to drive me and come back."

"Not in this lifetime, sweetheart. I know these streets. And I'll be damned if I'm going to let you leave here all...all *tipsy* on New Year's Eve, and trust in their mercy." He opened the first door they came to and shoved her inside. She stumbled a little, and he was instantly contrite.

"Sorry." He reached out fast to grab her elbow and steady her.

Her eyes came around to him, slowly and wide. "You're touching me again, Gunner," she said slowly, with something like wonder.

He snatched his hand away and cursed silently. What the hell had he gotten himself into here?

"Sorry," he said again. Hell, this was ridiculous. He'd only taken her *elbow*.

Then it dawned on him that she wasn't angry.

"Uh, the bathroom's right across the hall," he said, shaken. He moved past her into the room, yanking down the bedspread. "It's all yours, anytime you want it. Okay?"

"Okay," she whispered.

She decided to give up the fight. She was too tired—maybe even too tipsy—to argue with him. And something about him made her feel safe. No matter how many people there were downstairs, no matter how many of them might slink off later, looking for a bed to lay down in, she knew Gunner would make sure she had this room to herself.

She sank onto the edge of the bed. "You can go now," she said quietly. "I think I'll just...I've had enough."

Gunner hesitated. "Well, good. That's good."

"You can go back to Angela."

"Huh?"

"I saw you talking to her and watching me," she whispered.

"So?" Why did he have the sneaking suspicion they were entering that ozone layer again?

"So I'll get out of your way now," she said more firmly. "That's why you brought me up here, isn't it? So you didn't have to...you know, watch over me anymore. Go on, Gunner. Go back downstairs and enjoy yourself. You don't have to baby-sit me."

"I wasn't baby-sitting you," he snapped.

"Yes, you were. You've been watching me all night like you're waiting for me to change color."

He swore richly. And at that moment the shouts began erupting from downstairs.

It was midnight, or damn close. *Ten, nine, eight...*

He watched her come off the bed again like a shot. She turned around in a little half circle, looking wildly around the room.

"Tess—"

She whirled back to him. "Go on, Gunner, or you'll miss it."

Everything he wanted was right here. "Yeah, sure." He didn't move.

Seven, six, five...

"Tess?" His voice was odd, strained. "You okay, Princess?"

"Fine," she managed to say in a strangled voice. "Right as rain."

No, he thought. No. She was shaking like a leaf.

Ah, hell. He closed the distance between them again abruptly. "I'm sorry."

"For what?" she asked, confused.

Four, three, two...

He realized that the voices weren't quite in sync. The hollering in the street, filtering up to them from the open front door, was a half beat ahead of the voices rising in glee in the kitchen. Someone had left a radio on in one of the other bedrooms, and the announcer was saying there were still fifteen seconds to go.

This stroke of midnight was going to last about an hour, he reckoned grimly.

"I was trying to spare you this," he said hoarsely. "I just couldn't think of any way fast enough."

"Spare me?" Her voice broke. "Oh, Gunner." He was so kind inside that cocky, self-sure exterior, she thought. She could deal with him far more easily if he wasn't so...so *good*.

One...

She was safe with him. Somehow, impossibly, she was sure of that. He'd help her through this.

"Kiss me, Gunner," she whispered impulsively. "I don't want to think. And it's midnight. It's tradition."

He felt something cold and wary shoot through him. Then it was hot and amazed and oh, too willing.

"Come on, Tess," he said roughly. "You're drunk."

"Not really. No, I'm really not."

He swallowed a groan. His hands curled into fists at his sides. Tessa didn't notice. She didn't look down. She looked up slowly, into his face instead.

She'd been aware of him, starkly, titillatingly aware, for days now. She was alive. She hadn't died with Matt. And she'd felt little spasms inside every time she let herself notice the way Gunner moved. She melted a little every time he gave that crooked grin. But not once, she thought wildly, not once until now, had she really noticed his mouth.

It looked soft enough to kiss, his bottom lip slightly fuller than the top. It lost that appearance when he grinned the way he did, but he wasn't smiling now. Little lines bracketed the corners of his mouth—laugh lines, she thought. And there was something like a dimple at the lower right part of his jaw, only not quite a dimple because it was longer, less deep than that. Light from outside and from the hallway played over his face and left a shadow there.

"Go to bed, Princess," he said, his voice raw.

Happy New Year!

She flinched as though someone had struck her.

He was too close to miss the reaction. He hadn't intended to touch her. God, no. He hadn't once really considered it, hadn't allowed himself to. But then her mouth opened ever so slightly, and he felt her breath, sweet with the punch, and he was only a red-blooded, all-American male after all.

He let his hands find her hair. His fingers tunneled into it on either side of her head, slowly, almost of their own volition. He lowered his mouth to hers, agonizing inch by inch, watching her carefully the whole time, watching her eyes.

They just kept getting wider.

He was ready to move back if she gave even the slightest hint that she had changed her mind. She didn't.

He felt her shudder as his lips finally touched hers. Something incredible shot through him, nearly taking his legs out from under him.

He had all the finesse she had supposed. Oh, he was good at this. Experienced, she thought. It showed. His hands held her head still while he tilted his own, just so. And his mouth covered hers with so little pressure that she felt something ache inside her for more, needing more contact, something deeper, something harder. He would make her want, and want badly, before he finally gave.

He'd keep it chaste, Gunner decided. Pretend she was...oh, hell, he didn't know. Sort of his sister, maybe. Yeah, that would work. Easy. No big deal. Just a kiss. And then he felt her leaning into him and he realized that for full seconds now he'd been tracing her lower lip with his tongue. Tasting punch. Wanting to taste *her*. Needing it. It was agony. She was *not* his sister.

He felt her fingers dig into his waist, holding on as tightly as though she were being tossed around by a storm. His caution went out the window.

He pulled her sharply and suddenly toward him. His tongue left her lip and plunged into her mouth, desperate to find hers. He was just a man, only a man, after all. What the hell did she expect from him? Anger at himself, at his own weakness, made everything inside him burn even more.

She felt something ignite within him. Felt his urgency. His fingers clenched suddenly at her scalp. His chest was like granite, relentless pressure crushing her breasts as he held her to him, still with nothing more than his hands in her hair. She felt her nipples tighten at the contact even as she felt him getting hard. She had to pull away. Had to stop this insanity. She'd been wrong. It didn't stop her from thinking. It made her think too much.

But then one of his hands left her hair and went to her neck, and his thumb stroked the hollow at her throat, shooting frissons of pleasure through her from that point. And his tongue kept searching for hers, so she sought his with her own.

Stop! Oh, God, she wanted to feel her fingers in his hair. *Get control of yourself!* But it was bliss, not even really forgetfulness, but more a fullness. It was like being full of *him.* It was sweeping sensation blotting everything else out. Heat was spiraling inside her. He moved his hand from her neck. She didn't dare, couldn't dare, find out where it would go next.

She finally gasped and jerked away from him. Gunner swore richly and dragged a hand over his mouth.

"Your idea," he said hoarsely after a moment, then he grimaced at his own self-serving words. "My doing," he added harshly.

"No...I..." She couldn't finish. She watched him, wide-eyed, her heart thumping, wanting so badly to go back into his arms that it made her shake.

She took another little stumbling step away from him.

"I started it," she murmured.

"Only so you wouldn't remember." And damn it, it hurt. Oh, yeah, it hurt. He felt absurdly used—him, a man who had always maintained that kissing, loving, was a matter of pleasure, nothing more weighty and complicated than that.

"Or maybe so I would," she said in a very small voice. She spun away from him to look out the window, staring unseeingly at the people cavorting down there in the street. It hadn't worked.

"So you *would?*" He felt dazed. "You kissed *me* so you would remember *Matt?*"

"Yes...no. Oh, God, no. That's not it. Exactly."

"So tell me what it was," he said, suddenly angry. *"Exactly."*

She was silent for a long time. "When it happened, when he was shot..." Her voice trailed off as though the words were acid on her tongue. She licked her lips. Gunner waited.

"When I came through that restaurant door," she began again, "and saw..." She took a deep breath. "I would have done anything, Gunner. Anything to save him."

"You didn't have a gun—"

"Anything." She interrupted fervently.

"There was nothing. Nothing you could have done."

"If I had gotten out there a step sooner, I would have thrown myself in front of him."

That floored him.

Just as he had never loved anyone that totally, that consumingly, neither could he doubt that this woman had. That she would have done it. She would have taken a bullet meant for the man she loved, and she would have died smiling.

Her small cry snapped his attention back to her. "What?" he asked hoarsely.

"I loved him that much, but now I can't even remember him!"

He wasn't sure he had heard her right. Then she went on, and he knew he had.

"I can't really see his face anymore when I close my eyes, you know? Not easily. I can't remember how he smelled anymore, how he felt! *I can't remember!*"

Angela had been right. She was breaking his heart. And it wasn't a totally selfish pain.

"Tess..."

"I didn't want to *not* remember him at midnight! I didn't want to find out that I...that I couldn't. Do you understand?" It was what had been scaring her all day, she thought, what had brought her here to South Philly in the first place.

And it had happened.

She *hadn't* been able to remember Matt. It had been, for a moment there, as though Matt Bryant had never breathed, never laughed with her, never existed. Her senses, every one of her senses, had been filled with John Gunner.

She felt sick—with shame, with guilt, with too much punch.

"It's okay," she heard him say. "I don't care why...why you— why we did that."

"You should."

"Hell, Princess. I'm a mongrel. I have no pride."

Her gaze shot to him helplessly. She knew as well as she knew her own name that he was lying. He was doing it to make her feel better. Tessa knew suddenly that she was going to cry.

"Gunner."

"What?"

"Would you mind..." What? she thought frantically, her throat closing. All she knew was that she had to be alone now. "Would you mind getting me some more punch?"

There was a heartbeat of silence. "Yeah. Sure." And if there wasn't any left, he'd get his mother to make some.

He realized, not quite able to comprehend it, that he would do anything for this woman, anything in the world.

He stepped back into the hallway and closed the door quietly behind him. What the hell was he getting into here? What was she doing to him?

He didn't go for the punch. He was shaken. His whole body seemed to rock from what had happened in there. What she had done. What she had said. He leaned back against the door and scrubbed his hand over his mouth again.

It took a good five minutes for him to get himself under control. For his body to subside. For his heart to stop pounding like a snare drum. He eased his weight off the door and opened it again silently, just a crack, peering in to check on her.

She was curled up on her side on the bed. Tessa Hadley-Bryant had finally fallen asleep. He laughed, a raw, pained sound. His half-baked plan had worked.

Much, much too late.

Chapter 13

Tessa woke the following morning with the feeling that her tongue had cleaved permanently to the roof of her mouth. And she had a headache. She rolled over, looked at the ceiling and remembered where she was. Her voice escaped her in a little cry.

In an instant, her headache worsened. For a moment, she was overwhelmed with things to consider, with impressions and memories. Finally it occurred to her that no matter what had happened between them last night, Gunner had not taken advantage of the situation.

No, she thought sinkingly, he was not a mongrel. No matter what he might want people to think, he was a good, principled man.

Or maybe he'd preferred to spend the night with Angela.

Her heart lurched at that thought. Once again her head filled, this time with fragments of things he'd said to her over the days that had just passed. She reached up to press her fingers to her temples, groaning.

"I just don't like sloppy loving. I'll never take anything from you under the influence that you wouldn't give me sober." Suddenly that conversation seemed prophetic.

Tessa forced herself off the bed. There was a dresser against the far wall. She went to it and stared into the mirror there, pushing her hair back from her forehead, looking into her own eyes as though expecting to find a stranger peering out at her.

She pretty much did. She hadn't been all that drunk last night. Tipsy, certainly. But not enough for it to be an excuse. She knew she hadn't drunk a lot from that thermos. Too many people had swigged from it. Tonie's punch might be potent, but if she'd had as much as Gunner seemed to think she had, she would have passed out long before midnight. She wasn't used to drinking.

So where did that leave her?

It left her with a mild hangover, she thought, and the frightening, unavoidable necessity of leaving this room and facing him again.

Dear God, she had kissed him. Not because she was drunk. Oh, no, that excuse would be too easy, and she wouldn't be easy on herself. She had done it because she had wanted to.

Tears burned at her eyes again. Suddenly she was frantic.

She had to do something. *What?* Had to fix this. *How?* She wanted him. She was no more immune to John Gunner than any other woman in the department, and that was humbling, over- whelming. Because she *wasn't* any other woman, and it had noth- ing to do with who she was, but *what* she was. She didn't sleep around. Dear God, Matt had been her first and only lover! How could she deal with this? What in the name of heaven was she supposed to do?

Her pulse roared. She moved carefully back to the bed and sat on the edge, feeling as fragile as glass. Then she jumped, physi- cally starting, as a knock came on the door.

''Come in,'' she said weakly.

It was Gunner. She had known it would be.

He stuck his head inside. She looked up at him and couldn't read his eyes. Then he spoke, and his voice was remote, so much like it had been after they'd hidden in the bathtub that it made Tessa's skin turn cold.

''Hey,'' he said carefully. ''You're awake.'' He hesitated.

Her breath caught halfway in her throat. Was he going to men- tion last night?

No, she realized, no more than he had been eager to mention the bathtub until he thought she'd pushed him to it.

''You mind if we settle for watching the parade on the tube?'' he asked. ''It's snowing. I'm not in the mood to get wet and cold.

Let's just chill out here long enough for me to get my caffeine
level up to snuff, then I'll take you home.''

Her breath left her. ''Fine. Okay.''

''Good,'' he said, then the door cracked shut and he was gone
again.

Oh, God, Tessa thought, what was she supposed to do about
this? He seemed as uncomfortable as she felt.

But *why?* She would have thought he'd handle a kiss just fine.
Unless he hadn't wanted to do it. Unless it had just been a pity
kiss. She paled.

She went to find the bathroom. She located a tube of toothpaste
in the medicine cabinet and used her finger as Gunner had suggested, finding it a reasonably acceptable alternative. She washed
her face and straightened her clothing. She was wrinkled, rumpled,
tired, but she was less than an hour away from her own shower.
Surely that would make her feel better.

She went back to straighten the bed, and found Gunner there.

Her mouth went dry, as though she had never rinsed it out. He
was rummaging in a drawer. There must be a second bathroom in
the house, she realized, because he had showered. He wore jeans
and nothing else. They rode low on his hips. When he turned
around something happened to her insides. He'd zipped them, but
he hadn't done the button yet. A damp towel hung around his
neck, and his hair was wet and unruly.

He seemed surprised to see her.

''Just...uh, looking for a T-shirt,'' he said hoarsely. ''I thought
you were downstairs.''

''No. I was in the bathroom. I was going to fix the bed,'' she
whispered inanely. And she knew, in that moment, that this was
worse, so much worse than Monday morning after the bathtub
incident.

This hadn't been accidental, unavoidable. This had been done
with intent, with desire. *Her* intent and desire. Her throat closed
and her face burned.

Gunner slammed the drawer and she jumped. He dragged a
T-shirt over his head. She saw it out of the corner of her eye. The
broad expanse of his chest disappeared again. Tessa finally managed to swallow.

''Coffee's on,'' he said shortly. ''I'll catch you downstairs.'' He
left as quickly as if she had chased him.

She straightened out the bed and went reluctantly after him. He was sitting on the sofa in the living room, guzzling coffee from a mug. Everyone else seemed to have gone. The string band music of the Mummer's Parade, the too-cheerful voice of the announcer, filled the room. He looked back at her over his shoulder when he heard her pause on the steps, then he held up his mug.

"Help yourself," he said neutrally.

"Yes," she said quietly. "Thanks. I will."

Gunner watched her leave for the kitchen, wondering how this partnership had gone so far off course so fast. All morning long he had been torn up inside wondering what to do now. What did he *want* to do? Where did they go from here?

He didn't want to hurt her.

She would almost certainly expect something from him now, he thought. She was that kind of woman. He felt an unfamiliar kind of panic. That had never bothered him before. He'd simply explained as kindly as possible that it couldn't happen, that he had nothing to give, then he'd moved on.

When she came back, she sat down on the far side of the sofa. He tried to ignore her.

"Oh!" she said suddenly. "There's that guy on stilts! We saw him last night!"

"Mmm," Gunner said carefully. She seemed inordinately pleased to recognize him, to have known him however distantly and briefly before he had showed up on the tube. He wanted badly to smile. This was a politician's daughter?

Wrong, he thought. She was a politician's sister, granddaughter, niece. Close enough. It catapulted her right out of his world.

He felt her settle back against the cushions and refused to look her way.

"They're all men, right?" she asked finally, tentatively. "Even those people there?"

Gunner scowled as she pointed, doing his damnedest to concentrate on the television. One of the bands was doing a skit with a mouse coming out of a clock. He tried to make sense of that and realized he couldn't quite think this morning. A woman in a full skirt and apron was dancing around with a broom, trying to chase the mouse back inside.

The costumes were artful, some sequined, some feathered, the results of a full year's work. Tomorrow the members of the bands would rest and regroup, but the day after that they would already be organizing for next year's parade.

"Gunner?" Tessa said.

He jolted. "What?"

"I asked if they were all men."

"Uh, no," he mumbled. "Not anymore."

"I thought only men could be Mummers." She was sure she had heard that somewhere, and she was striving mightily for some safe, innocuous conversation.

"It used to be that way. They changed it a few years back." He stood suddenly. "Want more coffee?"

"No," she said weakly. "Thank you. I'm fine."

He left the room. She forced her attention grimly to the television. And then, as she stared at the parade almost unseeingly, something occurred to her.

She was reaching, she thought. She was probably reaching. But she remembered what Gale Storm had said about this being a game for Benami. How he would put any saved evidence in a clever and cunning place.

Gunner came back, swigging coffee.

"I just had a thought," she said.

He gave her a sharp look, but he was mostly relieved at her tone. It was less stilted, more genuine. He wondered if they could just possibly go on as though nothing had happened.

"Yeah?"

"About Benami," she said.

He had been sitting here picking at thoughts of the man, too, before she had come downstairs. Anything to keep his mind off her. But he hadn't come up with anything new. "What?"

"I was thinking about what Gale said about him being cunning and looking at this as a game. It's a long shot," she admitted, "but maybe whatever evidence Christian kept is hiding right in plain sight."

"Plain sight," he repeated thoughtfully. "So he could get a good laugh every time we pass by it, not knowing it's there?"

"Exactly!"

"So how come we're passing by it, not noticing it's there?"

"Because it's so obvious." She thought about it. "Or maybe it's obvious, yet somehow camouflaged."

"You're losing me, Tess."

"Where do you keep important papers, insurance policies, your divorce decree, that sort of thing?" she demanded suddenly.

"In my nightstand drawer."

"Oh." She let her air out. It wasn't what she had been getting at. But Gunner was Gunner; he probably *would* keep important papers in such an indifferent manner.

"Well, I keep mine in a safe-deposit box," she said. "At the bank."

She would, he thought. She would keep everything about her personal life in proper order.

"Okay," he answered. "So what's your point?"

"I was thinking that maybe Benami did that."

He shrugged. It was possible. They hadn't checked for that sort of thing with the banks yet. And it would be an obvious place, something Benami would get a charge out of them overlooking.

Except they wouldn't have overlooked it forever. It *was* obvious. "So why do you think that's so clever?"

"I was thinking about how the Mummers used to be all men, dressing up as women for those few female roles."

She was losing him. If not the ozone layer, then this was only one step down.

"Based on the psychological portrait that Gale painted of Christian, maybe he would do something like that, too," she explained, pointing at the television. "If only for the fun of it."

Gunner's eyes widened slowly. He was starting to catch on. "Put the box in a woman's name? His victim's name? *Daphne's* name?"

"Too close," she argued. "Too easy."

"Yeah." He scowled. "But something...some name...that offers us a clue."

Tessa nodded hard. Her eyes were alight again. "And then he'd sit back and wait to see if we catch on," she added.

Gunner downed the rest of his coffee. "I like it. It makes a sick sort of sense."

And that was when he realized that they were talking normally again. As if last night hadn't happened. As if he'd never tasted her and had never laid awake half the night thinking about it, wanting more, fighting the strongest urge he'd ever known to go back upstairs to that room and touch her again, to make love to her.

He was relieved. Of course he was. She didn't expect anything from him after all.

She was watching his expression closely. "I'll get my coat," she said, and her voice wasn't normal anymore.

He drove her home, and the closer they got to Elfreth's Alley, the more quiet Tessa became. She felt as though she was standing in mud up to her ankles—no matter that she had never, ever meant to step off solid ground. Every instinct she possessed screamed at her to move backward fast, onto dry land again, as quickly as possible. But the sense of his nearness was almost palpable in the car, and it wouldn't let her go. Memories of his mouth on hers, of his fingers in her hair, his thumb stroking her throat, seemed so real, so immediate, that they made her heart thud all over again.

She lowered her window suddenly, trying to take in the icy air outside. Gunner looked at her sharply, but said nothing.

"I want to ask for reassignment," she blurted suddenly, surprising even herself. "I can't do this," she said, her voice getting frantic, faster. "I can't function, I can't even think."

She was met with silence.

"Is that the way the Hadleys do it?" he asked finally. Tessa risked a glance over at him. His knuckles were white where his fingers gripped the wheel.

Damn it, he'd known this was coming. No matter how reasonable she'd sounded when they'd been discussing Benami earlier, some instinct inside him had kept howling that she wasn't a woman who could kiss her partner, then say, "Oops, wrong turn" and forget about it. What he *hadn't* anticipated was his reaction when she finally got around to saying the words aloud.

He didn't want complications. He *didn't*. But he felt as though she had punched him. He didn't want to make a big thing of last night, but neither did he want to end this partnership.

He grimaced. He wanted it all. He wanted the easy way out.

He had the strong sense that if he let her move on, he would be losing something great, something *precious*, something beyond a good working relationship. Something that maybe could have changed his life from lackadaisical and enjoyable to something meaningful and profound and *good*. And there wasn't a damn thing he could do about it. He couldn't try to grab it back and expect to maintain his pride. So he went with his temper instead.

"Something surprising happens, something that felt damn good, but because it wasn't planned, because it doesn't fit into your rules, you run and *hide* from it?'' he protested, his voice finally turning angry.

"Gunner, I'm being as honest with you as I can!''

"I can't do this," he mimicked, taking a corner too sharply. It tilted her against the door. "Tell you what, Princess, you didn't even give it a goddamn try.''

"I don't want to.'' *I'm afraid.*

This time he looked at her. Her eyes blazed even as her chin trembled, and it was a combination that knocked the air right out of him again.

"So we're adults here,'' he growled. "It doesn't have to happen again.''

Oh, God, Tessa thought, if only it were that easy.

It happened, was on the brink of happening, every time he touched her, she realized. Oh, yes, she was afraid. What she'd done last night rocked everything she'd thought she knew about herself.

There was a right way and a wrong way to do things. She'd always believed that, *always.* Taking the wrong way was a conscious choice. But she had nearly tumbled over the edge last night with no conscious rationality involved. She'd just been feeling. Swimming in sensation. Lost in it.

Turned on. Oh, God, she had been so turned on. And even if she could let go of Matt, even if she could accept that maybe it was time, she could not allow herself to get caught up with a man like Gunner. Love was *not* too stringent and confining for her tastes. She needed structure. She needed rules.

She didn't trust herself. And so, quite simply, she would remove herself from all temptation so that she would *not* take the wrong way, a way she knew wasn't right for herself at all.

When she didn't answer, his voice got harsher. "So you're just going to sail off and leave me holding this whole Benami thing on my own?''

"No, no.'' She shook her head. "I want Benami.''

"What?" He pulled off suddenly to the curb.

At least, she thought, he always had the good sense to do that when he was coming unglued.

"You heard me.'' She forced some starch into her voice.

Her chin didn't tremble anymore, Gunner noticed. Her eyes were pure fire. It fed his own anger.

At least she'd given him something to focus on now. Something impersonal, something he could deal with. "You want to rock the boat now, change everything around, with a case like this? This is all that jerk needs! It's all the bastard's been waiting for! We'll get sidetracked with our own problems, not be on our toes, and off he goes! A *murderer* is going to get off the hook because you can't handle a *kiss*." He laughed hoarsely, an ugly sound. "Grow up, Princess."

Tessa paled.

"Fine." He pulled angrily out into traffic again. "Do whatever the hell you have to do. I don't care."

She didn't believe him.

He didn't believe himself. He hated himself for being cruel. But damn it, this *hurt*. It hurt out of all proportion. He was shaken.

He stopped at the corner of Elfreth's Alley. Her brownstone was only three doors down, and no traffic was allowed on the narrow street.

"I'll talk to Kennery tomorrow," she said stiffly. "I just...I wanted you to know what I'd decided first."

"Thanks. That's big of you," he answered coldly. *Nothing like a little Hadley class to soften the blow.*

Why didn't she get the hell out of the car? He opened his mouth to say something rude and cutting again, then snapped it shut. His problem, he realized without much liking it, was that he'd never actually been *rejected* before. Hell, that was all it was. He would just keep it in perspective. It was almost funny.

Though it didn't feel funny.

"What do you want from me?" he snarled, looking over at her when she just sat there. "My blessing? Sorry, sweetheart, but I'm not that refined. I don't like this decision of yours, and I'm not going to kiss the air beside your cheek and wish you well. Now will you please get out of the car?"

She did it as though he had pushed her. She groped for the handle, jerked it and jumped out. He watched her walk up the alley, her spine straight, her hips moving gently if a little stiffly. He hurt some more.

He *had* been rejected before, he thought. By Elaine. By his own wife. She had been the one who had finally pointed out that their marriage wasn't working. He'd agreed and moved out. Case closed.

It hadn't hurt like this.

He was stymied. He put the car roughly into gear and peeled off into traffic with a squeal of rubber.

Tessa heard it and flinched, but she didn't let herself look back.

There were sixteen messages on her answering machine. Tessa took a shower and curled up on the sofa with another cup of coffee before she noticed it blinking at her. Her heart sank hard and fast. *She hadn't even remembered to call her family last night!*

She was not herself, she realized. She was totally out of control.

She went reluctantly to the machine and hit the button. Three of the messages were from her mother. Her father had left two, short and to the point. *Where are you? Why can't you show us a little consideration and let us know?*

Eleven of the messages were from Jesse. They were genuinely concerned, even frantic toward the end. Her brother was the one she decided she would call back. She felt most guilty where he was concerned. His current female companion du jour couldn't have had a very good time last night if Jesse had been continually running to the phone, worried about her.

"I'm fine," she breathed when he answered. "I'm sorry."

There was a short pause. "What happened?" Jesse demanded.

And she knew in that moment that she couldn't tell him.

Jesse was ten years her senior. They were close as adults because they battled much of the same problems with their family. But as children, they'd had little contact because he was so much older. By the time she was out of diapers, Jesse had been shipped off to prep school. She didn't think he could handle her pouring her heart out to him about this. And what could she say? *My life has been turned upside down because I'm sexually attracted to a man who isn't my type at all.*

Except he was. Oh, God, everything about him was.

She realized that she genuinely liked Gunner. It was his irreverence she couldn't handle. At least not when it involved her. She could watch it fine from a distance, but she could never adapt it to her own life.

"Hey, you're scaring me," came Jesse's voice. "Say something. You don't sound fine at all."

"I'm okay," she reassured quickly. "I just wanted to get away from it all last night." And oh, she had certainly done that.

"Bad, huh?"

"Not as bad as I thought it would be." And that was the whole problem, she thought dismally.

Jesse paused, then seemed to accept her explanation. "I heard through the grapevine what Baum did to you."

Tessa gratefully latched on to a subject that didn't hurt. "He's a worm, Jess. Christian's got to be paying him off."

"Maybe. Maybe not. Baum's always sided with the bad guys."

"Gunner and I are scrambling for more evidence, for probable cause to convince him to order a blood test."

"Well, when you get it, hand it over to my office. I'll take it to the old goat personally. We'll see how easily he can turn down the D.A."

It was what she had been hoping for. She'd never have asked for a special favor, of course, but she'd been reasonably sure that Jesse would volunteer. It was another reason why she wanted to keep the case when she and Gunner parted ways. She flinched in spite of herself, then told herself that whether Gunner liked it or not, she was the one with the connections. She was pretty sure Kennery would agree with that and give her the Benami file, but something strange and twisting happened in the area of her heart anyway.

"What?" she gasped. Jesse was still talking.

"I asked if you've got anything new so far, anything besides that stuff under Daphne's nail."

"I'm going to be working the cab companies today," she told him. "I'll try to get a trace on where he went and at what time." It would help her fill the day, help her get through this endless, quiet holiday that was suddenly yawning ahead of her. If she had learned one thing after Matt had died, it was that keeping busy made her feel better.

Then she realized that she was likening the situation with Matt to this one with Gunner, and she almost choked.

She dragged her mind back to Benami and told Jesse about Gale Storm's theory, too, and her gut instinct about the safe-deposit box.

"Put something together there, and I'm as good as in Baum's

office,'' Jesse replied. Then Tessa heard a female voice in the background, muffled quickly as her brother covered the phone. ''Keep me posted,'' he said into the receiver again suddenly. ''I've got to run.''

''Sure.'' Tessa smiled sadly, feeling lonely. ''Talk to you later.''

She hung up the phone slowly. *Keep busy.* Before she could get too much more lazy and comfortable on the sofa, she got up for another cup of coffee and the telephone directory. She opened it to the yellow page listings for cab companies and got to work.

Chapter 14

In contrast to Monday's silence, on Wednesday morning the Homicide floor of the Police Administration Building was bustling. People strode deliberately down the corridors, waving sheaves of paper, talking animatedly. Computer keyboards kept up a muted, distant tapping and printers hummed.

Tessa stopped to check on Igor first. Nothing. She hadn't really expected that the computer would produce anything over the holiday, not now that it was reduced to waiting for some other police department to notice the query she'd entered. She was stalling. She knew it, and didn't like herself for it.

The next order of business was Captain Kennery. She made it as far as the hallway again before she hesitated, clutching her briefcase to her chest. Her throat was suddenly, unaccountably tight.

Was she being naive and immature about this? No, she thought indignantly. It was a practical, logical move after what had happened between them. Surely he could see that they couldn't continue working together after the bathtub, after New Year's Eve. Things between them were just getting worse and worse, more and more tangled. Soon this...this attraction she felt for him would muddle their whole professional relationship.

Even so, stupidly, perhaps, she hadn't anticipated Gunner's anger. Even remembering it made something shrink inside her.

Her gaze slid to the left, to the door to the detectives' office. Then her eyes dropped to her watch. It was early, only a quarter past eight, but she knew he'd already be in there, at their desk.

The knot in her stomach turned to an ache.

Well, what was she supposed to do? she thought angrily. She could hardly keep trying to work with him just to placate him. She couldn't *believe* the things she'd done in the short time they'd been partnered—everything from breaking into a man's home to kissing him. *Oh, God.* No, she could not continue with this partnership. She had no true idea what she was liable to do next.

She laughed a little at that thought. Becky Trumball, Kennery's secretary, was just passing by in the hallway, and the woman gave Tessa a knowing look.

You won't stay immune to him for long.

No, she thought. She certainly hadn't.

That made her spine snap straight. "Is the captain available?" she demanded.

Becky held up the mug she was carrying. "Yeah, he just got in. I was taking his coffee to him."

"I'll do it." Tessa took the mug out of her hand and went to Kennery's office, knocking quietly. His voice barked out that she should enter.

She stuck her head in and tried to keep her voice light. "Got a minute? I come bearing gifts."

Kennery waved her into a chair. "Sure. Anything for royalty. Have a seat."

She put his coffee on his desk and sat stiffly. She cleared her throat.

"I need to get reassigned," she blurted on a breath. "I can't...it's not working out with John Gunner."

Kennery leaned back in his chair and hooked his hands behind his head. "Nope," he said after a thoughtful moment.

Tessa's jaw dropped. "I beg your pardon?"

"Nope," he repeated. "As in, not now. Can't do it."

"But you've always been such a stickler for partners getting along! You've always said that *not* getting along could jeopardize a case!" Tessa launched herself to her feet without even realizing she was doing it. She was frantic. "I can't work with him!" she almost shouted.

Kennery lowered his hands and dropped his meaty fists on the desk with a thump. "Fine. I'll try to change you around. *After* you bring me Benami on a silver platter."

"*I* want Benami!" She took a deep, steadying breath. This was her ace in the hole. It had to work. "I'll keep Benami myself," she said more quietly. "I don't intend to ditch that, too. I mean, I know that's why you brought me back, and of course I'll—"

"You're not listening, Princess."

Tessa sank into her chair again. "I'm sorry," she whispered.

"Okay. One more time. No. I can't do it right now. I'm not going to break up the team handling one of the biggest cases to come through this unit in years. Gunner's good. You're good. You've both got your areas of expertise, your strong points. I want you together on this. I want Christian Benami, regardless of all his new money and his connections. Am I making myself clear now?"

"Yes," she said softly, helplessly. *Now what?*

"I don't give a damn what happened with you guys in any bathtub."

Her eyes flew to Kennery's face, stricken.

"You're just going to have to get over it," he said. "If you want to go your separate ways when this is over, I'll see what I can do. Until then, put bathtubs and your other differences behind you and act like professionals."

Tessa felt her face flame. She was appalled to feel hot tears burn her eyes. No, they definitely could not continue to work together.

"How did you...never mind." Of course she had known their argument at the elevator would get all over the department. "I can't do this," she said helplessly. "I can't live like this."

"You want to go back to the Fifth?" Kennery demanded.

Her temper flared. It shot blessed heat into her system. Her eyes dried. "Is that a threat?"

"Yeah." Kennery swigged coffee. "It is. Because people in my unit work like adults. You want to play hanky-panky with Gunner on your own time, fine. But I'm not going to take either one of you off this particular case just to make your personal life easier."

Tessa shot out of her chair again. "Hanky-*panky?*" she fairly sputtered. "I'm not— I didn't—"

"Hey, that's your business, Detective. Notice I didn't ask *what* you guys were doing in a bathtub, or even whose bathtub you were in, although it does snag a guy's curiosity."

She suspected he knew. There was something in his eyes. And, of course, there'd been that phone call from Basil English about someone breaking into Benami's home.

She flushed, suddenly unable to meet the man's eyes.

"All I care about right now is nailing this sucker," Kennery breathed. "Bring me a conviction, and I'll be much more understanding about the birds and the bees and the flowers and the trees."

"Fine," she snapped. She turned on her heel, heading for the door. Kennery stopped her.

"In the meantime," he said, "you got anything new? I just asked Gunner a little while ago and he damn near took my head off. He said I should ask you."

Tessa swallowed carefully as she stepped out into the hall, then she leaned her back against the doorjamb and looked at Kennery helplessly.

"I *am* professional," she insisted, still stung.

"Yeah, you always used to be. Until this crazy request."

"He's just...wild. There are no lines with Gunner."

"Which is why I thought you two would work well together. You keep him in line, and he loosens you up."

Oh, he'd done that, Tessa thought helplessly.

Kennery's voice softened a little. "Give it some time, Tessa. Give it until the end of this case. If you still want reassignment then, come back in and see me. I'll do what I can. Although I've got to tell you, everybody else is paired off pretty happily right now, and no one is going to take kindly to being shuffled around."

"I hadn't thought of that," she admitted weakly.

Kennery slung his hands behind his head again, leaning back. "So answer my question about Benami."

"Oh." She filled him in on what she had learned yesterday from the cab companies. Kennery's eyes, tiny to begin with, narrowed even more.

"Good. I like that. There's something Baum can't ignore."

"I think my brother will agree." She told him of Jesse's offer of help.

Kennery rubbed a hand over his crew cut. "I knew all your connections were good for something, Princess."

She nodded woodenly. She told him of their conversation with Gale Storm, and of her hunch regarding where Benami might have stored any souvenirs of the crime. Kennery finally smiled.

"The unit pool gives two-to-one odds on you and Gunner putting this guy behind bars by Monday," he told her. "I think I'll put my money on you." He decided not to mention the other pool, the one that had nine-to-five odds on John Gunner asking the Hadley princess to marry him by Easter. Amazing odds, given that Gunner was no way, nohow the marrying kind. But he was as boggled by his new partner as anyone had ever seen him. The odds-makers firmly believed that the only place it could lead was the altar.

Tessa's jaw hardened. Her chin came up. "Take the bet," she advised shortly. "You'll double your money."

Kennery thought so. On both counts. If he just kept them working together a little longer.

Tessa left his office, trying to cling to her temper, her righteousness, and went to find Gunner. She thought maybe it was the hardest thing she had ever done in her life.

She stopped in front of their desk. "Hi," she said cautiously.

Her voice was a thin, piping squeak. She cleared her throat to try again. Oh, this was so hard. Should she apologize? No, that was ridiculous. She'd only tried to do the right thing. The fact that she hadn't been able to manage it, due to forces beyond her control, felt like penance enough at the moment.

Gunner replied without looking up from the notes he was making. "Hey," he answered inflectionlessly.

Right or wrong, he was still angry, she realized.

She found herself studying his hands, the fingers that ostensibly couldn't handle delicate work. He finally reached for the telephone, then he hung it from his shoulder and looked up at her.

"So what did Kennery say?" he asked shortly. "I guess you were in there talking about this partnership thing, huh?"

Tessa jolted. "How did you know I was in with him?"

I felt you in the building, he thought. *I sensed you, smelled you,*

something faintly floral filling my head. The air changed the mo-
ment you stepped into the hallway.

"Becky said."

"Oh." Tessa cleared her throat again. "Well, you're stuck with
me."

Gunner felt his breath leave him in a harsh little burst. He
coughed to cover it. So Kennery had said no. He shouldn't be
relieved. Where was his damn pride? She had *dumped* him—had
tried to at least. And all he could think of was that he had more
time, time to win her over or to win her back, time to...*what?*

He wasn't sure what he wanted from her. It was just that he
didn't want to lose her to a different partner.

Right, another voice chided him.

He wanted *her.* She was out of his league? Too damn bad. He
had no respect for that sort of thing anyway. She wanted rules,
lines? He'd shatter them, love her so hard and so well that she
wouldn't give them another thought. He'd—

Love her and leave her and move on, the way he always did.
No complications, no headaches, no letting himself, or anyone
else, down.

He slammed the phone down again without calling anyone. *He*
knew that nothing was forever. But Tessa Hadley-Bryant was the
type to dream of eternal stairways into the stars. She would have
died for Matt Bryant, he thought again. How the hell could he
compete with that, even if he wanted to?

"Gunner?"

Her voice dragged him back. "What?" he snapped.

"I...you just looked...odd for a minute there."

"Yeah, well, I've got things on my mind."

He looked tired, she thought. She wanted to touch away the
shadows under his eyes.

"What have you got?" he asked roughly.

"Where?" She jumped a little, then forced herself to rest a hip
against the corner of the desk.

"In that briefcase you're clutching to your chest like it contains
holy water to ward off Satan." He hesitated. Get it out, he thought,
get it behind them. Again.

They seemed to do a lot of that.

"I'm not *that* bad," he stated.

Something happened to her face. It crumbled. "Oh, Gunner,"

she said softly, and her voice was like velvet running over his skin. "It's not you. It's me. I just—"

"I know. You can't function and you can't think." Interesting, he thought. He'd given those words of hers a lot of play in his head yesterday. And last night. And this morning. And they had infuriated him even more because they pretty much made it clear that she wanted him. She didn't *want* to want him, but she did.

Funny, he thought. The only woman who'd made him stumble in years—maybe ever—didn't want him.

Leave it alone, he chided himself. Especially right now. He looked around and realized that at every desk, heads were swiveled toward them. Phones had been quietly put down again. Scribbling pens were forgotten.

"Don't you guys have work to do?" he snarled.

The eyes dropped in unison.

He glared at her. "Where were we?" Then he remembered that he'd been convincing himself to leave it alone, to leave their relationship as professional as it still could be after...well, after all that had happened.

He could still taste her.

"The *briefcase,* Tess," he said again. "What's in the briefcase?"

"Oh." She put it down and began dragging out papers. He wondered if her hands were really shaky or if it was just his imagination.

She looked as though she hadn't slept. And even that left her better looking than any woman in the department, than any woman he could think of off the top of his head.

"I worked on the cab companies yesterday," she explained, and he realized that her voice had sharpened a little. She had found something then, he thought. His own pulse kicked.

"Christian Benami took an All-City taxi from his town house to the Ball at 7:27 that evening," she said triumphantly. "That's when the guy picked him up. A Checker took him home again at nineteen minutes past twelve."

"Picked him up at nineteen after, or dropped him off then?" Gunner demanded.

"Picked him up. They time the point of origination."

"Wait a minute." Gunner grabbed the Benami file off the corner of their desk. "Wait just one damn minute here. He said he got home shortly before *one*."

"Yes." Tessa grinned widely.

"He tripped up. Here it is." He read the report of the original district officers and the 9-1-1 transcripts. "He called to report Daphne's hanging at one minute after one in the morning."

"I couldn't remember exactly, but I thought it was somewhere in that neighborhood."

"Even if he walked, even if he *strolled* home, he would have gotten home within ten minutes, by twelve-thirty at the latest. There's not so much pedestrian traffic at that time of night."

"And he didn't walk. The driver took him directly home."

"So he would have been inside no later than twenty-five after twelve."

"Right. And you can see into the dining room from the entry-way, so he couldn't have missed her when he came in, not easily. First of all, the table was pushed back and that was odd. And second, she would have been dangling right there from the chandelier."

"Yet he waited over half an hour to call it in. I'll be damned. So he's not *that* brilliant and cunning."

"There's something else. This guy..." Tessa's voice trailed off as she flipped through her notes. "Dhiry Patel, with Tri-State Taxi," she read. "He saw a man matching Christian's description—in evening clothes no less—walking up Eighteenth Street right around nine o'clock. I lucked out to have found him so quickly—he was working the holiday yesterday. As soon as I described Benami he thought of the guy he had seen."

Gunner looked up into her face slowly. His heart kicked. "Why didn't you call me with this last night, for God's sake?" Stupid question, he thought immediately.

Because I thought I'd be working this by myself from now on. Because I was having a hard enough time getting you off my mind without hearing your voice. "I didn't find out about Patel until he came into work at around midnight," she answered. "He was on the graveyard shift last night."

Gunner let it go. "Well, we've got to get him in here, get a statement from him."

"He'll be here at nine, as soon as he gets off work and can get over here."

Gunner swore.

"What?"

"I've got an appointment at Commercial Savings And Loan at nine. To go over their list of safe-deposit box rentals."

She realized with a perversely unpleasant feeling that they really had worked just fine without each other's cooperation.

"So change it," she suggested quietly. "You can do that this afternoon."

"Yeah, I'd rather take this taxi driver's statement and cram it down Baum's throat myself."

Tessa hesitated. "I thought we could get Jesse to do that."

Gunner's face hardened. "This is *our* baby, Tess."

"Don't be unreasonable," she snapped. "If we've got strings dangling in front of our faces, it's silly not to pull them."

"I don't need the damn D.A.! I've been getting compliance orders and convictions on my own for six years now. No strings."

"You're being ridiculous." And then she realized how good, how *very* good, it felt to argue with him over something so blessedly impersonal.

"Four days ago, it was macho," he snapped.

"Well, you're that, too. *Ridiculously* macho." She took a deep breath. "Okay, we'll compromise."

He looked at her warily. "How so?"

"First, we'll take Patel's statement."

"Okay."

"Then we'll take it over to Jesse."

"Not okay. How is that a compromise?"

"Will you just listen a minute? While Jesse's seeing Baum, we can cover the banks closest to Benami's home, see if we can come up with something there. Then, when we're armed with the taxi driver's statement, the compliance order, the 9-1-1 report that we know he called in much too late and anything else we can come up with at the banks—"

"Don't forget the knife," he interrupted suddenly. "Angela called this morning. There were traces of skin cells on that knife, so he used it to coerce her."

Tessa thought that English would say that Daphne had cut herself cooking. But *she* knew Daphne had never cooked a meal in her life. Her heart rate picked up.

"That too, then," she agreed. "Anyway, when we have all that, we can haul Benami's backside down here and you can put the screws to him. It just makes more sense to organize our time so we can get to him as soon as possible.''

Gunner was silent. She could tell he was thinking about it.

''Are you still feeling mean?'' she asked.

He flashed her a look. It didn't go right to her face. It started somewhere around her knees, where her legs were crossed as she sat on the desk. It danced to her hip, up over her breasts, and by the time it got to her face, she was breathless and blushing.

''More than you know, sweetheart,'' he said quietly.

Their plan didn't quite come off without a hitch.

Taking Patel's statement went fine, but everything went awry after that. They were able to ascertain that the cabdriver remembered seeing Benami because he had been on his way to pick up someone else for another formal function. Patel had had a flat and traffic had been a bear. He'd been late, and when he saw the guy dressed in evening clothes, he'd thought it was his own fare, disgusted with waiting, making the walk on foot.

''This is great,'' Gunner muttered after the man left and they went back to their desk.

Tessa nodded. ''Things are really breaking.'' She hesitated. ''I want this guy, Gunner. I want him so *badly.* I don't want to leave anything to chance. Jesse'll get that compliance order. With any luck, the judge will even allow us to hold Benami here until the blood results come back. Even if he doesn't, we can stall. Then maybe we can even charge him today.''

''Yeah.'' He still seemed disgruntled. ''It'll help if we have something from one of the banks, too.'' But they'd move on the bastard even without that, he decided. They had enough now.

Tessa nodded. ''I'll take Patel's statement over to my brother myself, and you can get started on the banks.'' She'd been thinking about that since they'd finished with Patel. It would send them in separate directions.

She was going to get some lines back here if it killed her.

She was trying. She was trying so very hard to be professional about this. And she needed to part ways with him for a little while, if only to get her breath back. She had resigned herself to their partnership for the time being. She hadn't resigned herself to being in Gunner's intriguing company every minute of every day until this case was wrapped up.

Gunner picked up the list of the banks he had made. There were sixteen branch offices within a reasonable distance of Benami's house. It was going to be long, tedious work, he thought, and they probably wouldn't finish it by the time her brother got the compliance order. They'd have to study every name on each rental list, then check out anyone with a name that sounded even remotely like it could be Benami—pretty much anyone with the initials *C.B.* Or *D.B.* Or *D.C.,* for Daphne Carlson. *Then,* assuming they found something, they'd need a search warrant to get into the box. That meant Baum again.

"Kennery should be willing to give us extra legs for this," he muttered. "We're close now."

He stood up and moved around behind her. Tessa stiffened. If he noticed, he made no comment. He only took his jacket from the back of the chair. Then he paused to scribble the name and address of the bank closest to Jesse Hadley's office.

"You take this one. We'll meet back here as soon as each of us is done. If Kennery won't give me extra legs, I'll quit anyway and come back here by three."

He went to the door, shrugging into his jacket as he walked. It settled over his shoulders and hugged them. Tess watched him go, then she went after him impulsively. She stopped in the doorway and watched him walk down the hall. His shoulders dipped a little with each stride. He fairly swaggered. Oh, yes, he was cocky, she thought. And arrogant. And macho. Strong and forgiving and kind.

Her throat tightened and she closed her eyes. She wasn't sure she'd have been so magnanimous with a partner who'd just tried to dump her.

She turned to go back to their desk to call her brother, then she realized that everyone who remained in the office was watching her again.

"Will you guys please get lives of your own?" she cried angrily. Then she heard her own shrill voice and sat down hard.

She was out of control.

Chapter 15

Jesse waved her into his office. He was on the phone, pacing while he talked, and Tessa settled down in a chair to wait.

They'd both inherited their mother's black hair. But Jesse—thank God—had been the one to get the Hadley nose. When she'd been a child, Tessa had just called it big. But the older he got, the more Jesse grew into it. Now it was aquiline, strong.

"What've you got?" he asked suddenly, hanging up. Tessa handed over a copy of Dhiry Patel's statement.

"I'll be damned," Jesse murmured, glancing over it, sitting again. "Good work. At least it's good enough for Baum."

She heard what he didn't say. "But not for the grand jury."

"Not yet. I might get past them—the burden of proof in that court isn't heavy. I'd just have to show probable guilt. But why bother when English would chew this up and spit it out at trial without anything else to back it up?"

Tessa nodded. Jesse's reputation was stellar, his indictment and conviction rates better than those of any of his predecessors, because he knew when to press charges and when to decline.

"We're going to bring Benami in for questioning this afternoon," she told him. "With a match on the blood type, we can at least start the wheels turning."

Jesse picked up the phone to call Baum, then he put it down again. "You look like hell, Tess."

She grimaced. "Thanks."

"I thought you were doing okay lately. What gives?"

John Gunner. She stood up. "I'm just getting my sea legs back. I lost my stamina up in the Fifth."

Once again, Jesse was too busy to do anything but accept her explanation at face value. She went back to the door and Jesse gave her a thumbs-up sign. He was already talking to Baum's secretary.

The vice president of the bank that Gunner had given her was not cooperative. It took Tessa the better part of forty-five minutes to convince him to let her see their list of safe-deposit box renters. She commandeered one of the privacy rooms and sat down to study it. They were in the order of sequential box numbers, not listed alphabetically.

William Connicella, Frank Mahon, Laurie Arnold. None of them seemed to have any link to Benami at all. Briefly she considered that the man might have chosen a name out of the blue, a name they *wouldn't* catch on to. But no, that would ruin the clue. If Gale Storm was right, then there had to be a hint somewhere.

Of course, that didn't necessarily mean that the hint pertained to a safe-deposit box. But where else would Benami hide something that he didn't want to keep in his house? The possibilities were endless, she realized sinkingly. It could be anything from an apartment he might have rented to a hole he'd dug in the ground.

She went for a cup of coffee and returned to go over the list a second time.

After he left Baum, Jesse Hadley strode aggressively into his office and flung his briefcase on the desk. He grabbed the phone to call the Homicide Unit.

His secretary strolled in and dropped a paper bag on his desk while he held on. He held up a finger to indicate that she should wait.

Roger Kennery finally came on the line. Jesse turned to look out the window as he identified himself.

"I've got that blood compliance order on Christian Benami,"

he told him shortly. "I'm sending the original over to the Ninth District so they can serve it on him. I'll fax you a copy." He hung up and looked across his desk again.

His secretary was gone.

Damn it. He didn't have time to be chasing these people all over the building. Jesse knew he was a tough taskmaster. God knew he went through enough help—secretaries especially—but he made it a point never to ask anyone to do anything he wouldn't roll up his shirtsleeves and do himself.

He popped open the paper bag as he stepped around the desk, grabbed half of the sandwich inside, and bit into it as he headed back to the outer office. Then he winced and coughed and veered for the men's room to spit the bite out.

Mustard. *Damn it.* He was allergic to mustard. Where was that woman's head? Then, to be fair, he considered that she'd worked for him less than a week now. Maybe he'd just never mentioned it to her.

"Where's Jeanie?" he demanded of the first person he spotted.

"Lunch. She just left."

Jesse swore and went back to his office for an antacid.

Tessa finally gave up on the bank list at a quarter to three. She was firmly convinced by then that Christian Benami was not any of the people who had rented a safe-deposit box with Penn National, at least not at this branch.

She tried to catch a cab back to the office, but the city was alive and bustling, the way it always was right after a holiday. She ended up walking, and she didn't make it back to the Homicide office until three-thirty.

Gunner was nowhere to be found.

She went to Kennery's office. He was on the phone. She sought out Becky. "Anything going on?"

"Your brother called. Baum finally coughed up that compliance order."

Tessa broke into a grin. "Yes!" she exclaimed.

"A couple of officers from the Ninth are out trying to serve it on Benami right now."

"Have you heard from Gunner?" Tessa asked excitedly.

Becky shook her head.

Where *was* he? Then she thought she knew. He'd probably gotten wrapped up in the bank lists and had lost track of the time.

Then she frowned. No, he wouldn't do that, Tessa thought. Not when he knew there was every possibility they'd be bringing Benami in for questioning today. Had something *else* broken, some new angle? Had he run off impulsively to chase it down without even leaving a message for her as to what was going on? Temper swished inside her.

"Hey, Tess," Melanie Kaminski's called from behind her. She whipped around to acknowledge the other detective.

"Igor's fax is spilling out paper left and right. It's all got your name on it."

Tessa's heart tripped. She forgot Gunner and literally ran to the computer room.

A moment later her pulse was roaring. The first page that had come through was a newspaper clipping from Lincoln, Nebraska. The picture was grainy, and the fax transmission hadn't improved upon it any. She carried it to a place of better light and studied it.

"Oh, my God," she whispered aloud. It was Benami. It was *definitely* Christian Benami.

He was being led into a building in handcuffs. The photographer must have called his name, or done something to snag his attention, because he'd looked back over his shoulder in the direction of the camera at the exact moment the picture was taken. His expression was one of angry surprise. But it was him—the perfectly coiffed blond hair, the pretty-boy looks. Tessa's eyes flew down to the caption beneath the photograph.

Conrad Benning.

He had called himself Conrad Benning in Nebraska. Maybe it was his real name. Maybe it was another alias. But it sure as the devil had nothing to do with Witness Protection. The caption said that he was about to be booked for Murder One for the premeditated death of his wife, Laurina Arnold Benning.

She knew that name. *Laurina Arnold.* She'd heard it recently. No, she realized. Not Laurina. *Laurie.* Laurie Arnold had been one of the names on Penn National's safe-deposit box list.

She snatched up the rest of the fax pages. *Where was Gunner?* She darted into Kennery's office, waving the pages.

"We've got him!" she cried. "Can you call Baum and get a search warrant over the phone?" She told him about the safe-deposit box, then she thrust most of the pages at him. She kept the one with the detective's name and number for herself.

"You want me to play devil's advocate here?" he asked, looking down at what she had given him.

"Of course." She stopped in the door and looked back at him. "All you've got is extradition to Nebraska."

She shrugged. She'd take it.

"They'll incarcerate him there."

"And if he ever gets parole, they'll send him back here," she said pointedly. "Either way, he's no longer a free man, and he *won't* be a free man for a long time to come. He won't be able to hurt anyone else."

Kennery nodded. "True. At the moment, however, the guys from the Ninth District still haven't found him to serve the compliance order on him."

Tessa's heart slugged. Did she imagine it, or did Kennery look worried for a second?

"It's after four o'clock on a Wednesday. Can't expect him to be sitting at home waiting for us," Kennery said.

"No," she said thoughtfully. "I suppose not." Actually, the delay was probably good, she decided. She wanted—*needed*—Gunner here when Benami arrived. How had she ever thought she could handle this case by herself? Her good-cop routine, the one she was most adept at, wouldn't shake Benami up enough to get results before Basil English arrived to protect him. Once a suspect's attorney was present, all tactics, the whole *tempo* of questioning, changed. It became wary, more careful, less productive.

She left Kennery's office to call the detective in Nebraska. She kept one worried eye on the clock, and finally sat back in her chair with a sigh at four-thirty. She returned to Kennery's office.

"Any word?" she asked.

"Nope." This time she was *sure* Kennery didn't look happy.

"Nebraska says Benami—their Conrad Benning—was released on bail pending trial," she said finally.

"For Murder *One?*"

"He held real estate. A lot of it. His wife was a railroad heiress." She snorted at that. "Sounds familiar, doesn't it? He hired a very good attorney, who convinced the judge that he wasn't a flight risk."

"Bet that judge feels stupid," Kennery muttered.

"Mmm. Benami—Benning—cleaned out his wife's bank accounts and immediately skipped town."

"And got lost in Philly."

"Eventually. Apparently he cooled his heels in Paris for a while." Tessa caught her breath. She was dying—absolutely *dying*—to tell Gunner of this development. She couldn't wait to see his expression. And a righteous, angry part of her—the part that kept remembering Daphne waiting, tied to that table leg—couldn't wait to watch him sink his teeth into Christian Benami now.

Where was he?

Kennery's phone began ringing. "I'll call Baum," he said, and answered it.

Tessa excused herself, then her footsteps faltered. Something prickled up her nape at Kennery's tone as he spoke into the phone. Physical reaction rammed into her as she heard the captain's half of the conversation. She whipped back to look at him again, wild-eyed, holding on to the doorjamb for support.

Kennery slammed down the receiver.

"What?" she demanded. "What did he do?" But she knew. It had been in the back of her mind all afternoon. The only reasonable explanation for Gunner's protracted absence was that something had happened to him, especially the longer it went on.

The captain swore a blue streak. Tessa's heart was whaling against her chest now, rushing her blood through her so fast she felt light-headed. *"What did he do?"*

"He's at Thomas Jefferson Hospital. He wrecked another car. Hey! Now where the hell are *you* going?"

Tessa leaned over into the front seat of the cab as it got mired in rush hour traffic at the light on Chestnut. "Go up on the sidewalk," she ordered the driver.

He looked at her in the rearview mirror. "What? Lady, are you *crazy?*"

"I'm a police officer." She fished frantically in her briefcase for her badge and flashed it at him. "Go!"

The cabbie went.

She sat back again, fear clawing at her chest. Tessa knew fear. She knew it intimately. It gouged with icy fingers. It snatched the breath right from your lungs, leaving you suspended in some frozen, horrified state. It made your skin tighten over your flesh in enraged and helpless protest at what was happening.

Always before, she had felt it for herself or for someone she loved. But it all came back to her now when she closed her eyes and envisioned Gunner's broken body.

It had been bad this time, she thought, nausea pressing up in her throat, her eyes burning with unshed tears. It must have been bad for them to have taken him to a hospital. She moaned and pressed her knuckles to her mouth. *Oh, Gunner, please don't die.*

Dying was so easy, so sneaky. It could happen in the blink of an eye. She couldn't lose him that way. She couldn't.

The taxi dropped her off at the emergency entrance of the hospital. She shoved money at the driver—probably too much, but he *had* driven up on the curb—and raced inside on legs that fought her control.

"John Gunner," she gasped when she reached the desk. "A car accident. He's a cop."

Something predictable happened to the nurse's face—a slight flush, a private smile. "Oh, sure," she responded. "I know who you mean. The good-looking guy who was cracking jokes."

Cracking *jokes?* "Can I see him?"

"That'd be tough. He's gone."

"*Gone?* Gone how?" Had he died? No, no, certainly not, not if he had been joking.

Still, the room tilted. Tessa's fingers clawed at the desk for support.

The nurse sprang to her feet. "Are you all right, ma'am?"

"Where is he?" Tessa croaked. "What happened?"

"He checked himself out AMA about five minutes ago. You just missed him."

"Checked...himself...out."

"You'd better sit down."

"Yes. I'd better." She stumbled back to a line of chairs and dropped into one gracelessly. Her breath finally came back in short, little bursts. Her fingers wrapped themselves around the arms of the chair. She held on as though it were likely to pitch her out at any moment.

The nurse brought her a cup of water. She looked up at her vacantly and managed to loosen the fingers of one hand to take it. She drank greedily.

"He only had a minor concussion," the woman said comfortingly. "Are you his wife?"

Tessa stared at her. "Of course not!" Why would she think *that?*

"Well, you seem so upset."

"He's my partner." And she was going to kill him. "Five minutes?" she repeated. "Just a minor concussion?"

"Well, a few cuts and bruises, too. We tried to keep him overnight, just for observation, but he'd have none of it."

AMA, Tessa remembered. Against medical advice.

"He's a dead man," she muttered, getting to her feet again.

"No," the nurse argued. "Like I said, it really wasn't all that bad."

"Dead," she repeated. "With my bare hands. Why can't he just drive like a normal human being? Can you tell me that? Gas pedal, brakes, steering wheel! It's not that damn hard to master!" she yelled at the woman.

"Uh, no," the nurse agreed warily.

"And he says *women* can't drive!"

She stalked out of the emergency ward again, leaving the dumbfounded woman to stare after her.

Sweet God, his head hurt.

Gunner stepped off the curb and waved a hand at an approaching cab. It slowed down for him, but then an old woman with two shopping bags scooted ahead of him and crawled inside, her bags bumping out behind her.

Gunner stared disbelievingly as the taxi sped off again. He stepped back up onto the curb and began jogging, dodging around people, pushing a few aside in his frantic haste.

Was Tess home, or was she still at the office?

He'd left his watch back at the hospital. He didn't even know what time it was, whether it was likely that she'd given up waiting for him and gone back to her brownstone, or if she was still at the office, chewing nails because he was late.

A phone, he thought.

He needed to find a telephone. Then he could send district officers to wherever she was. They would protect her until he could get to her.

He noticed a shop keeper, standing outside, closing up for the night. Gunner ran to him.

"Whoa there!" he shouted. "Let me in. I need to use your phone. What the hell?"

The man turned on him instantly, brandishing a billy club. Gunner jerked back out of range just in time to avoid being hit in the temple.

"Those things are illegal, damn it!" he snarled. "Give it to me!" The guy swung harder, more wildly. This was a dream. All a bad dream. Had to be.

Gunner's headache was killing him now. Still, he managed to snag the man's arm. He wrestled it behind him and held him a moment, trying to still the pain behind his eyes. The guy began bawling for the cops.

"I *am* the police, you idiot!" And then, abruptly, he let go of the man's arm. He realized what was happening here.

He didn't look like a cop. He looked like a sorry excuse for an aging hoodlum. His T-shirt was blood-spattered from the gash on his forehead. He'd left his jacket behind, so the blood stains were in plain view. They'd taken his clothing from him at the hospital, and he'd had a hell of a time getting it back. Sometime while it had been missing, his wallet had disappeared from his rear jeans' pocket, he discovered, fishing for it. So no badge, and no money.

He swore again, angrily.

This man was too frightened to let him inside, he realized. Gunner left the shop keeper and began running again. He was maybe eight blocks from the office. Eight long blocks. He prayed to God that he had enough time to make it on foot.

He'd had his seat belt on, maybe for the first and only time in years. He hated them and never bothered with them. But when he'd been getting into his car, a group of school kids had happened to walk past, and it had occurred to him, out of the blue, to set a good example. A few of them had been watching, so he'd done his good-citizen bit, latching his seat belt.

A few blocks later, driving the route he took every night, he'd been virtually broad-sided.

He'd been unconscious when they'd delivered him to the hospital. Then he'd woken up to find himself damn near naked on a very uncomfortable table with people peering down on him, shining penlights into his eyes. He'd reacted like a madman. He knew that but didn't care. It had taken him all of maybe five seconds of consciousness to assimilate what had happened and to realize that he hadn't had a run-of-the-mill traffic accident.

He'd had the green light at the intersection. He remembered that distinctly. Dusk had been starting to gather and it was overcast to begin with, but the car that had hit him hadn't had its headlights on. It had roared straight at him, through the red light, through the intersection, swerving at the last possible moment to neatly clip his right front fender. Gunner had lost control of the car briefly enough to take out the traffic light. Admittedly, he'd probably been speeding. The city car had cleaved to the metal pole.

It had been Benami's doing.

It was the only case he and Tess were active on right now. Somehow, the bastard had to know that they were closing in on him. *How?* A leak? Gunner's gut clenched. Ah, hell, was there a leak in the department? Or had Tess's brother merely gotten the compliance order? Maybe they'd tried to serve him with it, and the man had run. But it made more sense that Benami had access to inside information. Not that his routines were a big secret, Gunner thought. His co-workers, his friends, a whole handful of people were privy to them.

Either way, if Benami had made a move on him, then Tess was next on the man's agenda.

He reached the Administration Building, a stitch digging into his side and pulling tight. He reached over the reception desk in the lobby and grabbed the telephone from the startled man sitting there. Mel Kaminski answered upstairs.

"Is Tess there?" he gasped.

"*Gunner?* I thought you were in the hospital. Boy, is Kennery bugged at you."

"Later." He had to think. His head was muddled, and it hurt. "Where is she? Where's Tess?"

"She hightailed it out of here when we got the word on you. I think she went to the hospital. Kennery's not happy with her, either. He had to send another team to go peek into that safe-deposit box."

Gunner tried to make sense of that and failed.

Oh, hell. She had gone to the hospital. No matter what had happened between them, no matter how strained their relationship might be now, she was his partner and she was that kind of woman. She would find her way to his side through a firestorm if he was injured.

She had been willing to take a bullet for Matt Bryant. Why couldn't he get that out of his head, even now?

"We've got to find her, Mel," he said hoarsely. "Fast."

"Is something wrong?" Fear crept into Mel's voice.

"Real wrong. Listen, you've got to alert every pertinent district for the guys to keep their eyes open for her. If she's not upstairs with you, then she's either still at the hospital or making her way back from the hospital. Maybe she's gone home. Look everywhere. When she's found, tell the cops to stay with her and phone in their location. I'll get to her as soon as I can and explain."

To her credit, Mel didn't waste time with more questions. A fellow cop was in danger. That was enough.

Gunner hung up and briefly considered the time it would take him to cajole another car out of the parking lot attendant. He ran for the street again instead. When she left the hospital, she'd probably go straight home.

Tessa went to check the answering machine when she got home. She had no messages, so Gunner hadn't called her here.

She grabbed the receiver and phoned the office. Mel Kaminski answered.

"Have you heard from that crazy fool?" she demanded.

It took Mel a moment to recover. "Tessa? Where are you?"

"Home. He checked himself out against medical advice. Can you *believe* that?"

"I know." Mel caught her breath. "Listen, I'm supposed to send district officers over to you right away. I'm not sure, but I got the impression Gunner's headed there, too."

"Here? District cops?" What was going on? "Why?" Then her heart stalled. "Benami's still missing."

"As far as I know. I'm not sure if that's what has Gunner in an uproar or not. Look, you're supposed to stay put. I'll radio a car to get to you A.S.A.P."

"Mel, I *am* a cop!" Why did everyone still insist on babying her?

"Yeah, and in this day and age, cops always need backup," Mel said unperturbedly. The line clicked abruptly as she hung up.

Cops. Backup, Tessa thought.

She realized she was shivering. Cold. Suddenly she was so very cold. *What was going on?*

She fumbled in her purse for her revolver. Her hands were shaking. She made sure it was loaded, that the safety was off, and stepped into the hallway, her heart thudding instinctively with the threat of danger. Benami was missing. This had to have something to do with Benami.

Did Gunner have some reason to believe that the man was going to come after *her?* If only she had a clue as to what was happening here!

She moved down the darkened hallway into the kitchen, stepped into the room, and hit the light switch. The glass in the back door exploded with a barrage of bullets.

She had no more warning than that. Tessa screamed. And screamed.

Matt stepping toward the gunman, hands out, reaching, placating—no, no, don't do that!—and she left the restaurant door and stumbled in his direction. Her gun. She didn't have her gun. Bullets spit, cracked, whined. Too late. Matt falling, down, down, and that horrible gurgling sound he had made as he died—

"Oh, God," she whimpered. "Help me, please help me."

She had a gun. This time she had a gun.

She stood frozen, unable to bring it up as more gunfire came at her. A bullet pinged neatly into the refrigerator behind her. She screamed and dodged toward the table. Another bullet smashed the glass of the light fixture over it, plunging her into darkness again. Glass rained over her. Blood stung her eyes. She finally dove for the floor.

Her gun. This time she had a gun.

She meant to bring it up, had every intention of firing back, but it dropped clumsily from her nerveless hand. She fumbled for it. More bullets spat into the kitchen. The wine bottle on the counter exploded.

Tessa screamed again. She finally began crawling for the corner where the kitchen counters came together. Nobody could get her there, not shooting from outside.

Her gun. She needed her gun in case they came *inside.*

She went back for it, clutching it against her breasts as she crawled again, bracing herself on one hand. And she finally made it, into the corner, huddling there.

Distantly, almost absently, she realized that the gunfire had stopped.

Tessa put her head down against her updrawn knees and sobbed.

Gunner ran around the corner into Elfreth's Alley at the exact moment gunfire exploded. He never realized he was roaring her name.

He did know that his own life was suddenly passing before his eyes at the thought of losing her. That this was a woman he would kill and die for. He would do anything to save her, anything to the person who had hurt her. If he could get there in time. If only he could get there in time.

Her front door was locked.

He gave an enraged sound and drove his shoulder into it, using his full weight and every ounce of adrenaline that was pouring through his body as if it were fire. He hit it again and again. The wood finally split and cracked. The door swung open, creaking. Still bellowing, he raced down the hallway.

Somehow, his eyes saw and his mind registered. The living room was untouched. The dining room was fine. The kitchen then. He kept going.

The room was pitch-black. Glass crunched under his feet. He heard her crying.

"Tess," he croaked. *She was crying. She was alive. Hurt? Shot?*

A sob caught halfway in her throat. She said something that might have been his name. Gunner followed the sounds clumsily, moving into a corner of the cupboards, hunkering down, putting a hand out for her. He was shaking. He felt it, couldn't actually see it, but he was amazed. He'd always had nerves of steel.

"Tess," he said again, hoarsely. "Did you get hit? Can I touch you?"

This time her words were clearer. "Yes, please," she whispered.

Gunner groaned.

He moved around to sit beside her. He did it carefully, one arm moving slowly around her shoulders. She put up no resistance when he pulled her into the crook of his arm, against his chest.

"Shh. It's okay now. I'm here." He used his hand to ease her head down. Just until she stopped trembling, he told himself. Then he realized that his hand was sticky from where he had touched her. He rubbed his fingers together, and immediately knew the tackiness there for what it was.

Blood.

"Ah, Lord." His life seemed to stop. His heart stalled and every bit of breath in his lungs vanished. "Oh, God, you've been hit."

"No." Her voice was tiny, tremulous. "Glass. He shot the light out."

Just glass. Just cuts. Okay. He could deal with that.

No, he thought in the next breath, he was never going to be able to deal with anything normally again. Everything had changed. Everything he knew about himself had shattered, crashed, with a sniper's bullets. A woman mattered. *This* woman mattered. More than life itself.

"I c-couldn't shoot. Oh, Gunner, I couldn't do it, I *froze!* You should have let me get a new partner. I could get somebody k-k-killed. I could get *you* killed. Gale was right. Oh, God, Gale was right."

She started crying again. Each sob racked through his own chest, tightening around his heart.

"Shh," he said again. "It was the first time."

"Couldn't do it," she repeated, sobbing.

"It was the first time since Matt." God knew nobody had ever shot at her up in the Fifth. "It won't happen again. It's behind you now. You'll be fine next time."

"Maybe n-not."

No, Gunner thought helplessly, maybe not.

Maybe what had happened to Matt, what had happened tonight, would combine to scar her forever. Suddenly he realized that Ben-ami had gone directly for both of their weakest, most vulnerable points. It really was a game for the bastard. He'd known that even if he didn't manage to kill them, he'd still cause some serious complications in their lives.

Gunner knew he was neck deep in Internal Affairs alligators again. That city car was beyond repair. And Tessa. *Ah, Tess.*

The rage that filled him was unlike any he had ever known before. Because this was what everybody had expected her to do when she was fired at again. *He* knew she was stronger, better, steadier than this, but the bastard had ambushed her, taking her off guard in her own home, and Gunner knew that Tessa wasn't easily going to trust herself again.

Yes, Benami knew someone who was aware of general department gossip.

He swore aloud, then felt a fresh surge of adrenaline at the sound of sirens. "Come on," he urged. "Can you stand up?"

Tessa tried valiantly. Her legs were still weak. She clung to him for support.

"It's the district cops I asked for," he said quietly. "Come on, pull yourself together. We'll tell them you never had the chance to get off a shot."

Tessa swayed. "I can't...lie."

"Then I will." He wasn't even going to try to fight his urge to protect her anymore. He knew, finally and irrevocably, that it was beyond him.

"What happened here?" demanded a male voice from behind them as one of the district cops came down the hallway.

With dogged determination, Tessa dragged in a breath, swiped a hand over her wet cheeks and steadied herself.

"Benami found her before I could get here," Gunner said shortly. "Stay with her a minute."

"No," Tessa said flatly.

Gunner turned on her. "What do you mean, *no?*"

She had to get her pride back somehow. She choked on a low, moaning sound, unable to bear what Gunner must think of her right now.

"You're going outside, right?" she asked, and her voice was thin but stronger. "To see if there's any trace of him?"

"Yeah," Gunner said warily.

"So we'll all go. Three pairs of eyes are better than one."

"Four pairs of eyes." Another cop corrected her, coming into the kitchen. He looked at his district partner, then at Gunner. "Radio's buzzing off the dashboard. Every neighbor in a five-block radius called in about shots being fired."

"Good. We'll separate the area into quadrants, pick over every damn inch of concrete. Except you." He grabbed Tessa's hand "You're coming with me."

The two district cops went up the hallway ahead of them. Gunner detained Tessa.

"When we're done here, get that toothbrush you were all fired up about the other night," he said roughly. "Even if we pick up this guy, you're staying with me tonight. Your front door is all busted out."

Tessa shuddered deeply. Panic tried to scoot through her again. It couldn't quite get a grip.

In the end, she only nodded. There were worse terrors tonight than her own treacherous body and heart.

Chapter 16

They found no trace of the gunman except for some spent cartridge shells from his semiautomatic. Gunner examined one beneath a street light with gloved hands. His heart stopped all over again.

It had been a powerful gun. He went cold inside, then hot, when he considered that none of the bullets had hit her. They'd been calling her Princess. Maybe she was an angel. Either that, or she had one sitting on her shoulder.

"Might as well go back," he said roughly. "There's nothing else out here."

"No," Tessa whispered. He looked at her sharply. He didn't like her tone.

By the time they got back to the brownstone, her scratches had stopped bleeding. She washed up and they left Forensics rummaging around in the wreckage of her kitchen. She knew they wouldn't find anything.

They wouldn't even find discharged bullets from her own gun.

She cringed inwardly. Sooner or later, everyone would know that she hadn't fired. They would send her back to the Fifth, and maybe that was exactly where she belonged. She couldn't let Gunner lie for her. It just wasn't right.

She was silent as they drove to his apartment, too shaken to watch exactly where they were going. When he stopped on South Street again, she looked out the window vacantly.

Gunner watched her. He wasn't just worried about her, he realized. He was scared to death. Her face was as white as parchment in the streetlights. Her eyes were too big, and darker than their normal clear blue. Her hands were fisted tightly in her lap, and they had been that way since they had left her brownstone.

Fresh emotion surged through him. First there was rage again. He'd deal with that later, when he finally got his hands on Benami. Tenderness came second, so new, so strange, that he wasn't quite sure what to do with it. But he finally understood why he had reacted with such pure temper when she had tried to get reassigned, and why he had taken her home with him on New Year's in the first place. He knew why he had broken one of his cardinal rules and had kissed her when she asked him to, in spite of all his better judgment. He knew why she'd had him turned inside out from the start. She made thunder roll and lightning strike. And right now, she was making him ache.

"We're here," he said finally.

"Oh," she murmured. "You live *here?*" They were parked in front of a flat-fronted, brown brick tenement.

"No."

She finally pulled her eyes away from the street to look at him vacantly. "Pardon me?"

"This was the closest parking space I could find. We have to walk back around the corner onto Third Street."

"Oh," she said again simply.

She finally got out to stand on the sidewalk. Just as he joined her, a car backfired somewhere on the street behind them. Tessa jumped and gasped.

Gunner swore, and the rage came back. "This way." He took her arm harder than he had to, pointing her in the right direction, and decided that if she didn't like him touching her, then that was just too bad. He was finished with tiptoeing over and around her little lines.

But she didn't protest this time.

She remained unnaturally quiet as they walked back around the corner. He led her to a coffee shop and pushed his key into a door just to the side of the entrance. "Upstairs." He pointed.

He had the whole second floor of the building, Tessa realized. There was no foyer—in fact, there really wasn't much in the way of rooms. It was mostly open space, with nothing to hem him in. They stepped directly into an immense living area and she looked around. Something inside her began to squirm and come back to life.

It was so...Gunner.

The gray carpet was the color of his eyes. The whole east wall seemed to be windows. The blinds were rolled all the way up, letting in the lights of the city. On the north wall there was an entertainment center with every imaginable electronic appliance. Tessa stepped over to it.

A television, two VCRs, a stereo, CD player, turntable, speakers. And magazines. Lots and lots of magazines. Everything from *Bon Appetit* to *Field And Track,* to *Newsweek* and *Sports Illustrated.* They were everywhere, not just on the entertainment center. She looked around in wonder.

"You can't possibly be interested in all these subjects," she breathed.

"It's amazing how some odd tidbit of information can come in handy in this business. I like to learn."

She finally looked at him. He was watching her closely, looking uncomfortable. Funny, she thought, how as recently as a week ago, she would never have been able to imagine John Gunner feeling awkward about anything. She seemed to bring out the worst in him. She gave a short, high-pitched laugh.

"What?" he asked too quickly.

Tessa shook her head and hugged herself. "Nothing."

"I would have cleaned up if I'd known you were coming."

She looked around again and sighed. "It's wonderful. Someone lives here. My place used to look sort of like this."

Ah, he thought. So the neatness of her brownstone, the sterility, the lack of anything personal there, *had* been a reaction to her widowhood.

Gunner cleared his throat. "Hungry?"

Tessa grimaced. "If I ate anything right now, I don't think I could keep it down."

He flashed one of those crooked grins. It thawed the ice inside her a little more. She went to the sofa beneath the wall of windows and sank on to it with a tremulous sigh. Then she looked over her shoulder and jumped up again.

"He could shoot right through there!"

"Not unless he's on the roof of the building across the street," Gunner answered evenly.

"But he *could* be!"

Gunner moved around her and closed the blinds. "Better?"

"A little." She nodded, embarrassed, but she went to sit in a chair.

"Want a drink?"

Her gaze flashed up to him. "I don't think so. You know what happens when I drink."

"Yeah. And I loved every minute of it."

Her eyes widened. Twin spots of color came instantly, finally, to her cheeks.

That was better, Gunner thought.

"I don't want to talk about it," she gasped.

"I do."

Her eyes widened even more. Her heart began thundering. *Don't do this to me, not tonight, Gunner, I can't handle it.* She began looking around frantically, as though seeking escape. Gunner crossed slowly to the chair and leaned over to put a hand on the cushion on either side of her head, effectively trapping her.

"What are you doing?" she gasped.

"Keeping you from running."

"I'm not...I can't—"

"No, you can't go anywhere." He hesitated. "Not now. Not anymore."

His voice was like callused fingers on her skin. Tessa shivered and looked up at him helplessly. *Oh, God, she wanted him.* All he had to do was get close to her like this to start everything up inside her again, even now. And that was without even considering the implications of his words.

Gunner held her eyes and thought again of how he had felt when he had turned that corner and had heard gunfire. No more lines, he thought again. She didn't know it yet, but she was his.

His heart thudded briefly, then was calm.

Unfortunately, first things came first. He finally straightened away from her.

"I'm having a beer."

She watched him disappear into the kitchen and stood unsteadily to go after him. It terrified her to realize how unwilling she was to be alone right now.

"I also have brandy, bourbon and vodka," he said, peering into a cupboard. "You seemed to do okay with bourbon the other night. I think that was one of the things in the punch."

Tessa blushed, then she sighed. It wasn't worth arguing about. "Fine."

He rooted in the refrigerator and mixed it with ginger ale. Tessa peered over his shoulder at the shelves.

"Gunner, there are things *growing* in there."

He smiled privately. Now that sounded a lot more like the Tess he knew. "Yeah."

"What's that orange stuff?"

"Mold."

"Mold's green."

"Not when it used to be a carrot." He closed the refrigerator again and turned to look at her, then he sobered. "So," he began, "the first order of business is to figure out what set Benami off tonight."

Tessa shook her head emphatically. "No. The *first* order of business is how *could* you?"

Gunner blinked in surprise. "How could I what?"

"Wreck another car!" Impulsively, unable to stop herself, she touched a finger to the bandage on his forehead. "Oh, Gunner."

Yeah, he thought. This was going to turn out just fine. "Want to kiss and make it better?" he asked, grinning.

"No!"

He shrugged but kept smiling. "Maybe later then."

He changed gears fast enough to leave her dizzy, and she'd only had one sip of her drink.

"I was run off the road," he explained. "Benami came after me first. That's how I knew that you were probably in danger, too."

It was why he had checked himself out against medical advice, she realized suddenly. The room seemed to spin. He'd done it for *her,* to get to her, to save her.

Well, she was his partner. But still, it felt bigger, more momentous than that. If he had a concussion, he really should be in the hospital. Head injuries could be scary.

Tessa dragged a chair away from the kitchen table and sat down hard as other things occurred to her, her brain working fast and furiously now. "*Why?* Why would he suddenly start attacking us?" Her face paled again. "Gunner, he was trying to *kill* us!"

He nodded slowly. "Sure was."

"But how could he know? How could he know we were getting close?"

"Well, now, that's what's been bothering me all night. Because I came up with nothing at the banks. I managed to touch base with two of the other guys Kennery gave me. They didn't come up with anything, either. What nags me is that even if they *did* find something, how come Benami knew about it before I did?"

"I found something," she blurted. "Igor finally coughed something up. Benami is wanted in Nebraska for Murder One. Only he was Conrad Benning there. He killed his first wife, too. Her name was Laurie Arnold. And I found a safe deposit box under the name of—"

"Don't tell me. Laurie Arnold."

Tessa nodded. Gunner whistled. "Who knows this?"

She felt like crying. "Melanie, Kennery, Becky...just about the whole unit. I was running around with those fax papers like a lunatic." Then what he was intimating sunk in. "You think there's a leak in the department?" She shook her head frantically. "Gunner, I don't want to believe that. One of *us?* One of Homicide?"

He paced to the kitchen window. She was still jittery. It took everything she had not to cry out for him not to stand there. She fisted her hands again.

"Got to be," he said finally. "I can't come up with anything else. Hit me with another answer. Anything. Believe me, I'd be glad to entertain any other reasonable idea."

She was miserably silent, unable to come up with anything.

"Did your brother get the compliance order?" he asked finally.

Tessa nodded. "But the Ninth District guys haven't been able to find Benami to serve it." She hesitated, then went on bitterly, "Now we know why. He was busy running you off the road and shooting at me."

Gunner pounded a fist against the wall. Tessa jumped.

"Somebody told him," he snarled. "He *knew* that I had a rep with Internal Affairs for losing cars."

"It's no big secret, Gunner."

"That's my point. And neither is it a secret you spent nine months in the Fifth."

She flinched.

"He *knows* this stuff. Common departmental gossip."

"It's not just the police department," she said weakly. "Gunner, *everybody* knows that stuff—almost everybody connected with the city judicial system."

"Yeah, and everybody knows the compliance order came through, and that Igor finally panned out, and that you found that safe-deposit box. Or maybe even that Dhiry Patel saw him and gave us that statement."

"Baum?" she whispered.

"Sure. Why not? Like you said, it could be anybody connected with the city judicial system. Whatever, Benami knew he could throw his harassment tactics right out the window."

"I was standing in Kennery's doorway when I gave him the update," she said miserably. "Anybody could have walked past and heard me. I wasn't paying much attention. But even so, why didn't Christian just disappear again, like he did in Nebraska? Why try to *kill* us?"

Gunner shook his head. "Because he's ticked off?"

She looked bleakly out the kitchen window. "It's scary. He could be anywhere out there."

She wasn't going to like this part, Gunner thought, but he wanted to get it over with. "Yeah. So which do you prefer? Jersey or the Pocono Mountains?"

She looked at him wildly. "What in the world are you talking about?"

"We're out of here tomorrow morning, Princess. We're leaving the city until he's picked up. So which will it be? We can go north to my hunting cabin, but I don't have plumbing."

She kept staring at him as though he had lost his mind.

"Somehow you don't strike me as the type who would enjoy roughing it without a toilet," he agreed as though she had said something. "Jersey, then. My father's got a fishing cabin on Still Run. *That* has a bathroom."

"Gunner!"

"What?"

"I'm *not* going anywhere! Are you crazy?" She was furious. She realized that it felt a whole lot better than the fear. "I finally worked my way out of the Fifth! I'm not going to run for cover now that my first case is heating up, no matter what happened to me tonight!''

"Yeah," he said quietly. "You are."

"No...I...am...not!"

"Tess, it's only fair to tell you that if you won't go willingly, I'll just pick you up and carry you."

"You egotistical, macho, chauvinistic, arrogant, crazy..." She trailed off, running out of words.

"Done?" he asked.

"Just taking a breath."

He caught her face in his hands. She flinched but didn't pull away this time. Yeah, he thought again, this was all going to work out just fine.

He had to get her alone for a while. Whisking her out of town would serve the dual purpose of keeping her clear of Benami while he put his mind to convincing her that she was his, that there was nothing about him worth running from, hiding from, and a lot worth hanging around for. He hoped.

Admittedly he had his work cut out for him.

"Hear me out," he said quietly.

She nodded stiffly. He hadn't expected anything more. Inbred manners would make her listen, but she wouldn't like it.

"I honest to God believe that now that you've been shot at once, you'll be fine the next time." He felt her go rigid beneath his hands. Her bottom lip trembled. It took every ounce of will-power he possessed not to cover it, to soften it, with his own.

Later. First things first, he thought again.

"And there *will* be a next time," he assured her. "The longer you're a cop, the more likely it is to happen again. But to tell you the truth, I'm much more confident of my ability to protect you right now than I am of your ability to protect yourself. Not—" He almost shouted the word as she tried to pull away. He held her tighter, his strong fingers digging in. "Not because I think you're going to fall apart again," he said more quietly, "but because *you* think you're going to fall apart again."

He saw tears brim in her eyes. He felt like hell for doing this to her. But it was something that had to be addressed if he was going to keep her safe.

"Hell, Tess, going for your gun has to be a split-second, rational decision. When a cop hesitates, the way Matt did, he's *down*. No second chances.''

She blanched.

''I just don't know how quickly you're going to be able to make that instinctive move for your weapon right now. Not while all this is fresh in your mind.''

Tessa opened her mouth angrily.

''Give it *time*, Tess!''

''I gave it a year,'' she argued weakly, sagging a little as the fight went out of her. ''It didn't make any difference tonight.''

''Because it had to happen again,'' he said patiently. ''In that year, the most violence you probably came up against was someone banging their fist on your desk.''

She tried to gather her pride back. ''If what you're saying is true, then I'll be fine now. I'll be fine if I get shot at tonight, or tomorrow, or next week.''

''Yeah, but tonight and tomorrow we know the most likely direction the bullet's going to come from. Only a fool would deliberately stand in its way.''

''I'm a cop!'' she cried. ''It's my *job* to stand there and face it!''

His hands dropped to her shoulders and tightened. ''Our job is done, Tess. We did what the city hired us to do. We got the evidence. *We're done now.* There's nothing else for us to do until Benami's in custody. Then, I swear to God, we'll come back and go for his throat.''

He was right, she thought dismally. They had no more immediate leads to chase down. She just couldn't bear the thought of *hiding*. Like a coward, she thought. Like a frightened woman who couldn't fire her gun. She shook her head helplessly.

''Sleep on it, Princess,'' he said quietly. He thought that by morning her common sense would probably prevail. At the moment, there was nothing else he could do where Christian Benami was concerned. But he still had a few unresolved personal issues of his own.

Her face was tilted to the side as she frowned at the window.

''Look at me, Tess.''

Her eyes snapped around.

''That's better.''

''Better for what?'' Her heart hitched. No, he wouldn't, she thought. Of course he wouldn't kiss her. Not after all the trouble New Year's Eve had caused between them.

He would. His mouth lowered slowly to hers. But then he stopped and simply watched her. It was, she thought helplessly, almost as devastating as another kiss. He was so *close,* and the anticipation was almost as arousing as the actual contact.

"Tell me what scares you," he murmured.

She knew he wasn't talking about Benami now. She started to shake her head. But then his choice of words struck her. He hadn't said, "What are you afraid of?" That would have sounded chiding. He hadn't said, "You're scared." That would have come off as accusatory. He'd just said, "Tell me."

And because of that, she could.

"I can't be like you," she whispered fervently.

"How am I?"

She waved a hand and only managed to skim it over his chest, over muscles made even harder by tension. She snatched it back.

"Casual," she blurted. "It doesn't mean anything to you!"

"What doesn't?"

"Kissing!"

Oh, if only she knew.

He slid his hands down to her hips. He leaned back against the refrigerator, drawing her with him with a heavy sigh. And now she found herself tucked between his thighs, and her heart erupted into thunder. Air filled her chest and her limbs, a suspended sense of awareness, and she felt tingly, warm.

"Gunner, I don't think—"

"Let's get to the bottom of this," he said, interrupting her, "once and for all."

Yes, they should do that. If they established lines again, rules, if they understood each other, then they really made decent partners. Maybe there would be no reason to get reassigned after all, to put Kennery through all that trouble.

She took a breath. "It's all tactile pleasure to you. It doesn't have any emotional import."

"And how do you know this?" he asked reasonably.

Everybody says so. She realized just in time how stupid that sounded. She bit her lip uncertainly.

"Let's set the record straight here, Princess. I have never—

repeat, *never*—gone out with anyone who works with the city. Well, Angela. But we didn't work for the city then."

Her heart twisted with something perversely like jealousy. "You *did* date Angela?"

"For God's sake, Tess, I was seventeen. It doesn't seem to me like that ought to count. There ought to be a statute of limitations here somewhere."

She wondered, in spite of herself, if he had been to bed with her. And she wondered why that hurt. "But—"

"As for everybody else, how the hell should *I* know why they say what they say about me?"

"They all claim to have been with you."

"They wish," he said tightly.

Tessa almost laughed. It turned out to be a strangled sound. "Gunner, you've really got to work on that low self-esteem."

He finally dropped one hand from her hip to press his thumb between his eyes. Damn, he had a headache. But this was too important to put on hold. He had to clear this up before he could go on to anything else.

And, oh, did he have places to go.

"The department is a community unto itself," he said slowly. "I'm single. I flirt periodically."

"Periodically?" It came as naturally to him as breathing, she thought.

"Yeah. And somewhere along the line I guess it became a contest to see who could finally grab me, because nobody could. It's human nature. Everyone wants what nobody can have, and I told you how I felt about relationships." Felt, he thought. Past tense. Would she pick up on that?

She didn't seem to. He blew out his breath and looked up at the overhead light fixture in exasperation.

And that was when it really hit her what he was saying.

"You haven't been running around kissing everyone in city hall and the Administration Building. Then why *me?*" The answer came to her almost as soon as the words came out of her mouth. *Because I asked him to.* Color flew into her face. *A pity kiss.* She tried to pull away, but he held her.

"Because you're different," he said quietly.

She closed her eyes, her heart thudding again. Even if what he said was true—even if this attraction between them *was* different for him—she wasn't ready for it. Even if he had been the type to settle down into a relationship, she couldn't let herself touch him, fall for him. If she got involved with him, then Matt would finally, irrevocably be gone.

Her breath snagged.

She remembered what Gale had said about loving someone new, and she knew suddenly that the woman had been right about that, too. Loving again would erase the last of the pain. Loving again would finally, completely heal her. She could so easily lose herself in John Gunner, and then everything she'd had with Matt would be forgotten, lost to her.

And she needed to remember him. She *needed* it. She could not let herself forget the sweetness, because it reminded her of the pain. As long as she remembered the horror of his death, she would not be tempted to love again. She knew instinctively that she could not endure loss like that twice in one lifetime. And death was a specter that hung over every cop's life, a palpable shroud.

She thought of the magazines again. John Gunner was a cop as deep as his bones.

No. She shook her head frantically, not even realizing that she did it. *She couldn't.* She couldn't love John Gunner.

She couldn't tell him that, of course. She couldn't explain, because there was certainly no issue of love between them. They were talking sexual attraction here. That was all. He wanted her. That was exciting and flattering, but she could never, would never, do anything about it.

''No,'' she whispered.

''You've got to let it go, sweetheart.'' It was as though he read her mind. ''You buried a part of yourself with Matt, and you're too young to die.''

''So was he!'' she protested, her voice strangled.

He went on as though he hadn't heard her. ''When it's done, when that vicious mess is really over and behind you, you'll be able to shoot again,'' he murmured, realizing it. ''It's all tied together somehow.''

''It's not!''

''You saw him tonight, saw it happen all over again, didn't you?''

Her heart was roaring. ''Gunner—''

''Sooner or later, you're going to have to pick up the pieces and go on.'' *With me.* "You haven't yet, not really. You're pretending. You're even kidding yourself.''

But she was close, he realized. She was almost there. What had she said to him the other night? *I can't see his face anymore when I close my eyes.* Yeah, she was ready, on the brink, so close...and terrified by it. Her heart was telling her she was ready to go on, but she wasn't hearing it, wouldn't listen.

Well, he would be there to catch her when she fell over the edge. And maybe, just maybe, he would give her a gentle nudge in that direction.

He dropped his hand from her hip. A little breath of surprise escaped her that he had finally let her go. But before she relaxed too much, he leaned forward, capturing her mouth with his.

She could have moved away. She could have simply taken a single step backward. He made no other move to touch her. His hands remained by his sides. But she froze as sensation plunged through her again, as he brushed his lips over hers, feather-light and easy, and then his tongue was back, teasing the corner of her mouth.

So good, she thought. *So sweet. So dangerous.*

She dug her fingers into the front of his T-shirt almost tentatively. It was the sign he'd been waiting for, a holding on rather than a pulling away. He straightened away from the refrigerator and caught one hand around the back of her neck, dragging her closer.

He wanted to touch her. He wanted more of her, all of her. It was a pounding, aching need. He had never needed like this, not with any of the women who had given of themselves eagerly, trying to hold him. They hadn't made him feel necessary. One of this woman's tremulous smiles could make him feel like a king.

He fisted his other, free hand to keep control over it, so it wouldn't go to her breast of its own volition. She was kissing him back. That was enough—for now.

He let his tongue slip into her mouth, and she met it with a little groan. They sparred for a moment, and something happened to his gut. A sweet tension, a rolling over, something almost painful that he'd never felt before.

He realized with some surprise that the next groan he heard was his own. He traced her teeth, teased her tongue, bit her lower lip gently where it trembled. He covered her mouth fully again with more restraint than he had known he was capable of. He was trembling with it.

Just a little more, Tessa thought. She'd pull away in a moment. And he'd let her go. She'd made it clear, hadn't she, where she stood on this issue? But first she needed to run her fingers through his hair the way she had wanted to from the first time she saw him. Her hand reached, sliding over his temple, finding his dark locks soft and thick as the strands threaded between her fingers.

She cried out when his free hand shot up and caught hers, imprisoning it against the side of his head. Their fingers tangled together and his kiss deepened, the pressure of his mouth getting harder. It was hungry now, hot. His tongue began sweeping. Need sliced through her, cutting through her resolve. She made another wordless sound as something liquid and warm gathered at key points of her body, pooling, aching. Oh, how she wanted him to touch her. How she wanted his hands on her body. She needed with crazed intensity.

He's right, I'm not dead, I didn't die, too, I'm right here and I need him to love me. Unshed tears burned her eyes.

With a last groaning nip at her lip, Gunner pulled away. She looked at him dazedly, her eyes unfocused.

"You can have the bedroom," he said. "I'll take the sofa."

He left the kitchen. Just like that. Tessa stared after him, shaken and amazed.

He heard her gasp and couldn't look back. She'd never know what this had cost him.

Chapter 17

She was grateful that he hadn't pressed his edge. Of course, she was. But Tessa still couldn't seem to relax enough to sleep. It was the day, she told herself. It was everything that had happened. She was amazed to realize that it had been only this morning that she had asked Kennery for reassignment.

It was the haunting truth that she hadn't been able to pull the trigger, any more than she'd been able to pull away when Gunner had kissed her again. It was Gunner's bed, and Gunner's body, right out there in the other room, as close as a breath and a million miles away, on the other side of her fear.

She rolled onto her side and trapped her hands between her knees, but that wasn't good, either. With her cheek pressed into his pillow, his lingering scent filled her head. Something started throbbing deep inside her, something unfinished, frustrated, needy.

She flipped over onto her back and saw his grin in her mind's eye, crooked and confident. She closed her eyes, but the image remained.

She wanted him.

If he hadn't stopped kissing her so abruptly, she might have found the courage to slide her hands over his shoulders, to finally touch them, too, to explore the way they moved when he walked. Thank goodness he had stopped kissing her.

What was she going to do about tomorrow?

She knew that he fully intended to whisk her out of town. She realized she could go away with him without too much fear, and that was stunning in and of itself. No matter what his reputation implied, he was a gentleman. But she couldn't walk away from Christian Benami. She owed it to Daphne to see this through.

Except Gunner was right. What, really, was there left to do?

Still, her last conscious thought wasn't of the case at all. It was a realization that Gunner didn't seem to snore.

She woke to the very strong smell of coffee. Tessa jolted upright, almost knocking into Gunner's hand as he held the mug under her nose. He put a hand on her shoulder to steady her.

"Easy there, Princess."

"What time is it?" she mumbled, scraping hair out of her eyes.

"Seven-thirty. And we've got places to go."

So they were back to that again. Already. She grabbed the coffee and eyed him warily. This was absurd, she thought wildly. She couldn't even seem to look at him. She couldn't lay her eyes on him without her pulse taking off and something warm pooling in crucial places in her body. She stared down into the mug and felt his gaze anyway.

He'd given her a T-shirt to sleep in and it was several sizes too big, even with her height. She dragged the hem down over her knees, and heard his soft laughter.

Her eyes flew up to him again. "What?" she asked breathlessly.

"You remember that little conversation we had about wriggling and breathing, Princess? Don't push me."

She realized she was squirming and abruptly stilled.

"You're still breathing," he said softly.

Her eyes finally met his. And what she saw there told her as clearly as a shout that she'd been enjoying a false sense of security. He hadn't pressed his advantage. Yet. He hadn't pushed her. Yet. But he knew that she wanted him—she just wasn't able to hide it. Sooner or later he would do something about it. Her heart knocked.

"Gunner, you're doing a real good job of talking me out of going to Jersey," she said.

"Oh, you're going." He finally got off the bed and went to the door. "I just want you to know what to expect."

She put her coffee down, and leaped off the bed. "Gunner, get back here!"

He stepped into the doorway again so quickly she almost ran him over. She took a quick, guarded step backward.

"Didn't you hear anything I said last night?" she demanded.

He braced a hand on either side of the door frame and looked down at her. "Princess, I hate to break it to you, but you didn't *say* much of anything."

She hadn't, she realized helplessly. She'd decided she *couldn't* tell him. She couldn't tell him how horribly close she was to falling in love with him, because love wasn't the issue here. Sexual attraction, she told herself again. That was all it was. Pure and simple. And sex without love had no place in her world.

It didn't matter that his macho arrogance made her feel safer and more protected than she'd ever felt, that it had been that way from almost the first day they'd worked together. It couldn't matter that when his gaze moved over her body, it made her feel beautiful and cherished. It didn't even matter that she admired his idealism and his strength and his goodness or that he could make her laugh at times when she would have sworn it was impossible. *It was just sexual attraction.* Period.

"I can't do this," she said again.

He seemed to think about that, then he grinned. "Actually I'd say you're doing just fine. Come on, let's get out of here."

"What?" she asked, dazed.

"I have to stop by my folks' house and pick up the key to the cabin first."

He finally went back to the living area and she ran after him. "Gunner, I can't do this." Be firm, she thought, just...be firm. He'd always respected her wishes. Eventually. Sooner or later. Most of the time.

"Sure you can."

"Then we need rules," she insisted. "If I'm going to go away with you, we have to establish a few things right from the start."

He went to a closet near the front door and pulled a duffel bag off the top shelf. "More fun to just make them up as we go along."

"Gunner!"

He looked at her innocently.

"I am *not* going to sleep with you!"

He grinned. "Did I say anything about sleeping? Go on, Princess. Get dressed."

She fought the urge to stomp her foot. "You're not taking me seriously."

He came back to her slowly. Suddenly his face was so intent it sent something warm through her blood.

"I don't think you have any idea how seriously I'm taking this," he said finally.

She opened her mouth and closed it again. She swallowed very carefully and searched for her voice. Then she changed the subject. Discretion suddenly seemed the better part of valor.

"We can't just cruise off into the sunset here, Gunner," she tried. "We can't just *disappear*. Kennery will be furious."

He scrubbed a hand over his jaw and scowled.

"And we can't just take off until we know what's going on. Maybe they've even found Benami by now."

"We would have heard." He paused. "I don't want to talk to Kennery. But you're right. Somebody needs to know what we're up to. We need a contact to keep our finger on the pulse back here."

Her hand flew to her mouth as she understood what he was saying. "Kennery?" she whispered. "You think *Kennery* is leaking information to Benami?"

"I don't know what to think, Tess. And to be real honest, I don't trust a soul right now. Call your brother," he decided finally.

Tessa blinked. "Jesse?"

"Let *him* know where we are. And tell him why we're not telling anyone else and to keep it under his hat. Then we're covered. Can't do much better than having the D.A. on our side."

Tessa paled. "You really think Benami is going to come after us again? You think he'd chase us into *Jersey?*"

He put his gun into the duffel bag and shot her a look. "Anything's possible. He's nuts."

She flinched, then she squared her shoulders and nodded. He

watched, fascinated by the transformation from panic to courage. Then she slumped a little again.

"I still feel like a coward, running this way," she muttered.

"Yeah," he agreed. "I'm not real comfortable with it, either. But there's no help for it."

And that was when she realized that it was just as hard for him to walk away from Benami right now. *He's doing it for me.* Because he knew that if he just sent her away somewhere, she'd only come back. He was slinking off himself to keep her safe, not only from Benami, but from herself.

This man was so much more than anything she had ever bargained for.

"I'll call Jesse," she said, shaken. And she knew, as she went to the kitchen phone, that she was agreeing to much, much more than hiding for a day or two, more than laying low until Benami was found.

They were going to New Jersey, and they had never managed to establish those rules after all.

It took them over an hour to get across the bridge. Tessa had to stop and pick up clothes and they had to exchange the patrol car that Gunner had commandeered from the district officers the night before, and the garage attendant wasn't happy about giving them another unmarked.

"Man, I'll get called on the carpet for this," the kid said. "Everybody knows what you did yesterday, Gunner. *Another* one. Jeez."

"It's all right, Ernie. Yesterday's smashup wasn't my fault."

"That was what you said about the bomb!" Ernie complained.

"And Internal Affairs didn't put that one on my record, either, did they?" He tried to reach over the kid's shoulder into the little booth for the keyboard there. Ernie moved fast to block his way.

"Man, I can't. Not until Internal Affairs says it's okay."

"Check it out to me, then," Tessa suggested.

Ernie looked at her as though seeing her for the first time. "I don't know." He hesitated. "I mean, technically, you're partners, right? So giving it to you would be as bad as giving it to him."

"Not when I've never had a traffic accident in my life, much less in a city car," she declared, then she sent a smug look to Gunner. "I promise I'll drive."

"Around the block," Gunner mouthed at her as Ernie finally turned his back to reach for a set of keys.

"That depends on which block," she whispered sweetly.

Tessa could only be amazed at the way the tension seeped out of her as she turned the city car onto Route 676. They headed for the bridge and a sense of relaxation began to fill her in its stead. Relaxation...or peace.

Right or wrong, she'd made a decision. She couldn't, in all honesty, say that she had changed her mind about hiding from Benami, but she knew Gunner was right. It was the safest, only sensible thing they could do under the circumstances. And she was still frightened of what was happening between them— terrified by what might *yet* happen—but a sweet resignation seemed to have taken her over, a feeling of inevitability.

No matter how many times she told herself that she didn't want him, she knew she did. And no matter how much she thought she wanted to keep her distance from him, to establish lines, she kept finding excuses to step over them and inch a little closer to him. She couldn't fight herself anymore.

"Which way?" she asked a little breathlessly as they came down off the bridge onto the New Jersey side of the river.

"Right here. Pull over."

She felt herself grinning. "Nope."

He swore creatively enough to make her eyes widen.

"I can't even imagine that," she mused. "How could a person *do* that? Is it possible?"

"Is that a roundabout way of telling me to watch my language?"

"Your intellect constantly amazes me."

"Pull over."

"No."

"I can't just sit here," he complained. "It's emasculating."

"This is the nineties, Gunner. It's okay for men to be sensitive. It's okay to let women be strong. Get with the program."

A challenge like that, he thought, could not be ignored.

"Which one?" he asked quietly, and his voice should have

alerted her, if only because it got closer. "Which program? This one?" His mouth touched a vulnerable spot on her neck, right below her ear.

Tessa jumped, then everything inside her went instantly liquid and warm. It left her with a feeling almost like an ache. She wanted this. She did. God help her.

Still, she tried. "Wrong program," she whispered.

"Pull over," he said again.

"No."

Gunner grinned. There was something interesting going on here, he realized. Yesterday she would have given him the wheel, if only to stop him from touching her. He had no choice but to go on, to search out her new breaking point.

He took the diamond stud out of her ear and dropped it into the ashtray.

"What are you doing?" she gasped.

"Too crunchy."

She felt his teeth close gently on her earlobe. The ache inside her bloomed. She shrugged her shoulder in a halfhearted effort to push him away.

"Stop...it. Gunner, I can't—"

"Drive? No problem. Let me do it."

"No."

He was amazed. And thrilled. "You realize, of course, that this refusal relieves me of all responsibility for my subsequent actions."

Her heart thrummed painfully. She couldn't get air. She couldn't answer.

"Well, then," he murmured into her ear. He moved closer and his broad hand came down on her thigh.

Tessa jumped again and the car swerved. "If you make *me* crash, I'll kill you."

"I'm already dying, sweetheart, a slow, painful death over all these lines of yours. You don't know how they make me suffer."

Oh, God, she thought helplessly. He was *good*. Were they just smooth, polished words, ones he had used a thousand times before? Maybe not on anyone who worked for the city, she allowed, but on some women, many women, somewhere? She tried to believe it. Tried one last time to get a grip on herself and on what she had always thought to be right and wrong. *Sex without love.* It couldn't work, wasn't part of her world.

There were other reasons this couldn't work, other reasons she shouldn't allow him to touch her. His hand moved up her hip. She sucked in breath. What were her reasons? She had important ones, *immense* ones.

Matt. Of course, there was Matt.

Gunner's hand was under her sweater, sliding over her skin. She was losing Matt, couldn't find him, couldn't call him to mind at the moment at all, and that should have shot sense back into her system like cold water. But she couldn't possibly be sensible when she couldn't even think clearly.

"You wouldn't dare," she gasped as his hand stroked higher, enjoying her skin.

He dared. Oh, of course he dared. A groan escaped her as his hand closed over her breast.

"You feel like heaven," he said quietly.

If she fell in love with this man—*another cop*—if she did that, then she lost him, it would destroy her. She was afraid.

"Gunner." If she told him to stop, he would stop. She knew that.

She couldn't bring the words up in her throat.

"Front or back?" he asked.

"What?" she croaked. Already his fingers were moving, skimming, searching.

"Is the hook in the front or the back?"

She couldn't have answered if she had wanted to. It didn't matter; he found it on his own.

With the first caress of his callused palm on her bare skin, her heart stalled and she wanted desperately to close her eyes, to revel in it. *Finally.* It was so delicious, so intimate, almost a sweet breath of relief to have him finally touch her this way. For a moment he simply cupped the weight of her breast in his palm, but then his fingers tightened over her.

"Do you have any idea how long I've wanted to do this?" he asked quietly. "And more, so much more."

Everything coiled suddenly at the core of her, a tense ache between her legs, a need so demanding that she couldn't bear it. She felt something almost like a sob work up in her throat.

Gunner cracked one eye open as his mouth worked on her ear again. He watched her knuckles go white on the steering wheel.

Too bad. He no longer wanted to drive.

His mouth roamed down her neck, to her collar bone, and his thumb found her nipple, teasing gentle, lazy circles around it. She cried out wordlessly.

"Better pull over," he said again.

"Yes," she whispered. "Maybe I should."

But she didn't want to. If she pulled over, he would stop.

"Take this exit," he told her.

She veered for it blindly. Horns blared behind them.

"I want to look at you, Tess. I want to see where my hands are. I want to watch them cover you, touch you, stroke you."

Wanting burned, hurt, inside her. She had never wanted this way before. Never. Was it him? Or was it her? Was it the way she felt about him? Was she already in love with him? Surely not. *Sexual attraction.* It was just something...chemical. She had loved Matt with all her heart and soul, and he had never said things like this, had never made her feel this way.

That was blasphemy, she realized. And God help her, it was true.

Gunner pushed her sweater up. His hand slid over her other breast, easing her bra away from there, too. She almost missed the stop sign at the end of the exit ramp and had to hit the brakes hard.

"Oh, Lord," she whimpered.

"Pull over."

"Yes." She dragged in breath. "Was this all...just to get me... to stop driving?"

"No."

"No," she repeated, her voice quivering.

"But this is."

"What? *Oh.*"

His tongue, warm and rough, slid up the side of her bared breast just as his hand went back to her thigh again, inching higher, and then he was urging her to move her legs apart, and she couldn't do that, not here on a secondary highway.

She finally managed to stop the car. There was a wooded picnic area beyond a spattering of service places—a gas station, a fast-food joint, a convenience store. She scarcely saw them, but something about the trees and the gravel parking lot beckoned to her just in time, and she swerved into it.

She moved her legs apart without conscious thought, yielding to his will as it seemed she had done from the first time she had met him. Her head fell back against the headrest. He touched her intimately, rubbing and stroking, and even through her jeans, it made her moan and yearn for more. She turned into him and his head dipped to take her breast into his mouth.

She pushed herself into him. She was melting in his hands. And that told him more, so much more than anything she had said, any words she had spoken. This was not a woman whose body would melt unless her heart was already his.

The knowledge exploded inside him, shattering restraint. He wanted her here, now, as badly as he had ever wanted anything in life. *Not here, not the first time, not with her.* A voice inside him kept trying to shout reason at him, but her eyes were half closed and smoky, and her breath had become short, little pants.

He finally straightened. *Not here.* "Come here."

She flowed into him, flattening him against the opposite door. And then his hands were in her hair again, and his mouth found hers with an urgency that stunned him. Their hands groped, and their mouths slid as tongues explored fervently. He moved one hand to find her breast again, covering it, feeling the warm fullness of her. Her skin was rich, smooth, like satin.

"Gunner..." One of her own hands dragged at the front of his T-shirt, searching for something she couldn't seem to find, something she needed more than she needed air to breathe, something he had to give her. She jerked the cotton free of his jeans and drove her hand underneath it, her palm sliding over his torso, his chest, over the pelt of soft hair there.

"Please," she whispered. *Not here.*

"Wait," he growled.

She couldn't. She changed her mind. *Yes, here. Now.*

But he wasn't kissing her anymore. He put her away from him gently, with gritted teeth, and framed her face in his hands.

"Okay, this is how we're going to do this," he said hoarsely. His own breath was coming fast and hard. Had she done that to him?

Tessa managed to nod. She licked her lip nervously.

It almost undid him, that little darting of her tongue, almost made him lose his grip on his resolve. It was a tenuous hold to begin with. He closed his eyes and fortified himself with a breath.

"I'm going to drive," he told her.

She let out her breath and nodded again.

"I drive fast."

She certainly would never argue that.

"We'll be there in less than an hour."

"Okay," she whispered.

"You have just that long to change your mind. And if you don't, I can pretty much guarantee you that you'll be naked before we hit the front door."

He forced himself to let her go, and he got out of the car.

No, Tessa thought wildly, scooting over nervously into the passenger seat as he got behind the wheel. She had an hour to make sure she could live with the repercussions.

Chapter 18

It took them considerably less than an hour.

Thirty-five minutes later, Gunner turned off the main road onto a rutted, narrow lane. They drove several more minutes in the same thick, tense silence that had gripped them since they had left the picnic area. Finally Gunner spoke again.

"You change your mind?"

Her voice wouldn't come to her throat. She finally managed to shake her head.

Gunner let out the breath that he hadn't been aware of holding. He was stunned by how terrified, how desperately unwilling, he was to hear that she had. Because he didn't know anymore where he would find the willpower to respect her wishes. He'd taken a step too close to easily pull back this time.

"Okay," he said hoarsely. "All right. Will you please take that sweater off?"

That brought her voice back. She looked at him quickly, blushing again. "What? *Here?*"

"We're here."

He turned the car suddenly onto a gravel path. There was a tiny cabin at the end of it, all rough-wood siding and a steep roof. A chimney shot up from one side. She could just make out a thin ribbon of cold, gray water behind it.

Gunner stopped the car. Her gaze swung back to him. His eyes burned into hers.

"I mean it, Princess. Last call. Last chance for those lines of yours."

"I know," she whispered.

She was at the mercy of a stranger inside herself, she realized. Not Gunner, no, he would never twist her arm. But that gremlin inside her was hungry now, desperate. Perhaps if Gunner had never touched her the way he had when she had been driving, she might have been able to turn away from what he offered. But he *had* touched her, and that changed everything.

If she loved him, if that was what this was, then she would just have to tuck it away somewhere inside herself and try to live with it. She had the strong feeling that if she told him so, she would lose him. And she would pray, oh, yes, she would definitely pray, that he would live to an arrogant, macho old age, with or without her.

Another cop.

She closed her eyes briefly and wondered if she was out of her mind, then knew that she didn't have much of a choice. If she didn't go with her heart, she would be miserable. She tried to recall Matt's beloved face, needing to say goodbye to him before she did what she knew she was about to do.

But of course he wouldn't come to her. Not now. He had already been slipping away from her before she had been partnered with Gunner and her world had been turned upside down.

She reached for the hem of her sweater. He was out of the car before she could barely touch it. She looked around, startled, just as he wrenched the passenger door open. He caught her hand, pulling her out as he dug into his pockets for the key.

He couldn't find it. Ah, well. He had tried, Gunner thought. He had gotten them this far. And he had never been of the mind that a bed was necessarily the most romantic place in the world.

She was suddenly in his arms again, and her hands were everywhere, in his hair, stroking down his face. He pulled up on her sweater himself, and a heartbeat later he felt like a fumbling teenager. It tangled at her neck, unable to go any higher unless he lifted his mouth from hers.

He was not aware of having started to kiss her again, before they even took a step away from the car. He eased away from her and pulled the sweater the rest of the way over her head. Her bra was all caught up with it. She had never hooked it again.

That hit him like a fist, that she, too, should feel this hunger, this immediate necessity. She had simply been holding her breath, he realized, waiting for this place, this moment.

She began pulling at his T-shirt and he managed to shrug out of it before dragging her back to him. Tessa breathed in the scent of him and couldn't be quite sure this time where his cologne ended, and where the smells and sounds of the forest began.

How right this was, she thought shakily. How fitting that they should come together here, in woods like those she had thought of every time he had gotten close enough to her that she could smell his cologne.

She pressed herself to his chest, rubbing against him and shuddering as skin touched skin, at the friction of masculine hair against her nipples. It felt so good to be held. *By him.* It felt so good to be kissed. *By him.* His arms were hard across her back, holding her against him, and his mouth demanded. Still, she wanted more.

His tongue swept past her teeth and somehow the kiss felt deeper than any other time he had touched his mouth to hers. Or maybe it was just that this time she knew he wasn't going to stop. *She* wasn't going to stop. And knowing that changed everything. Instead of worrying that she should put an end to this before it got out of hand, instead of fighting herself, she savored him.

She did what she had wanted to do from the first time she had watched him walk. She slid her hands up to his shoulders, feeling muscles knotted with the last of his restraint. She ran her hands down his ribs, his skin seeming to burn beneath her palms despite the cold, winter air.

He realized he had waited forever for this, for her. He had waited even before he had known he was waiting. Everything inside him throbbed. The way she explored his body with a sort of desperate determination made it threaten to explode.

He kept her mouth even as he stepped back from her, teasing her tongue with his own. He caught her hand and pulled her away from the car. Her eyes opened and focused on him dazedly.

"Where are we going? I can't walk, Gunner," she admitted shakily.

"Right here, Princess. Right about here."

They moved to a towering tree near the house. A mattress was one thing, a bed of pine needles something else entirely.

He scooped an arm beneath her legs and lowered her to it. And then, with a blow that he hadn't been expecting, urgency rammed into him again.

She laid beneath him, her hair all black curls tucked behind her ears, with one diamond missing. Her eyes were wide on his face, pleading with him, and he wasn't entirely sure what she wanted but he knew he would move heaven and earth to find it and give it to her. She was breathing in quick, short gasps again that made her bared breasts rise and fall. Her nipples tightened even as he watched, turning a dusky rose, maybe from the cold, maybe from need. Either way, it was all the invitation he needed.

He lowered his head slowly and took one nipple into his mouth and she cried out. Her arms came up, groping for him. He used his tongue, teasing the puckered tip, and she drove one hand into his hair, pressing his head there. He half smiled and moved to her other breast, his tongue trailing a warm, wet path. He would use every bit of knowledge he had ever learned about women, and make up new, intriguing ideas as he went along. He would brand her, mark her, change her so she could not live without this, without him, ever again. He would give her pleasure that would make her ache for more throughout the rest of her days.

His palm covered her breast as he left it behind, as though protecting and warming her. He sucked in breath as he felt her fingers brush the skin at his waist, fumbling for the snap on his jeans. He didn't help her but popped the one free on her own jeans instead, working the zipper down. He spread the denim and found midnight blue lace—but then, he had known it would be something like that, something feminine and pretty, a scrap of sexy, yet somehow demure, womanhood. Black curls crept over the top of the blue, and it undid him.

"Ah, Tess." His mouth went back to hers as he slid his hand beneath the lace, his fingers searching for the center of her. And he found her slick and hot and needy. He groaned into her mouth and heard her breath escape her on a sob.

Gunner froze.

"You want me to stop." The words would kill him.

"No. Oh, no," she gasped. "I need you so much."

Relief flooded him. He was amazed that he could still chuckle. He pulled back a little to look down at her. "You can have me anytime, sweetheart."

"Now, then. Please...now."

"Soon," he promised. "Soon."

As soon as he got tired of the way her body closed over his fingers in eager acceptance. Would he ever? He finally removed his hand to work her jeans down over her hips, then he took down the midnight blue panties.

"Your jeans," she gasped.

"In a minute."

The jeans were safety, he thought, a much needed barrier. Without them he would find himself inside her with no further thought, succumbing to something he was sure he had wanted since time began. Not yet. Not now. Not quite.

The fact that she was naked when he wasn't left her feeling momentarily abashed, vulnerable, shaky. The way he gazed down at her made her skin flush with heat. She felt it creep over her breasts, up her neck. But then he was kissing her again and it didn't seem to matter.

She was dizzy, her mind spinning. One moment he had her mouth captured with his own, his tongue moving deep, leaving her unaware of almost any other sensation but the way it teased and swept past her teeth. She tried to catch it with her own. Then his lips were at her breast again, suckling, and his magic fingers were back between her legs, so easily this time with no barriers to conquer. She felt herself opening for them unabashedly, and yes, oh, yes, they were good with delicate work.

She had known, of course. She had known from the time he had mentioned it that they would be. They slid inside her again and she arched into him uncontrollably, her body moving almost without conscious thought. She did not know the woman who was clawing at him, trying to bring his mouth back to her breast. His thumb found the nub at the center of her, and she cried out loudly enough to startle some birds in the tree above them. They took flight, their calls drowning out her own voice.

"Please," she begged. "I need."

I need. It was as simple as that, and all that was inside her. A rampaging hunger. A painful desire. She did not want to be alone any longer. She wanted to be with him, joined with him, and only then would she feel sated and whole.

"Please," she said again, and she felt him pull away from her. She looked up, panicked, and realized that he was pulling out of his jeans. Her heart seemed to thunder as she waited, but then he stopped and swore.

"What?" she cried.

"I'll be back in a minute." His voice was strangled.

"Back?" She sat up fast. "No! Gunner, *no!* Why?"

He came down on one knee again with a pained laugh, hooking an arm around her neck, drawing her head to his chest. She felt his mouth on her hair, then his chin as he rested it on the top of her head. She could imagine him closing his eyes. She felt his labored breathing beneath her cheek and heard his heartbeat, thunderous.

"No," she said again, confused. "Don't go anywhere. Don't do that to me. Why?"

"Princess, you've been alone in your ivory tower for a long time," he said finally, his voice raw. *And,* he thought, *I've been out of circulation twice as long as that.* He couldn't believe he hadn't thought, hadn't planned ahead. *Some Don Juan.*

He couldn't expect her to believe that. Not given what the women at the office said about him. Not given what she had heard. But he would protect her from a threat that didn't exist, and one that did. He knew as well as he knew his own heart right now that she would not have been taking any precautions against pregnancy all these many months since Matt had died. Not this woman, this princess peering out warily from her castle.

His princess. His own. And damned if there wasn't responsibility tangled all up with that. He groaned.

"I've got to go back to the drugstore," he said and finally reluctantly, let her go.

Tessa watched him disbelievingly as he stood again. He would do that? For her? *Now?* She felt hot tears burn her eyes. There were no recriminations that she might have thought of this herself. There would be no equal sharing of the responsibility. He was macho to the bone, taking it all upon himself, taking care of her...when he had finally remembered.

In that moment, she stopped hiding from herself. She stopped believing in a reputation that hadn't really seemed to fit him at all once she'd gotten to know him. She stopped telling herself that she didn't love him.

"No." She shook her head slowly. "John, come back."

He was amazed and overwhelmed. Not so much that she had finally used his given name, though it came off her lips as if it were a prayer. That she didn't seem to care that this act, this moment in time, might end up binding her to him forever.

He knelt again slowly. For the first time in his life, even through the short span that had been his marriage, he didn't care, either.

She opened her mouth to say something more. He caught her lips before she could find her voice. He eased her back onto the pine needles again.

"Okay," he whispered. "I'll stay. I'm not going anywhere. Shh."

This time when she reached for his zipper, he helped her. No more barriers. He was past needing them. He struggled out of his jeans and eased his weight down on top of her, finally naked, finally body to body, skin to skin. Her legs tangled with his, then came up around him. His hips moved, and the rigid hardness of him pressed against her, seeking entrance.

"Please," she whispered. *Make me whole. Make me yours.* She couldn't wait anymore, wouldn't wait. Her hand caught him, encircling him, to guide him inside.

He made a choking sound at her touch, of need too raw, too new, to be conquered. His hips jerked again, if only to press himself into her palm, but she lifted her hips and caught him.

He slid into her slowly, easing his way home, watching her eyes change. She welcomed him and moaned his name again.

Matt's face finally came to her. Briefly, fleetingly, then he was gone. There was only Gunner's eyes, his voice.

"Tess, I can't...all that waiting." With a guttural groan, he thrust hard and deep, with a suddenness that made her cry out. Pleasure and sensation filled all the aching emptiness inside her. It happened so fast, so completely, it brought a shudder to her as deep as her soul.

Gunner felt it and went still. "I hurt you," he rasped.

"No." And her body told him that she spoke the truth as she tightened over him.

He began moving inside her again. Tess was torn between the

sweetness of him filling her, and the sight of him, the way his jaw had gone rigid, the way the taut cords of his neck stood out. His arms trembled as he braced his weight upon them.

He thrust deeper, and she lifted her legs instinctively to take him in. And that was the moment when sensation won out, when need overcame curiosity, when there was only the fullness of him inside her. She closed her eyes and let pleasure build and coil.

His mouth brushed her forehead, and she was vaguely aware of him finally settling down on top of her. His thrusts became harder, more desperate, even as he tangled one hand in her hair and found her mouth again.

He had to kiss her at this moment, he realized. Had to be with her, part of her, when she went over the edge.

Her hips rose rhythmically to meet him. And then he felt something in the tension of her body change, spasming, erupting. He let himself go with her.

She nearly wept with the power of it, the *force,* as wave after wave pummeled her body. She clawed her fingers into his skin and held on. Then suddenly his hands were beneath her, molding her hips to his through that moment when his own body arched and shuddered.

And she knew, even as he collapsed on top of her, that she was forever and irrevocably changed. She would never be able to live without this, without him, again.

She heard him murmur her name and turned her face to the side to find his. She thought he would kiss her again, needed him to kiss her again. But his mouth only caught the single, hot tear that slid from her eye.

She was lethargic, dazed. And cold, she realized. She was very, very cold.

Gunner had rolled a little to his side, though his arm was still around her, holding her close. She tried to scoot even nearer to him for his body warmth, and he muttered something that might have been a curse. It was inarticulate, as bemused as she felt.

"Where the hell is that key?" he mumbled, finally sitting up.

It was right in his front jeans pocket. Had it been there all along? he wondered. Possibly. Probably. He shook his head and laughed at himself.

He got up and took her hand, holding on to it even as he began to grab up their clothing. She watched him, feeling warm inside all over again. His body was lean and hard, and she loved the way his muscles slid beneath his skin when he stretched.

"Let's go inside and get warm." He tugged on her hand again.

Unfortunately, it was as cold inside the cabin as it was out. Gunner went to turn on the furnace, then he disappeared into a bedroom. Tessa stood in the main room, hugging herself, looking around.

It struck her then that she had never actually set foot in a cabin before. But this was exactly how she would have expected one to look. There were sliding glass doors over a narrow, back deck. Just beyond it, the wooded land plunged steeply to the water. Tucked to one side of the doors was a tiny kitchen, separated from the main room by a breakfast bar. The fireplace was bigger than she had first thought, taking up much of one wall. A bearskin rug was centered on the floor in front of it, topping dark, hardwood floors.

Gunner came back and dropped a pile of blankets on the rug, then he opened the fireplace and set to work. Tessa looked dazedly at the blankets.

"We could always get dressed," she murmured, shivering.

He looked back over his shoulder at her. "What for?" he asked blankly.

She laughed.

It was a breathy sound at first, a sound almost startled by its own existence. He had been able to do that to her from the first.

"Do me a favor, Princess. There should be a cord of wood on the back porch. Bring me a couple more logs?"

She started automatically for the sliding glass doors, then she stopped cold. Her laughter got fuller. She finally had to lean against the breakfast bar to catch her breath.

Gunner looked up at her curiously. "What am I missing here?"

"Me," she gasped. "This."

Ozone layer, he thought.

"It just struck me how ever since I've known you, I keep finding myself doing things I would never have *dreamed* of before." Like breaking into Benami's house. Like what had just happened between them outside. She couldn't regret it, she realized. How could she regret something so sweet, so perfect? And now, she thought, now she was about to stroll outside onto the back porch of this cabin buck naked.

It didn't matter that he didn't quite understand, Gunner realized. Her laughter was alive. Her face lit with it. But his eyes didn't stay on her face for long. They moved down the length of her, over her full breasts and narrow waist, and the black nest of hair that held secrets he had waited his whole life for.

Something inside him quickened all over again. "Hurry up," he said hoarsely.

Her heart kicked at his look. "I'll be right back," she said softly, and went outside.

When she returned with the wood, the fire was already blazing. He threw an extra log onto it anyway, and shook out one of the blankets. Tess dropped to her knees beside him. His strong hands caught her waist and tumbled her beneath him. He pulled the blanket over them.

She was still shivering, but not with cold. "You do something to me," she whispered. "You make everything...new, an adventure."

He looked down into her wide, bemused eyes. He wanted to tell her that he always would, that he'd always try to do just that. He thought of telling her that he loved her, that he'd been waiting his entire life for her, knowing she was out there somewhere, never quite able to find anyone else to fit the bill. And so he had stayed alone, dating but never loving, never able to, never wanting anything or anyone so much that he couldn't walk away.

Until her.

The need to do something about that was stronger than ever. Making love to her had only been the first, sweetest step.

But it was all she was ready for. He knew that intuitively. That she had moved this close to him, that she had abandoned so many of her lines, was astounding enough as it was.

He brushed his mouth over hers again and she shifted her weight beneath him. Wriggling. His eyes narrowed.

"That time was on purpose," she admitted breathlessly.

And just like that, it started again.

Wishful thinking flared into raging need. A distant, uncertain future zeroed down into an immediate moment of demand. She locked an arm around his neck almost shyly and drew him back toward her, and he was gone.

He realized she owned him, body and soul. Though he was a man who hated confines, he gave himself over to the web she had spun around him.

As cold as it had been outside, now the heat of the fire beat at them. Tessa pushed the blanket away from them with her free hand, still clinging to his mouth. She was stunned to realize that his hand trembled as it slid up her ribs to her breasts again.

No, she realized, this was not practiced, not something he had done many times before. Or perhaps he had, but it had not had this import. She was suddenly ashamed of what she had said to him last night. *It's all tactile pleasure to you.* How could she ever have believed that? She should have known, should have sensed it, from the first time he had kissed her, when she had asked him to but he had still done it so slowly, giving her time to pull away. If he was the man they said he was, he would have raged into it. But he had given her such gentle care all along.

"Oh, Gunner," she moaned.

He touched her almost reverently, his tongue flicking over a nipple, urging it to a rigid peak, his strong hands stroking, first at her hip, then closing over her thigh. His fingers slid through the black curls between her legs and stroked gently.

Her hips began to move of their own accord. His name was a moan on her lips. She called him John again. Nothing had ever sounded so sweet.

"Easy," he whispered.

"I want you inside me," she gasped, then she blushed again. Since when did she become so *wanton?*

"I want to be there, too." He chuckled. "In a minute."

He had said that before, she remembered, and it had been worth waiting for. It was again.

His mouth trailed down over her belly, following his fingers. At the first touch of his lips and tongue at the center of her, her whole body spasmed and fire rained through her. Oh, yes, this was new. She felt no shame, no desire to pull away, and couldn't think about it, couldn't even dwell on that at all.

He savored the way she gasped each time his tongue flicked over the nub at the center of her, and he had to tighten his hands on her hips to keep her reasonably still. Her pleasure was so real, so simple and genuine. He felt her fingers in his hair again and

let his tongue slide. She was ready, writhing. For him. He finally
came up over her again.

"Now?" she gasped raggedly.

"Now," he growled.

He covered her body again then he rolled, taking her with him.
Then he felt her suddenly pull back. Gunner went instantly wary,
then his breath left him on a harsh burst.

Her mouth roamed, her hands following. "You're so beautiful,"
she whispered.

He fought the urge to buck into her. *Take it easy,* he told himself. *Don't scare her.* But his fingers drove into her hair of their
own accord, holding her, as she tasted him with a sweet curiosity
that unraveled him. A moment more, and he wasn't going to be
able to keep his promise. It would be all over before it started.

"Now," he said again, hoarsely. *"Now."*

He lifted her before she could protest, fitting her over him. He
throbbed with need. Her back arched and she groaned as she welcomed him in again.

He drove himself almost violently upward, into her. Princess or
not, she didn't shatter. She rode him with hard, fierce pleasure. He
was vaguely aware of her fingers digging into his shoulders, his
skin. He caught her hips, to hold her, certainly not to stop her, but
to maintain some control over this. And that was when he realized
that he'd never been the one in control of what was happening
between them at all. She had merely let him think he was.

He found his hands tightening, grinding her harder against him.
And he heard his own voice murmuring her name, again and again
in a litany.

Tess felt everything bursting inside her again and she bent toward him quickly, taking his mouth. He rose a little to meet her,
slanting his mouth over hers, and they fell over the edge together.

Chapter 19

She couldn't resist him, Tessa thought later.

It was amazing. Two weeks ago, she would have thought that he'd gotten exactly what he'd wanted from her, so he could relax now. But his charm just kept on coming. He wooed her, teased her, made her laugh. Some treacherous part of her began to wonder if living with him would be like this, if he went through every day of his life happy and joking, attentive and kind.

Oh, he had a temper. She had seen it, and it had ignited her own. But it was quicksilver. Even when he had quit smoking, he hadn't stayed angry or irritated by it for long.

Maybe he knew, too, that life was just too short.

They drove back into town in the afternoon to see to various errands. The market was really little more than a convenience store. There was a plastic basket near the checkout counter filled with some limp, pseudo-silk roses, and he grabbed one and put it on top of their pile of groceries. After the clerk had rung it up, he tucked it behind her ear.

"What's that for?" she asked, startled.

He met her eyes. "I figure you've had enough ugliness in your life, Princess. It's long past time for something pretty." He scowled briefly at the rose. "However dubious," he added.

She realized she would probably cherish the dusty thing forever. Her heart melted and her hand went to it.

It was a purely feminine, Tessa-like gesture that made it the best buck-fifty Gunner had ever spent. He refused to consider that she had probably acquired tons of the genuine article in her lifetime.

Back at the cabin, they ate cheese and crackers and shared a bottle of wine in front of the fireplace. They made love again and they talked. Of silly things and sensible things, but not, she noticed, of Benami.

Ugliness, she thought. Christian Benami was all ugliness, and for a little while at least, neither of them wanted to entertain that. The closest they came to the subject was a brief discussion about Maxwell.

Gunner fed her a piece of cheese and scowled. "By the way, did that cat make it?"

"Make it?"

"It wouldn't have gotten shot by any chance?"

"Oh. No." Tessa shook her head. "He was hiding underneath my bed. He's still alive and well. My housekeeper's keeping an eye on him."

"Too bad."

"Gunner!"

"Maybe what he needs is a woman," he mused. "You've done wonders for me."

She smiled with pleasure. "But Maxwell wouldn't be able to do anything with one. I had him neutered."

Gunner grimaced. "Ouch." Then his brows went up. "Maybe *that's* what's wrong with his disposition."

Tessa laughed and settled her back against the sofa. He was laying with his head against it, bolstered by some of the cushions that had somehow ended up on the floor. She traced a hand down his ribs, to his hip. Gunner followed it with his eyes and caught her hand suddenly.

"That's it."

"It certainly is," she murmured. She was thrilled and a little overwhelmed that she could arouse him so easily.

"I meant the mole."

"What mole?"

He moved her hand to it, just inside his left hip. "I defy you to find another woman in the department who knows that's there."

"Gunner, *I* didn't know it was there until you pointed it out."

"Oh."

"Besides, I believe you," she said quietly. "About the rumors."

"You do?" He hadn't known relief could be so sweet. "In that case, I think there's another one down there somewhere. But you'd probably have to look close to find it."

Which, of course, she did.

At some point she made up the bed—he left such a "woman's chore" to her unabashedly while he settled the fire and checked the windows and doors. At some point they even slept. But the morning sun had barely begun to steal in through the window when she felt his mouth on her nape, and an unmistakable hardness pressing against her from behind.

"Gunner, I'm not a morning person," she pleaded.

"Inside every night owl, there's a rooster waiting to get out," he murmured, and she realized he could be right. Need stirred inside her again—sleepily, true, but it was there. She snuggled backward, into him, and heard him groan into her ear.

"I'm not a night owl, either," she whispered. "I just like my eight hours."

No time to waste sleeping. The thought jumped at him with buckling urgency. He didn't understand it. They had time. He wasn't going anywhere, and he wasn't going to let her get away. But the instinct was there, needling him, goading him on.

He turned her toward him and claimed her mouth. She pressed her hands against his chest.

"I need coffee, a toothbrush—"

"No time." *No time.*

He took her suddenly, without warning, and was instantly remorseful. For a moment. For a heartbeat. It took him that long to realize that she had been ready for him all along. She cried out, not in pain, but with pleasure. He bucked into her and she met him thrust for thrust, clinging to him.

Sometime, as their bodies tangled, she began to feel his panic, too. Yesterday had been a short, brief respite. The ugliness was pressing in on them again.

Her climax was nearly one of desperation. She gripped his shoulders and kept moving long after he had finally gone still. She felt him stir inside her again, but this time he didn't pursue it.

"We've got to call in, don't we?" she asked finally. She was surprised at how long it took him to answer. She'd expected immediate agreement.

"I've got to know," he said eventually. "I've got to know what's going on back there."

They had been away for nearly twenty-four hours now. "Surely someone's found him."

"Let's hope so."

He gave her a final squeeze, his arms hard around her, and brushed his mouth over her forehead. "First one into the shower gets to drive to the nearest pay phone."

He was off the bed like a shot. She scrambled after him, but not quickly enough. She dove into the shower right after him, and the needles of spray were icy. She squealed and tried to scramble back out of the tub but he caught her, pinning her against the wall.

"*Now* I'm ready again."

And he was. But even as she felt him slide into her, even as she lifted her legs to wrap them around his hips, something was missing this time.

No, not missing, she thought wildly. Something was added. Tension. Worry. His mouth clung to hers, and the heat of their joining mingled with the cold water in a way that was exquisite, that brought all her nerve endings alive. But when they finally toweled off, his eyes were vaguely distant.

He was worried.

They drove back to the convenience store. There was no phone booth outside, and a sign taped in the window said that the one inside wasn't for public use. Gunner let the engine idle for a moment before turning the key off.

"I'll make them let me use the one behind the counter," he decided.

"We have no jurisdiction here."

"Hell, it's just a long-distance call. I'm not asking them to unload their cash register. Besides, I'm persuasive."

She couldn't argue that.

She watched him go into the store, watched his delicious walk, smiling at the way he swung open the door and stepped inside. Then her smile faltered.

What now? she wondered.

Her rules and lines were gone. But she realized she still *needed* them, or some semblance of them, anyway. She knew—was reasonably certain—that nothing would immediately change between them when they went back to the city. She didn't honestly believe that whatever they shared was all that fleeting. It was too good, too pure.

What an odd way of describing it, she thought, but it fit. What they had shared last night had been elemental, sometimes staggering in its force, but there was no badness, nothing wrong in it anywhere.

No, she didn't believe the attraction would end when they went back to work. It would just be easier for her if they could *define* what this relationship was. Then again, John Gunner was not a man who was long on definitions.

Don't think about it, she told herself. *It'll work out. For once in your life, just go with the flow.* Having him healthy, whole, warm and laughing in her world, even without definition, was far better than not having him at all.

She closed her eyes and leaned back. She loved him. She thought it was quite possible that she had been tumbling head over heels in love with him from the first moment he had made her laugh with his outrageous irreverence.

What was taking him so long? she wondered finally. Her heart lurched. Obviously something had happened. Something had broken back home. If the status quo had remained unchanged, it would take him only a moment to learn that.

She pushed open the passenger door, and it thudded against something. She looked up, startled, into Christian Benami's cold, unsmiling eyes.

She didn't have time to scream.

She opened her mouth, but before anything could come out, she dove instinctively sidewards, toward the floor, for her purse. *Her gun.* Christian leaned inside and wrenched her purse out of the car just as her hand closed on the strap, twisting it violently away from her. In the next moment she felt something hard and unyielding against her ribs.

"Gunner will be a while," Benami said in that smooth, not-quite-cultured voice. "Phone trouble." He pressed the gun into her with more force. "Move over. You're driving."

She had one clear, lucid thought, relatively untouched by her terror. No matter what Benami might have done to the phone, Gunner was just inside. She dragged a breath in and screamed for him. Benami cracked the butt of his gun against the side of her head. The pain was incredible. It brought instant stinging tears to her eyes. *Stars.* Red and blue, some white, like a fireworks display, she thought, slumping into the wheel, moaning.

"Drive," Benami said again.

"Can't," she mumbled. *Stall. Wait for Gunner.* Something hot and almost caustic burned her right eye. She put a hand there. Blood.

"*Drive.*"

Why wouldn't he do it? Then she knew. Because driving would mean he would be less able to keep the gun trained on her.

She laughed shrilly. At least she didn't have to worry about using her own. Christian had it. She looked wildly at her purse still clutched in his hand.

He shoved her again roughly. Tessa finally got an arm on the door and levered herself up, grasping the wheel. *Stall,* she thought again. Gunner had to come out soon. Surely, please God, he would come out of that store at any moment.

Then something inside her stiffened, hardened, got blessedly angry. She was a cop, not a damsel in distress. *Princess.* Oh, how she hated that tag! She shouldn't, *wouldn't* snivel, praying for rescue.

Think. Pain was jagged and sharp in her head.

She turned the key in the ignition. Her hands were uncooperative, trembling claws. She turned automatically for the cabin.

The gun came back, a sharp jab in her ribs that made her cry out. "Not that way," Benami snapped. "Back to the city."

The city. No, no, that wasn't good. "Why?" she gasped.

"More of a challenge," he said pointedly, and his grin was cold when she managed to glance at him. It froze her blood. "It'll make it harder for him to find us," he said. "But he will."

"Gunner will kill you for this," she whispered. "He'll make you wish for the gas chamber." And she was suddenly sure that Gunner would. She'd been sitting here fretting about their relationship when the truth had been staring her in the face all along.

John Gunner loved her.

She moaned. The truth exploded inside her head, making her feel even more dizzy and faint. It had been there in a million little telltale ways, almost from the beginning. He had nearly throttled this man simply for making her remember Matt's death.

There was no time to savor the sweeping, tender, amazed feeling that filled her. Yes, Gunner would kill Benami for this. Or he would die trying.

She had to do something.

But first she had to make sense of it, had to know. "How?" she asked. "How did you know where to find us?" If he was truly psychopathic, he would want to tell her, she thought. He would want to gloat.

She was right.

"Your brother. It was kind of you to tell him where you were going."

Jesse? She almost drove off the road. "No!" she howled. Jesse? Sweet God, no!

"Kind of him, too, to keep going through secretaries the way he does."

She didn't understand. Her heart was thudding and nausea pressed up in her throat. "Secretaries?" she repeated in a whisper.

"He lost another one two weeks ago. Just in time for a very good friend of mine to step up and apply for the job. She'll be leaving with me when this is over. She'll get her just reward."

He would kill that woman, too, Tessa thought wildly. Whoever she was, she had helped him trustingly, maybe even loving him the way Daphne had, but he would dispose of her, too.

Her thoughts raced on. The leak was in Jesse's office. That staggered her and relieved her all at once. Because Jesse would never have suspected. Why should he? Why should he be careful of what mundane details his secretary overheard?

It seemed that no time at all had passed, but suddenly Tessa realized she was seeing signs for the bridge. She panicked. Her palms went slick. Once they were back in Philadelphia, she was as good as dead. Or, at least, Christian would make her wish she was.

Drive off the bridge? A traffic accident? If she drove erratically, would someone notice—at best, a patrol car, or even another driver who might notify the police? It was the only chance she had.

She glanced in the side mirror and saw a car inching up behind her. She swerved suddenly into that lane. The driver leaned on his horn. She did it again, wildly, whipping back and forth.

Benami's fingers dug painfully into her arm to hold it still. "One more time," he snarled, "and I will shoot you right here."

"You'd die, too!" she cried desperately. "You can't kill me while I'm driving!"

"If I let you do this to me, I'm as good as dead," he sneered. "Haven't you wondered why this is necessary? There's no way I can disappear twice, from two states. Even the F.B.I. would be looking for me. You had to go and complicate things with your sickening, rich-girl virtue. I thought that when they brought you back for the case, I'd be fine. I had Jeanie in your brother's office, and I had Basil English. But then you turned into a bloodhound. You wouldn't leave it alone."

His eyes were turning less cold. They were heated now with some inner fire.

"I'll back off," she said helplessly, knowing he'd never believe it. "I won't push the investigation."

"No, you won't. And neither will your caveman partner. I warned him he'd pay for touching me. I think I'll let him watch you die."

They were on the bridge.

"Where are you taking me?"

"I'm not sure yet. You came to the store sooner than I'd expected."

"The *store?*" And then she understood. He'd known they were in New Jersey all along.

"I followed you from his house. I thought the two of you might stay holed up in that cabin for days yet." His expression made her skin crawl. "Who needed food and drink when you had each other? I couldn't take you there. There was no way I could get in without him waiting for me with his gun drawn. But the store...ah, the store. Sooner or later, one of you would have to show up there. And I have all the patience in the world."

"Gunner—"

"He's coming. We'll go somewhere he'll think of. Somewhere he'll find. I want both of you together, of course. He'll come after you, and then I'll have him, too. I'll get rid of both of you together."

He shouldn't have said that, Tessa realized almost dispassionately. Looking her own death in the eye was terrifying. But considering Gunner's was beyond endurance. *Not again.* She thought crazily that she was the kiss of death for men she loved. *Not again.* She started down the Pennsylvania side of the bridge.

She had not been able to save Matt, and she knew, suddenly, that God was giving her a second chance, a way to atone, a way to make things right. She began shaking uncontrollably. Her heart began beating harder. Her hands tightened even more on the steering wheel.

She had to get it right this time. *Had* to.

Maybe she would die, but God bless her, Christian Benami would die with her, long before Gunner ever found them. *He would not kill John.*

There were no tollbooths on the westbound lane of the bridge—they were all back on the Jersey side. They had already gone through one with absurd nonchalance, the gun hidden but pressed into her side in case she tried to call out for help. She searched for one on the other side of the highway divide. *Surely one would be empty.*

She realized she was sobbing. Her last desperate thought was that Internal Affairs would probably think Gunner's knack for wrecking cars was contagious. Ernie, the garage attendant, would be apoplectic.

She veered suddenly for the approaching line of traffic. She had to get into the other lane. Christian bellowed a protest as he realized what she was doing. He waved the gun wildly, and his finger was on the trigger.

It was the people! she despaired. *So many innocent people.* The car thumped and lurched over the median and she almost lost control of the wheel. For a moment they were airborne. Christian pulled the trigger, but the crazy rocking of the unmarked made the shot go astray. The windshield shattered into spraying glass and she screamed again—and then, there was a break in traffic just when she needed it.

Tessa sped through and rammed the city car deliberately into a tollbooth.

"Oh, for God's sake!" Gunner shouted in frustration.

The phone was dead. The clerk had insisted that sometimes he unwittingly tripped over the cord and it got unplugged from the wall. The young man had spent the better part of five minutes now digging beneath cartons of cigarettes and various other boxes behind the counter, following the cord to some unseen spot. Every few inches he had to stop and remove another obstacle.

He was moving as slowly as though someone had paid him to do it.

Suddenly, with that thought, Gunner knew.

He roared in a fit of rage, planted a hand on the counter, and vaulted over it. The man shouted in panic and backed up, but not quickly enough. Gunner caught the front of his smock and lifted him half off the floor as if he were a madman.

"Where is he?"

"I didn't— I don't—"

Gunner hauled back with a white-knuckled fist. *"Where?"*

"He left!" the kid bleated, his eyes glued to Gunner's hand. "Out the back way when you came in! He's been waiting for you for a couple of days. He just said to stall you! He said—"

Gunner literally threw him away from him.

The kid landed, sprawling, in the boxes. Gunner shouted Tessa's name as he leaped over the counter again. He raced outside. Their unmarked was gone.

Another car was just pulling out of the lot. He ran for it, slamming his fist down on the hood. The driver hit the brakes, his eyes bugging. Gunner ran around and wrenched open the driver's side door, dragging the man out.

"Which way?" he snarled.

"Which way *what?*" the man hollered in angry alarm.

"There was another car here. Right there." He pointed to where he had left the unmarked. "Which way did it go?"

"That way." He pointed west, toward the city. "Hey, that's my car! You can't—"

Gunner didn't hear him. He was already behind the wheel when the man started speaking, burning rubber before he broke off.

She had her gun.

He knew it was in her purse, knew she had her purse with her because he had had to wait for her while she went back into the cabin to get it. *Sweet Jesus, what if she couldn't use it?*

He yelled with pure anguish and pressed down on the accelerator. He had to catch up with them before they got back to the bridge. Once they reached the Philadelphia city limits, he would lose them.

Not indefinitely. Hell, no, not indefinitely. Benami *wanted* both of them. He hadn't just shot into Tessa's kitchen. He'd tried to run him off the road, too. And as long as even one of them was alive, he'd have to keep looking back over his shoulder. He'd leave a trail of clues, luring Gunner in. But it would take a while, a sweet, precious while, for Gunner to figure those clues out. And in the meantime, the bastard had her.

He would make the waiting torturous for her. There was no telling what he might do to her in the meantime.

"I'm coming, sweetheart, hold on, hold on. You don't need to shoot anybody. He won't have you."

It became a chant. When he finally hit the bridge, the car was bulleting along at nearly a hundred miles an hour. He leaned steadily on the horn to clear traffic and urged the car faster.

The air bags. *She had forgotten the air bags.*

Tessa jerked the wheel to the left so that Benami's side of the car would be the one to crack into the tollbooth at nearly sixty miles an hour. She couldn't get up any more speed in the traffic. The unmarked came to a sudden, lurching, screaming stop. It tossed her around and drove the steering wheel into her ribs in that split second it took for the air bags to release. Then there was white everywhere.

She fought it frantically, sobbing, thrashing, and heard the distant tinkling of broken glass and somebody shouting.

Then gunfire.

She hadn't killed him. *No, no, no!* Benami was alive, still trying to shoot her. Could still shoot her, because of the air bags. *Oh, God, give me another chance, one more chance.* Gunner would almost certainly catch up with them now that they had stopped.

Her door had sprung open with the impact when the front of the car had folded. There was the hiss of steam and it seemed to burn her eyes as she crawled out onto the concrete. Sharp, jagged glass cut into her hands and knees, even through her jeans. She was bleeding everywhere. There was a groaning sound overhead, and when she looked up she realized that her eyes burned because she was crying. She could barely see for her tears.

One more chance, please, one more chance.

The tollbooth had crumpled in upon itself. An insipid siren whined—the signal that someone had gone through without paying. She laughed giddily and began moving, keeping low. She heard the groaning sound again; the roof of the toll plaza was sagging dangerously without the full support of the booth.

She saw her purse. Christian had lost it when the car had crashed. Tessa pushed shakily to her feet. Pain screamed through her side and she pressed her arm down against her ribs, crying out.

Get the gun.

A bullet pinged off something nearby. Now that she was upright, the pain was more than she could bear. Her vision went red, then cloudy, and she swayed.

She dropped to her knees again and almost blacked out as bone ground together with the impact. She'd broken her ribs. Didn't matter, couldn't matter, because she had to kill Benami before Gunner got here.

Too late.

She heard Gunner roaring her name and cried out in panic and despair. How had he gotten here so fast? Stupid question. He drove like a maniac.

Where was Benami? She saw his heels disappearing around the back of the car. He was on his hands and knees, too. She must have hurt him at least a little. But he was moving in the direction of Gunner's voice.

She got to her purse and dug into it for her gun. Her fingers closed around the cold metal. She had the safety free before she dragged herself to her feet again, slowly, too slowly. The siren was somehow getting louder. She looked around crazily.

State cops. Someone had called the police.

"Get back!" she snarled when a bystander reached a hand out to help her. "I'm okay." She stepped shakily past the man.

A car she didn't recognize was skewed sideways, stopped, snarling traffic in the westbound lane. And Gunner was running away from it, toward them, shouting, his gun drawn. Not placating. Not with his hands outstretched in a plea. No, no, she had known he would never do that.

Yet memory seemed to superimpose over her vision. Something gripped her muscles in icy hands. *No, no, she couldn't let it happen again.* Gunner brought his gun up, firing as he ran.

And then he spun around and dropped hard onto the macadam.

"Noooo!" She didn't recognize her own voice. "I have a gun this time! *I have one!"*

And then, somehow, she had it up, in front of her, and her finger was on the trigger. She caught sight of Benami again out of the corner of her eye and whipped around to aim at him. He was coming to his feet just beyond the mangled wreckage of the un-marked car. Moving toward Gunner. His revolver came up again.

"Stop!" she screamed.

Christian looked over at her calmly and actually smiled. "You won't shoot."

She pulled the trigger.

Bam! The gun recoiled in her hand. She wrapped her left fingers around her right wrist automatically, instinctively, without thought, just the way she had been taught. Benami took a step backward, and at first she thought she had merely surprised him. But then she saw blood spreading at his right shoulder.

"Lay down, you bastard! *Lay down! Drop the gun!"*

Somehow, impossibly, he stayed upright. He turned, teetering, aiming at Gunner again. He knew that if he killed Gunner, she would crumble, so he'd go for him first, finish him off.

Big mistake.

Tessa screamed and kept shooting. *Bam! Bam!* He staggered a little the other way, then he finally went down.

Her legs gave out at the same time. Someone caught her. "I did it," she whispered, struggling against the hands that wanted to hold her. She looked wildly over her shoulder. It was a State Police officer.

"I'd say so, lady." He dragged her arms roughly behind her back to cuff her.

"I'm a cop!" she protested, struggling with him. "My badge is in my purse." *I'm a cop. I deserve to be a cop.*

Then her brain cleared a little. *"Gunner!"*

Somehow she managed to wrench away from the officer. She staggered at first, then she got her legs to work. She ran.

She heard a horrible keening sound and realized it was her own voice. She collapsed beside Gunner. His eyes were open. Her heart stopped. *Staring, seeing nothing, just like Matt, oh God, no!* Then they moved and tried to focus on her.

"Great...shot, sweetheart."

Tessa sobbed, and incredibly, heard her laughter bubble over her tears. He always made her laugh.

"You're alive," she gasped.

For the moment, Gunner thought. And he had plenty of reasons for staying that way. "Better...call me...an ambulance."

Chapter 20

Tessa sipped coffee and grimaced. It was cold.

She clutched the cup between both hands to keep them from trembling. She leaned forward in the hard, plastic seat in the hospital waiting room, her elbows braced on her thighs. The position put unwarranted pressure on her ribs, but they were bandaged now, and the pain kept her going. It kept her brain clear, sharp, focused.

She looked up when Becky Trumball pried the cup out of her hands and replaced it with a hot one. "Thanks," she murmured.

"He'll be fine," Mel Kaminski said for the thousandth time.

Mel was seated on Tessa's other side. Before she even finished speaking, Roger Kennery came up behind her and put a comforting hand on her shoulder.

They were all here. Nearly all of Homicide and a few other officers besides. Plus a good portion of the State Police who had caught the incredible shoot-out. Gunner's parents were a few seats down, and Angela Byerly paced wherever there was room, all long legs in a mint green miniskirt. A cop had gone down, and everyone who could possibly get here would keep the vigil.

Tessa drank hot coffee, and her gut churned.

It wouldn't happen again. It wasn't like before. Matt had died on the sidewalk. Gunner had been alive and reasonably full of wit and repartee when they had loaded him into the ambulance.

She had frozen when Matt had died, hadn't had a weapon to do anything with even if she had been able to. She had been armed this time, had shot Benami, had kept him from pulling the trigger with the bullet that would have finished John Gunner off.

Something moved painfully inside her again, but this time at least a little bit of it was satisfaction. *Pride.* If Gunner would only live—*please, God*—then she would be thrilled with the way things turned out. Benami was in another operating room. If *he* made it, Nebraska and Pennsylvania would scramble around for a while over jurisdiction, but he'd probably end up being tried in Pennsylvania. They could get him on more charges here and aggravate his sentence. He would not only be charged with murder, but with deadly assault on two police officers as well.

It wasn't like before. She had done something.

It wasn't like before. This was a thousand times better and worse, she realized, and she flinched. *I'm sorry, Matt,* she thought automatically, and for a moment she was sure she heard her husband's easy laughter.

He had been her best friend, and that had been the whole tone of their marriage. There had been such a warmth between them, a certain camaraderie. It had been a partnership in the fullest sense of the word—more so than her relationship with Gunner. She and Matt had shared everything, from household chores to...well, to driving. Matt had never been an arrogant chauvinist.

And she had never, ever shared with him the kind of passion, the kind of longing, that Gunner incited in her. She accepted that now.

She wondered what Matt, with his quiet, reasonable wisdom, would tell her in this moment. And suddenly she knew. He would tell her that she was a very lucky woman. A woman God had blessed with two strong loves in a single lifetime. Different loves, certainly. But a man like Matt would never have been able to urge her past her fear, her rules, her lines. He'd been far too easygoing, too accepting of any decision she made, even if he didn't agree with it. He would never have coerced her, teased her, pushed her, until she was free again.

Her love for a man like Matt would not have been powerful enough to make her shoot again, to finally pull that trigger. Only a love that was raging, elemental, immense had been enough to get her over that final hurdle, to make her put herself to the test, to do *something* to try to save Gunner's life.

She would never know if she would have been able to shoot in defense of her own life, but she had been able to do it for his.

A doctor came through the swinging doors into the waiting room. She was on her feet even before the doors closed behind him.

"He's as good as new," the man said proudly.

There was a collective murmur of relief from those gathered. Tessa felt herself sway.

"Luckily he's in great physical condition," the doctor disclosed.

I know.

"He took the bullet just inside his left hip. It didn't tear up anything he can't live without."

No more mole, she thought crazily.

"Our biggest problem was his shock, and a fairly significant blood loss. Once we got him over that, we were able to operate. He's out of recovery now. Who wants to see him first?"

Tessa took an automatic step, then she remembered his parents, Angela, a scattering of people who had loved him and known him forever. She held back.

Tonie Gunner nodded at her and urged her toward the door. Somehow Angela had stopped pacing and had ended up behind her. She gave Tessa's shoulder a gentle push.

Tessa took off like a shot. She was well down the hallway before the doctor even came through the doors behind her.

"Right there," he called out after her. "The door to your left."

Tessa darted inside, then her footsteps slowed. She approached the bed cautiously and groaned. He was so pale. He was sleeping. She put a trembling hand to his cheek and one of his eyes cracked open. She finally breathed. She hadn't believed it, couldn't really believe he was reasonably okay, until she saw it with her own eyes.

"Guess...this...proves it," he said, and his voice was like sandpaper.

What was he talking about now? "Proves what?" she asked dazedly as her eyes and hands frantically sought other wounds, other bruises, something a plethora of doctors might have missed.

"You're different, Princess. I never took...a bullet...for a woman before."

Her eyes filled. "Oh, Gunner."

"I surely do love you, Tess," And in the end, he thought, it was so easy to say.

Her heart swelled until it ached. She had been right. A tear spilled over. Funny how, from the time they had put him in the ambulance, she had not been able to cry.

Gunner's eyes closed again.

There was so much she had to tell him, everything she had realized in these past few interminable hours. But now wasn't the time.

"Don't you die, John. Don't you dare die on me before we finish this, or I'll kill you."

He held his arms out to her without opening his eyes. She bent and went into them carefully, avoiding tubes and cables and moles that were no more.

Her head was tucked against his shoulder, and she didn't see his smug half smile.

Kennery called them into his office almost as soon as Gunner was out of the hospital. Tessa bit her lip and glanced nervously over at him as Kennery picked up a pile of papers from his desk.

Their captain took the first stapled bunch and slapped it down hard. "Twelve thousand, nine hundred and eighty six dollars for the unmarked that got wrapped around a traffic light," he said harshly. He took the next bunch and his gaze swiveled directly to Tessa. "And *you.* Thirteen thousand and fifty four dollars for the one that took out the tollbooth! Both of them beyond repair. Totaled. Which is not to mention *this* little estimate." He waved another paper. "Thirty some odd thousand for the tollbooth. And this one." He smacked his big hand down on the last bunch of papers. "Over six thousand for a civilian's car—*a citizen's* car— left in the middle of oncoming traffic, smashed six ways to Sunday. So what have you got to say for yourselves?"

Gunner cocked a brow and shifted his weight uncomfortably in the opposite chair. "Good work?" he suggested mildly, and Tessa laughed, earning a glower from Kennery.

Then, finally, Kennery cracked a smile, too.

He was feeling mellow. Benami was behind bars, and it had happened before Monday. Kennery touched his wallet, satisfied.

"The safe-deposit box in question contained a second rope, which Forensics is currently working on, trying to match it to the fibers found on Daphne's body. It also held various memorabilia from both wives, and lots and lots of Bemami's fingerprints."

"That's great!" Tessa breathed.

"The guy actually dressed up as a woman to get into it. Can you believe that?" Kennery was grinning widely now. "A bank clerk managed to identify him by way of some clever work on the part of our police artist. Faced with that—and the bloodwork that matches what was under Daphne's nail—The Great Basil English The Fourth has resigned from the case."

Gunner laughed aloud. "No wonder he's so good. He doesn't take cases he can't win."

Kennery nodded. "So that leaves me with the last, little problem of what I'm supposed to do about you two." He paused, his gaze swinging between them. "Internal Affairs is irritated, to put it mildly, although they can't in good conscience put any of these cars on your records. But you might end up working on foot from here on in, assuming you're still partners."

"Yes," Tessa said immediately.

"Nope," Gunner said at the same time.

"No?" Her gaze jumped to him. "What do you mean, no?"

"Protocol," he said.

"Protocol," she repeated, confused. "What *kind* of protocol? What are you talking about? And since when have you cared about protocol?"

Gunner looked at Kennery. "Don't we have some rule that says partners can't be married?"

"Married?" Tessa lost her breath. Her eyes widened. She stared at him.

Kennery grinned and touched his wallet again. Easter? He'd put his money on Valentine's Day, and baby, was he going to collect.

"Don't know," he said enigmatically. "I'd have to look into it. It hasn't come up in my unit before."

"Well, it's up now."

Tessa shot to her feet. "Gunner!"

"What's the matter, Princess?"

"What's the *matter?*" Was this his idea of a proposal?

No, she thought, getting a grip on herself. It certainly couldn't be. She had obviously misunderstood. *Nobody* caught John Gunner. The rumors hadn't even turned out to be true. No one in city hall had even *dated* him.

She knew that, had no expectations otherwise. She'd spent many of the past nights in his arms, and she was content with that, knowing him, knowing it wasn't ever likely to become anything more.

Love's just too confined, too stringent for my tastes. He'd said that. He'd said those very words. Okay, she thought, so they had both climbed over some fences, had both come to terms with the toppling of a few tried and firm beliefs. He loved her. She loved him. Profoundly.

But he wouldn't want to marry her. He wasn't the marrying kind.

Except he was looking at her, watching her, with that grin. And it would be just like him, it would be so purely John Gunner, to do something like this here, now. No traditional and romantic champagne and candlelight. No bended knee. He would do it here, now, where it had almost immediately started the moment Kennery had assigned them as partners.

Her heart began slamming.

"What exactly is it that you're saying?" she asked carefully.

"Marry me."

Kennery grinned hugely and got up from his desk to lumber to the door. "Somebody get their backside in here!" he yelled. "I need a witness."

Tessa looked after their captain wildly. "A witness? A *witness?* I'm not going to marry him here!"

"I got five hundred bucks says you're going to do it some-where," Kennery answered, then he looked out into the hall again. "Becky? Where the devil are you? Mel, come here, you'll do."

This was absurd, Tessa thought helplessly. They'd had a pool about what would happen with her and Gunner? She knew there was always some kind of bet going on in the unit, but *her and Gunner?* Had the depth of their friendship been that obvious to everyone but her?

"Say something," Gunner said, watching her carefully. For the first time, he was overcome with doubts.

Was he pushing too fast, too soon? Scaring her? Matt, he

thought again dismally. The guy she'd been going to take a bullet for. He'd honestly believed that when she'd shot Benami, she'd put that behind her, was ready to move on again. He'd believed from the beginning that she was strong enough to do it, and that putting her in the Fifth had been a big mistake. She'd needed to face things, to deal with it all head-on. He'd believed he could work her over the memories, and in the end win her for his own.

Maybe not.

Maybe, with a nice, traditional, hardworking cop like Matt Bryant, a cop who didn't destroy cars, a woman never put him behind her.

"I love you," she whispered, oblivious now to the people crowding into Kennery's office.

Gunner got slowly and stiffly to his feet. His heart moved hard and painfully. "That's good. That's a start."

Actually, he thought, it was more than good. It was damn fine. It threatened to buckle his knees and it did something odd to his throat. He'd known it, of course, from the moment on the roadside when she'd flowed into his arms. Had hoped so. Had believed it with a desperate fear that he might be wrong. But until now, she'd never actually said so.

Unfortunately she didn't say anything else.

"But?" he prompted carefully.

You're a cop, Tessa thought helplessly. She had come to terms with a lot of things, but her fear of that was bone-deep.

It would never go away. She knew that. Not after what had happened with Matt, not after she and Gunner had nearly died at a toll plaza, all in the space of one short year. No, it would not go away, but she could learn to live with it.

If she married him, she would live with the fear every day of her life, every time he was late coming off shift, coming home. But she could control it.

Because she would feel fear whether she married him or not.

"But nothing," she said. She'd buy him a bullet-proof vest. And if that was too confining and stringent for him, then...well, too damn bad. But he would wear it, she realized. No matter how silly and confining it was, he would do it for her. Because he had always protected her from hurt, from herself.

He was her knight in tarnished armor.

She watched his expression as her words sank in and wondered if she could milk this enough to get him to permanently hand over the car keys. Probably not.

"Call if you're going to be late coming home," she insisted. "Always. *Always.*"

"I can handle that."

"It's stringent. It's confined. But I need rules."

"We'll make them up as we go along."

Of course they would. That was what made every moment with him new, an adventure.

Someone clapped. A second person demanded, "Is that a yes? Damn it, my hundred said it would never happen."

"It's a yes," Tess whispered, and then she was in his arms.

He kissed her long and hard and fully. And someone else clapped, a singular sharp, staccato beat before other hands joined in and someone whistled.

"I don't believe this," she murmured against his mouth. "Are you *sure?*"

He smiled and put his forehead to hers. "Yeah. Oh, yeah."

"But you said—"

"I said I was twenty-five when I married Elaine, and I didn't know love from baloney. And you asked me if I did now."

Yes, she thought, he certainly did have a mind like a steel trap. She couldn't believe he remembered.

"I said I hadn't had cause to think about it in a good, long time," he reminded, "and that I doubted if I'd ever been in it. And then you blushed when I mentioned my fingers, and it jumped up and bit me on the nose."

"Oh." She grinned, blushing again. "Well, they're great fingers."

"Thank you."

Someone was pounding him on the back. He finally let her go and went to talk to Kennery. Becky Trumball caught Tessa's arm.

"So," she said wistfully. "What about his *pants?*"

Tessa looked at her. "His *pants?*"

"Yeah. You know, does he put them on one leg at a time?"

Tessa looked back at him, her heart swelling. She smiled slowly.

"No," she said quietly. "John Gunner's definitely not like any other man."

* * * * *